A *Tint* of **Murder**

A PAINT BY MURDER MYSTERY

Bailee Abbott

A
Tint
of
Murder

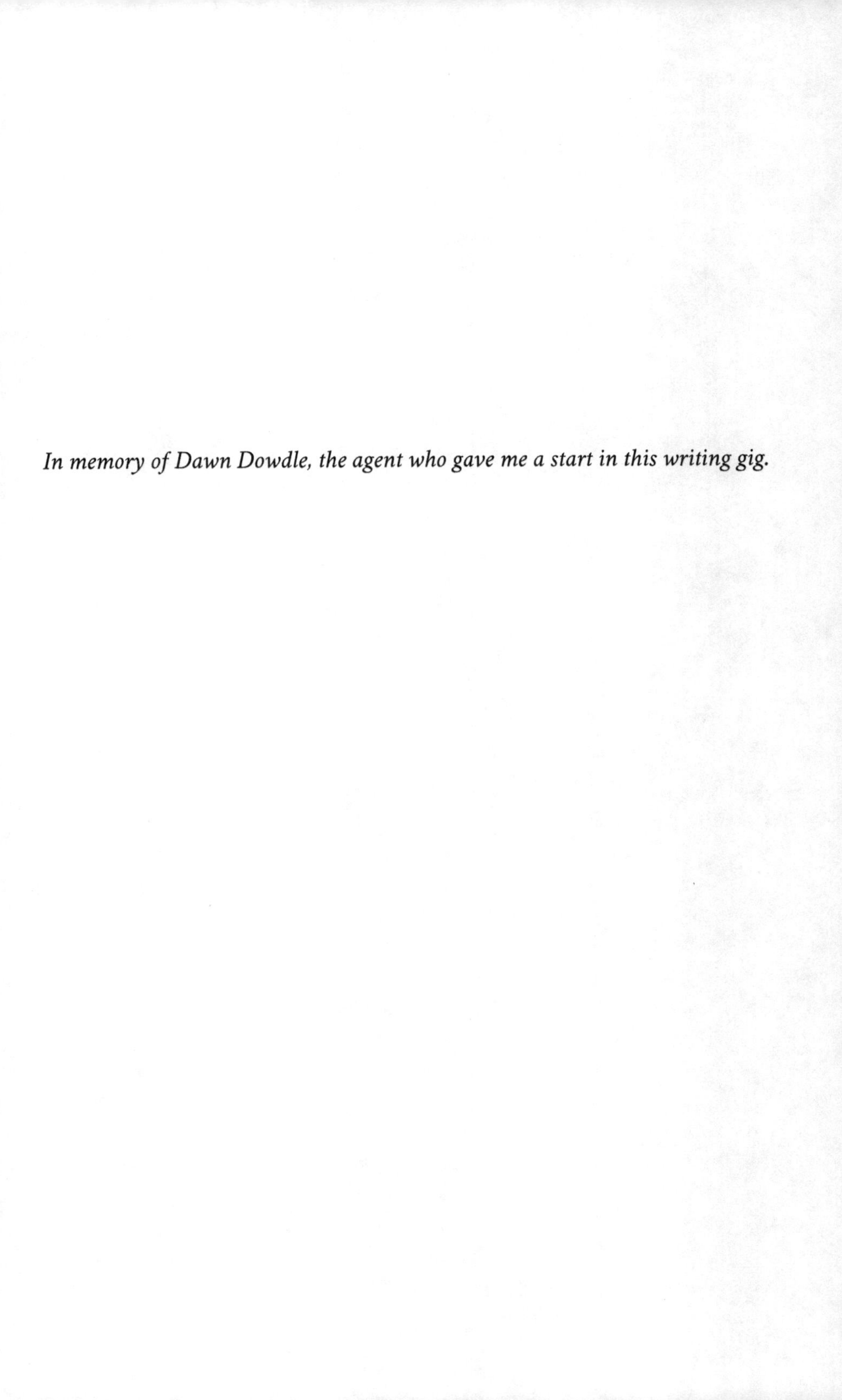

In memory of Dawn Dowdle, the agent who gave me a start in this writing gig.

Praise for the Paint by Murder Mysteries

For #1 – *A BRUSH WITH MURDER:*

"Plenty of local color blends with romance, an intrepid detective, and a tricky mystery."—*Kirkus Reviews*

"Bailee Abbott paints a charming lakeside town filled with colorful suspects and an unexpected protagonist in artist Chloe in her new novel *A Brush with Murder*."—Sherry Harris, Agatha Award-nominated author of the Sarah Winston Garage Sale mysteries

For #2 – *KILL THEM WITH CANVAS:*

"The Abbington sisters continue to display a talent for art and murder...with pleasant characters and a light romantic touch."—*Kirkus Reviews*

"Beautifully constructed and original 'whodunnit'."—*Midwest Book Review*

For #3 – *EASIER DEAD THAN DRAWN:*

"*Easier Dead Than Drawn* is an experience that will captivate even the most skeptical of mystery readers. With its intricately woven character arcs, you'll find yourself deeply invested in each character's lives, secrets, and motivations. The plot unfolds at a thrilling pace, and unexpected twists will keep you on the edge of your seat, guessing until the very last moment."—*Midwest Book Review*

"In *Easier Dead than Drawn*, Abbot paints a delightful mystery with a beautiful lakeside setting, complex characters, plenty of twists, and a smart heroine you'll want to root for and befriend. Readers will enjoy their visit to Whisper Cove and long to return."—Ayla Rose, author of *Murder on Devil's Pond*

"A lively sleuth, delightful characters, a singular setting and a twisty collection of motives make this cozy mystery a standout. The community Abbott has created is utterly engaging and I hope to get a chance to visit it again in future mysteries."—R.J. Koreto, author of the Wren Fontaine Historic Homes Series

For #4 – *A TINT OF MURDER:*

"I loved the warm, easy relationships in this story: The sisters work as a team to manage their business and solve crimes on the side…I recommend this series for readers who like strong, female amateur sleuths and a touch of art crime."—Sharon Marchisello, author of the DeeLo Myer Cat Rescue Mysteries

Chapter One

"Home. Never thought I'd be so glad to leave skyscrapers, traffic, and all of the rude New Yorkers." I wiggled my toes to relieve the cramping while waiting for the light to turn. "Nine hours of driving makes my body ache and head hurt."

"Four hours, you mean. We took turns," Izzie said. She gestured with a flip of her hand. "Besides, only ten more minutes and we'll be on Sail Shore Drive, looking at the most beautiful town and home in the whole world." She settled back in her seat with a long sigh.

"Absolutely. I can't wait to sit on the lake shore and dig my feet in the sand." I pushed down on the gas pedal. "Would be nice if Mom and Dad would take us for a sail someday soon. I can't believe it's September already. Before you know it, ice will be covering Chautauqua Lake."

Izzie chuckled. "Let's not race through autumn. Lots to do before the first snowfall hits us."

I glimpsed her for a quick second. The smile brightened her face. She turned away then to lean her head out of the window. Locks of her hair blew wildly in the breeze. I concentrated on the road once more as I flipped on the turn signal and maneuvered the car into our drive.

The majestic white clapboard, two-story structure made a proud statement. It definitely stood out from all the other houses on our road, and not just because of the size. The cement swan sitting in the front yard, as well as the porch swing and our mailbox, were painted a bright tangerine orange. No one could say Kate Abbington lacked flair in her choice of colors. Guess that was part of the artist's personality, as all of us Abbingtons knew well.

Looking in the side mirror, I ran my fingers through the wide stripe of pink hair, then tucked it behind one ear and frowned. Maybe impulsive flair wasn't such a wise move.

"I think it looks beautiful," Izzie tugged on strands of pink. "Makes a statement. Like 'I'm not getting old. I'm trending.'"

I yanked my head sideways, out of her hand's reach. "I'm not trending. I'm—how about you get out of the car and help me with the bags." I mumbled something about people being fixated on age as I pressed the trunk release and slid out of my seat. In exactly three weeks, I'd turn twenty-eight. The idea of inching closer to thirty made memories of my college years swoop in like an invasion of my brain. Those all-night parties, impulse purchases, my year in Paris traipsing through the French artist district with not a care in the world, and definitely no worries about getting closer to thirty.

"The art exhibit in Soho was so much fun. Thank you for letting me tag along." Izzie hefted her carryall over one shoulder and tugged at the handle of her luggage case as she set it on the ground. "And all those shops. I mean, you showed me the best time. Thanks again." At once, she released a long and labored sigh. "Okay. I know what's bothering you. Seeing those galleries, all the fantastic paintings on exhibit, made you feel a little down. Right? Like that could've been you one day, if you had stayed in New York."

"No. Well, maybe a little, but I'm so happy here. I can't imagine what my life would be without you, the paint party shop, Mom, Dad, Hunter." I waved an arm, spanning the house and the lake. "All of this included. I'm happy, Izzie." I lifted my bag out of the trunk.

Izzie frowned. "You don't sound happy. What gives?" She stepped alongside me as we headed up the drive.

"Twenty-eight." I shrugged.

"Twenty—oh!" Her eyes widened, then she heaved her shoulders. "Birthdays."

"Birthdays." I echoed. "Hey, you want to head over to Duckies this evening? I mean after unpacking, showering—"

"And the paint event we need to get ready for. Don't forget that. Plus, I need to make some calls. Business duties never end." Izzie twisted her mouth.

"Yeah, I want to call Hunter to catch up and cuddle with Max." I chuckled with a headshake. "Maybe tomorrow evening."

"Sure. Why not? I don't have any plans." Izzie opened the front door. "Mom. Dad. Your lovely, exceptionally talented daughters are home!"

A tiny ball of curly white fur came scurrying down the hallway with a high-pitched mix of yips and squeaks. Max hopped up and down at my feet, trying to reach me.

"Hey, buddy! Boy, did I miss you." I swept him up in my arms and welcomed all the wet, sloppy kisses. The warm, cuddle moment was the perfect pick-me-up. I refused to admit Izzie was right. At least not out loud. I didn't want her to feel guilty or think my decision to accept her offer in the business was my way of settling for second best. Another life in another time, the Big Apple had been a life's career dream. I wanted that validation of my talent to make myself known and praised in the art world, become a household name, so to speak, where all those who visited a gallery exhibit of my work would be in awe of my talent. Yeah, gotta dream big, I'd told myself. Only that didn't happen. Izzie called and asked for my help opening a paint party shop in our hometown, Whisper Cove. My dream wasn't happening, I had boyfriend problems, which was a whole other issue I didn't like to think about, so I packed my stuff and drove across state to arrive on the doorstep of our parents' home where all four of us, plus one dog, lived happily ever after.

Seriously, the move turned out to be a good choice. I loved becoming Izzie's partner in Paint with a View, our cute little cottage on Artisan Alley that skirted Chautauqua Lake, along with a few other craft shops. We had fun creating paint parties with theme titles like "Paint Your Pet" that customers loved. Business was thriving, and I was truly happy. Even my love life took a nice turn after being thrown into a downward emotional spiral over my breakup. Detective Hunter Barrett had grown on me and filled my lonely heart. Life felt complete, even if seeing those art galleries stirred thoughts of what I'd worked so hard in the past year to dismiss. The idea or hope that I still could or might give that dream one more try in the future lingered somewhere deep inside. And that was fine by me, too.

My brows curled as I shifted attention to a rather large crate resting against the front wall next to the coatrack. I set Max on the floor. "Did you notice this?" I eyed Izzie for a second.

Izzie hung her jacket and leaned closer to view the crate. "It's labeled with my name and our address. I wonder who—Mom! Dad! Are you home?" She stepped away from the crate.

"Goodness. What's all the shouting about?" Kate Abbington appeared in the hallway entrance to the kitchen wearing a paisley print apron from neck to hips. Her hands were covered with red and green shades of paint. She wiped them with the cloth she'd held. "Had a tiny mishap in my studio." She grinned sheepishly as she hurried forward.

"Hi, Mom." I wrapped my arm around her waist and gazed up at her face.

Kate had nearly five inches on my short stature. She and Izzie were a match. Long and willowy like models. Except for the auburn hair trailing in a braid down Kate's back, that contrasted with Izzie's brown waves. All of us had the vibrant green eyes and fair skin, though.

Joe Abbington followed behind his wife, walking out of the study holding a pipe.

I grinned at the plaid robe and matching slippers. "What's this? Trying on a new look?"

He coughed and set the pipe in a dish on the hall table. "Did you know Van Gogh smoked a pipe? He said it gave him peace during troubling times in his life." He glimpsed Mom for a split second while the corners of his mouth pulled into a frown.

Mom waved dismissively. "Oh, stop. I told you the room needed some cheering up. A great improvement, if you ask me."

I met Izzie's puzzled glance and shrugged. "Cheering up?"

"What room improved?" Izzie echoed.

"Improved is a matter of opinion," Dad mumbled and picked up the pipe and shoved the stem in his mouth.

Mom sat on the bottom step. "I decided to paint our bedroom a beautiful shade of lavender. Your father doesn't like it." There went the arm wave again as it seemed to voice its own opinion of his comments.

I puffed my cheeks with air, then let it release. "So, we had a nice time in New York. Can't wait to show you the photos we took."

"And how about this surprise delivery waiting for me? I don't suppose you can tell me about that instead of how you're painting rooms lavender, which by the way, sounds gorgeous, Mom." Izzie butted in as she patted the top of the crate.

"Oh! Of course." Mom popped up from the stairs. "The crate. A man delivered it Friday, soon after you two left on your trip. He drove a van that had a logo on the side. Speedy Delivery. Yes, that's what it said."

"I'm too curious to wait. Dad, would you get me a crowbar? I think we'll need one." Izzie circled the crate.

I estimated the dimensions to be more than three feet high and probably over four feet wide. "No return address?"

"Nope. Maybe there's a note inside." Izzie turned to face Mom. "Did the courier say anything?"

Mom shook her head. "He handed off the crate to your dad and nodded before jogging back to his vehicle."

"Huh. So weird." Izzie chewed on her bottom lip. "I didn't order anything for the shop. Did you?" She directed her inquisitive gaze at me.

"Not recently. Nothing that would be this size and shape, anyway." I squatted down to examine the bottom edge of the crate. Styrofoam bits had lodged in the cracks. I picked at a piece and held it up. "Packed like this, the contents might be fragile. I'd be careful opening the crate."

Dad had returned with the crowbar and offered to take over. He wiggled and pulled the claw end of the bar to loosen the nails until the crate easily pulled apart.

I mimicked Izzie's response and stared at the contents in silence. The painting was a gorgeous seascape, beautiful but somewhat haunting, with an ocean view, cresting waves, and an orangish-red sky at sunset. A lighthouse off to the right side appeared weathered and without its beacon, as if it was abandoned. The only sign of life appeared far off in the distance on the ocean's surface. I narrowed my gaze, but without a magnifier, I could barely make out the outline of a ship. All in all, the artwork was fine but hardly exceptional. Unlike most paintings, this canvas had no signature scrawled across the bottom. I glanced at Izzie. "For whatever reason, it could be the artist wants anonymity."

"Possibly." Izzie stepped in back of the canvas and pulled off a note taped to the surface. "Here's a clue." In seconds, she grinned. "It's from Martin." She paused to read silently. A frown creased her brow. "Seems he wants me to deliver the painting to Fine Art Storage in Buffalo, but he doesn't say why." She glanced up. "That's odd, isn't it?"

Martin Steele was a dear friend and also an investor in our paint party business. He had an impressive collection of art and negotiated quite a few deals for clients, acquiring paintings they wished to own. Izzie had known him for several years and, on occasion, completed a few projects for him. She even painted a reproduction of an original Steele owned. Rembrandt's *The Night Watch*. His suspicions had seemed rather dramatic to me, but Izzie believed him. He wanted to protect his priceless possession by storing it someplace safe while the copy hung on display in his home. He insisted some very unscrupulous people in his circle had sticky fingers and were not to be trusted. This time, his request was a bit unusual. He'd never asked Izzie to run errands. I wasn't sure how she'd take it.

"Odd is right. Does he say in his note who the artist is?" I stepped next to her to peek.

"Nope. Guess I'll have to wait and find out when I speak with him." She carried the painting into Dad's study that was mostly used as the family den, and leaned it against the sofa. "Should we hang it in here? It fits perfectly." She tapped her lip with one pink polished fingernail.

"I vote taking it to your shop. Display the canvas in your window, why don't you? Maybe add a beach theme to one of your painting events." Dad wagged his pipe that still remained unlit.

Izzie laughed. "Don't worry, Dad. I was only teasing you."

The tension in his set jaw relaxed. We all knew Dad's taste leaned more toward the western landscapes of the American photographer, Ansel Adams. Or paintings by Frederick Remington and Thomas Moran. This seascape hardly fit.

"I'll leave it here until tomorrow morning, if that's okay. Meantime, Chloe and I have a date with Gwen Finch and a kite painting event at the park in a couple of hours." Izzie returned to the hallway and grabbed the handle of her luggage case.

We left Mom and Dad in the den, gazing at the painting. Dad's fingers cupped his chin while Mom crossed her arms. They exchanged words with each other under mumbled breaths.

I shook my head and whistled for Max to follow as both Izzie and I headed upstairs. Admittedly, our parents acted a bit quirky when it came to art, often obsessed with analyzing a painting or sculpture, interpreting the work, right down to the tiniest detail. I had no doubt when we came downstairs to leave for our event, they'd still be in the room staring at the painting, trying to decide who the artist was, and betting on which of them would end up with the correct answer.

I dumped everything from my luggage case on the bed. Sorting what needed washing would have to wait until this evening. I had an hour to shower and get ready. No time to call Hunter and catch up on any news I'd missed over the weekend. I knew he'd been working on a murder case, which understandably caused me worry. After I returned home last summer, the life I expected, one with calm and quiet moments, was hardly that. No more than a few days passed when I stumbled upon the body of the Whisper Cove Gazette's editor, right behind our shop. Then, a few months later, another body turned up floating in the lake. Only this past spring, there'd been yet a third incident, but I didn't like being reminded of that one. No wonder I cringed at the mere mention of murder, which happened pretty often since I was dating a homicide detective. "Nothing like adding too much excitement to our lives. Right, Max?"

He sat up and pawed the air before punctuating that gesture with a *woof*.

"Glad you agree." I patted his head, then headed to one of the bathrooms to shower. Thoughts of the painting crept back into my head. Why couldn't Steele deliver it to the storage facility himself? And why didn't he mention the artist's name? "Maybe he doesn't know who painted it. More to figure out. Guess that will have to wait, too."

***

I set up rows of easels while Izzie unfolded and placed chairs by each one. Taking a deep breath of the crisp fall air, I gazed at the view. The park was beautiful this time of year. Marigolds formed a colorful border along the walking paths while benches and tables had been given a fresh coat of forest green paint. Children laughed and chattered as they sailed down the slide and twirled on the merry-go-round at the newly built playground, which sat closer to the lake and near our floating amphitheater. The town citizens had our B&B owner, Frank Benworthy, to thank. His ideas to improve the park and attract all ages of visitors were a huge success. He'd fought hard to petition for this project and even took over as production manager of the amphitheater. Good things happen to good people, as Granddad Abbington used to say.

"Ladies! I'm so sorry for being a bit late. Winston and I stopped for a quick bite to eat." Gwen Finch stopped midway across the lawn and heaved her chest to take a breath. "Thank goodness he offered to help me set up." She turned, cupping the sides of her mouth with her hands. "Winston! Wave to Izzie and Chloe."

I grinned. Fifty-something and acting like lovestruck teens. How refreshing to see. "Hi Winston!"

As he waved, a kite escaped his hand and sailed upward, tail streamers twisting in the wind. He ran and made attempts to grab a hold of the trailing string, but it was no use. Like a bird with bright colored feathers, the kite soared across the lake, gradually becoming a tiny blue dot. "Sorry, Gwennie. This one got away," he shouted.

"No matter. I've packed plenty of kites in the trunk." Gwen wiped the loose curls from her face. "Sweet how he tries so hard, isn't it?"

"Absolutely is, Gwen. I'm glad you found someone who makes you happy." Izzie patted her shoulder.

When I'd first met Gwen, her life seemed sad and lonely. A bottle of wine kept her company on a Friday night, and the shop, Go Fly a Kite, filled the daylight hours. Still, that wasn't enough. Then Winston came along. Life couldn't have been more different from that point.

"I am. I truly am. Happy, that is." She pulled a planner out of her satchel. "Now, this is what I've come up with that should move the event along."

With heads together, Izzie and I scanned Gwen's notes. Most of the agenda worked, but it appeared obvious Gwen was new to the process of a paint party.

"We need to tweak this a bit, but thank you." Izzie handed back the planner, keeping her tone light and cheerful.

However, I caught the twitch at the corner of her eye, hinting that she didn't totally mean what she said.

"How about you start off with a five-minute introduction by explaining your business and maybe a short description on how to make a kite, or something like that? Do you have a sale planned in the near future? That would attract customers." My voice trailed off at the end like I'd lost air to speak as Gwen's face puckered into a frown.

All at once, she raised her arm to point and lifted her chin. "Wonderful idea! Thanks, Chloe. I mean about the sale. I hadn't thought about having one. Five minutes, though? I could maybe shorten what I planned on saying to about ten. Would that be okay?"

Izzie tipped her head as if in thought. Her tongue trailed across her bottom lip. "Ten should work. I'll just tell everyone that the event might run over an hour, and when Chloe and I finish our part, they're welcome to stop by and chat with you."

Gwen bobbed her head. "Yes, that's perfect." She turned her wristwatch to check the time. "I should go help Winston. He's not very graceful when it comes to putting things together." She smiled, making her plump cheeks more pronounced.

Izzie anchored her hands to either hip, waiting until Gwen stood next to Winston. "We can shorten our part with a quick intro."

"It'll be fine, Izzie. How about we hand out the flyers for upcoming events and skip talking about them? That'll save a couple of minutes. I don't think guests will mind if we run over the hour a bit."

"I just don't want to start a habit. People have agendas and schedules and appointments to get to." She groaned.

"Do you think it's time to attend one of those yoga classes with Mom?" I suggested with the click of my tongue and a playful jab at her arm. For the past several months, Izzie had been using yoga—Mom's suggestion—to calm her nerves and anxiety. That therapy seemed to work well, but she struggled at times. Like now, when she worried about having control over the paint event.

She relaxed her shoulders and hugged me. "How about shopping, instead? I've been wanting to visit those new businesses opening in Buffalo. New clothes are therapy, too."

"Yes. Yes, they are." I squeezed her arm. "Now, we have a little over twenty minutes to set out plates, brushes, and cups, organize the paints, set up the projector—"

"Stop. I know the drill." Izzie laughed, then held up her finger when her cell rang. She stepped away as she answered.

I took over distributing supplies while casting a side glance at Izzie, who paced back and forth, giving the occasional nod. The creased forehead and her mouth stretched in a thin line suggested the conversation wasn't an upbeat or happy one.

All at once, she rolled her arm, beckoning me, then pointed to her cell. I dropped the roll of paper towels in the box and stepped in to join her. "What gives?"

She pressed the speaker button and mouthed the word *listen*.

Immediately, a man's voice spoke. Looking at Izzie, I shrugged with both palms facing upward.

"It's Martin," she whispered.

"I'm glad the painting arrived safely. A huge relief, really. One of my college roommates sent it to me a few weeks ago. We've kept in touch over the years, getting together every so often, but I hadn't heard from him in quite a while. So it caught me by surprise when I received the painting. He included a brief note of thanks. I'd helped him with closing a couple of art deals in the past. Anyway, he wanted to show me how well his efforts at painting were coming along and to ask for my opinion. I knew he'd finished a couple of other works, even displaying them in the gallery the family owns. Seems he's most proud of this one, though. Of course, a photo would've done, and I've been puzzling over his actions ever since…well, ever since I'd heard—"

"But why? Why send it to me?" Izzie interrupted. "It's not that I mind taking it to the storage place for you. Really. But wouldn't the task have been quicker and easier for your assistant to handle?"

"Yes. Yes. I'm guessing lots of questions are running through your mind, but it's wise if I don't share too many details. As for my request, I trust you. I can't say that about very many people in my inner circle. Secondly, I've been very careful to keep our relationship private. Being an unnamed investor in your paint shop is an example of that. Izzie, if I wasn't fully certain of your safety, I wouldn't ask for your help. As for the situation I'm in, I think…no, that's not it. I'm certain someone has been watching me. This all started soon after receiving my friend's gift. Though it's unlikely, I can't help thinking there's a connection. Being paranoid has made me extra cautious, I guess."

Izzie straightened. "Watching you? Martin, are you safe?"

"Yes, of course I'm safe, but I need you to help me with this one thing. Take the painting to the location. I'd do it myself, but if I'm right, I can't give anyone the opportunity to steal it."

"I don't understand. Who is this college roommate I've never heard you talk about? What's so special about his painting?" Izzie's voice strained, ignoring Martin's request not to ask questions.

"For now, I think it's better if his name remains anonymous. I have a hunch or two about his actions, but no proof. That's why I need time to search for answers. Give me that time, Izzie. Please."

Doing a fast replay of everything Martin had said, I came up with one question that seemed pretty important. "Hi Martin. It's me, Chloe. Hope you don't mind me listening in. Can you at least tell us why, all of a sudden, you want to hide the painting? That's what putting it in storage means, right? Someplace safe where no one, including whoever you think is watching you, can get to it. So, what changed?"

"It's my college friend. He was killed in a car accident a month ago. And more and more, I'm convinced his death was not an accident. I think someone meant for him to crash his car. I believe he was murdered."

Chapter Two

I tucked my knees under my chin and sipped tea from a mug, trying to prevent the trembling in my hands from spilling any. Thoughts of relaxing this evening to watch a romcom or play my favorite game of movie trivia with the family vanished with the word *murder* as it came out of Martin's mouth, then repeated in Izzie's high-pitched tone.

Izzie, of course, had fired off a few dozen questions to answer the what, where, when, and why of it all, but Martin had sealed his lips tightly, promising to tell her everything she begged to know, *after* he had found those answers himself. She wasn't satisfied, and neither was I.

Meanwhile, we sat in the den, staring at nothing but thinking about everything. Or at least, I was. Like how this situation could turn into plenty of trouble. I knew from past experience that having any connection or association with murder brought nothing good into our lives. I cast Izzie a weary glance, knowing she'd insist on helping Martin in any way she could.

Unfortunately, that sort of intense loyalty of hers could get out of hand. When Izzie set out on one of her missions, she had tunnel vision. With fierce determination, she'd never quit. I sighed into my mug while steam bathed my face. As always, I'd be right there alongside her, every step of the way.

"We can't let him do this alone. We should help somehow," Izzie said. At once, she stood up from the sofa and paced. "I know Martin. He'll put himself in danger, just to find answers."

I tightened my jaw. Two peas in a friendship pod. Did she realize how alike they were? I blew air out of puffed-up cheeks. "Somehow help. In what way, Izzie? We don't know anything about what's going on."

"You heard him. He's being followed. And how about the fact his friend, the artist whose painting is sitting right there, was murdered?" She stabbed one finger at the canvas, which still rested against the wall.

"Allegedly murdered." I nodded. "Besides, without a name, where would we begin to look?" My body parts were growing numb with tingles running up and down my legs. I stood to stretch.

Max trotted over to me with his squeaky ladybug toy and dropped it at my feet. Taking a few steps back, he woofed with his tail wagging playfully.

I leaned over and grabbed the toy. "Shouldn't we wait until he gives you more information? No rush, is there? I mean, since his friend is dead." I flung the ball across the room, and Max scurried after it.

"No, but what if Martin playing detective puts him in danger? Waiting wouldn't be such a smart thing to do." Izzie tapped her lip with one fingernail.

I blinked. Reason and common sense weren't exactly on her mind right now. Why bother saying how us snooping would be no different? I threw the ball again and chuckled at Max, whose enthusiasm over the game of fetch propelled him into action. With a deep growl, he lowered his head and took off. An unintended gasp caused me to choke on my laughter because now he was sliding across the plank wood floor, out of control, and right into the dead artist's canvas. He yelped and limped a few steps back.

"Oh! Max. Sweetie, are you okay?" I hurried to scoop him up in my arms and examine his front paws. The tension in my shoulders eased. Nothing was torn or bleeding, thank goodness.

"This is horrible." Izzie's voice edged with a quivering tone as she knelt down close to the painting.

"What? No, Max is fine. He—" My eyes widened. I set Max on the sofa. Stepping next to Izzie, I noticed the tear in the bottom corner of the canvas. At least three inches long. I winced. "That's not good."

"No kidding." Izzie's finger ran along the edge of the tear. "I don't even know if it could be mended well enough to keep from being noticed. Martin will be so upset." She leaned back to sit on the floor.

"It was an accident. He'll understand." I frowned at Max. I imagined his eyes filled with regret. As if he guessed what I was thinking, he lay down, resting his chin on both paws and whimpering softly. I took another step toward the painting to get a closer look at the damage.

"What's all the noise about? Dad and I can hear you from the patio." Mom entered the den, wearing the colorful floor-length silk muumuu she'd brought home from Hawaii. "Oh my." Her brow wrinkled as she lifted the sides of her dress and leaned in to peer at the canvas. "How did that happen?"

"Max." Izzie and I chimed in at once.

"That's odd." She fingered the tear and lifted one flap to the side.

"Mom, you'll make it worse." Izzie reached out to pull her hand away, but stopped suddenly. "Is that…?"

Mom nodded. "Another painting hiding behind this one, it seems."

Nothing was said for several seconds as all of us stared at the seascape with a tear, revealing shades of black and brown that contrasted with the lighter colors on top.

"Why so glum, you three?" Dad stood in the entrance to the den, pipe pointing at each of us.

"The painting is torn." I pointed.

"There's another one hidden underneath," Mom added.

"What should we do?" Izzie chewed on her fingernail and hiccuped.

"Maybe take a look at the hidden one? Could be stolen and valuable." Dad's eyes gleamed with enthusiasm.

"No." Izzie stepped in front of the painting with arms splayed side to side. "Let's slow down a minute."

"Izzie's right. Martin sent us the painting and wants us to secure it in some vault for safekeeping. Maybe he knows about the hidden painting, or maybe he doesn't. Either way, it doesn't seem right to do anything before knowing what he'd want us to do." I lifted my voice near the end of my speech, like I was asking them to agree.

"Yeah, we shouldn't mess with the painting until I speak with Martin." Izzie marched across the room and snatched her phone off the sofa. "In fact, I'm calling him this instant." She punched buttons while we all waited in silence.

Even Max sat up and tilted his head, the whimpering gone silent.

"Voicemail." Her shoulders slumped as she set the phone on the end table. The worry lines in her forehead deepened. "What if he isn't aware? I mean, maybe if we take a look at the hidden painting…"

I eyed the seascape before turning to gaze at her. "And then we'd have a better idea of how to move forward." I had to agree with Dad's comment. Stolen art was criminal but a very lucrative business. One of the most common ways for thieves to smuggle a painting would be to hide it behind another. I didn't mention my worry that we could be charged as accessories to a crime for having the painting in our possession, even if only for a few hours.

"You have a point." Izzie tapped her shoe on the hardwood floor. "So, we take a quick peek, see what's hidden, and then decide." She sighed. "But unless it's something as famous and valuable as the Mona Lisa, both paintings go back into the crate, on their way to the storage place in Buffalo, just as Martin wanted."

Without asking, I took out my phone and clicked a few pictures of our mystery artist's painting. The seascape was definitely mysterious, as if the lighthouse and ship were put there as some sort of clues. I stepped forward. "In case these help us."

Izzie frowned. "What?"

I rolled my eyes. "You know. If things turn out the way they seem to do for us, every detail is important."

She grinned. "You mean if you help me investigate? That's…" She set the canvas against the wall once more and wrapped her arms around my shoulders. "Thank you. Together again. The snoop sisters reunited." She punched the air with one fist.

"Yeah, yeah. Let's get to this unveiling." I didn't rise to her level of enthusiasm, but at the same time, I couldn't help but smile. I liked working with her. Whether it was a paint party event or dangerous sleuthing, those moments brought us closer. After spending two years away while living in Manhattan, missing too many family events and not sharing special bonding time with Izzie, I grabbed a hold of every chance I could.

"Okay. Here goes." Izzie took a deep breath and held it as she carefully slid the painting out of its hiding place.

We all stood in silence, studying the image. A woman sat in a chair, looking out of a window, as if daydreaming. Light streamed through the glass panes to cast a glow on her face, and as if reluctant to do so, a smile turned up the corners of her lips ever so slightly.

A washtub sat at her feet, and a basket of clothes next to it. Her dress of dark colors was simply styled and painted with rather harsh brush strokes. What contrasted with the plain look, however, was the wreath of jewels crowning her head. Still, the details gave enough clues. I nodded. "It's like Vermeer's work. Seventeenth-century working woman. He was famous for that."

Izzie pointed. "Light and dark contrasts. Firm brush strokes. And oh, those expensive paints he used."

"Expensive and not easy to come by, back in those times. What about the jeweled crown? I don't get it." I glanced at Izzie. She had more background in art history than I did.

She gasped. "It's a tronie!"

"A who?" I sat in my chair. It seemed I was about to get an art history lesson from Izzie.

Izzie paced the floor while Mom, Dad, and I listened. "Vermeer painted four tronies. The idea was to take a young woman and dress her in some sort of costume, frivolous, fancy, and totally unreal." She kneeled to study the painting once more. "This one's different in a way. The woman isn't in total costume. It's almost like the jeweled crown was meant to send a message. I'm not sure, but I don't think it's a Vermeer."

"As if the artist was imitating Vermeer?" I suggested.

"Yes. Something like that." She stood again.

"Is it valuable, though?" Mom asked. "Why else hide it?"

"Even if it is valuable and stolen, I'd think we'd have a tough time finding out. For instance, this could've been painted recently and not centuries ago," Dad leaned down and gently touched the canvas backing. "An expert would be able to tell."

"Which we don't have time to find. Without knowing more about the painting and how it came to be hidden behind the seascape, that makes me even more anxious to speak with Martin." Izzie fretted.

"No name on this one either." I circled around the painting.

"I say we turn it over to the police. If it's stolen, it's not safe or wise keeping it here a minute longer." Mom's jaw tightened.

"Look. We don't know that." Izzie argued. "I want to help Martin. I trust him. If he says to put the painting in storage for safekeeping, then that's what I'm going to do."

I knew Izzie well enough that convincing her to do what Mom suggested wouldn't work. "Okay, then. First thing tomorrow, we deliver the painting and get it out of our house and hands." I snapped a few more photos. Just in case, I told myself.

After hammering the last nail into the crate and sliding it into the hall closet, Dad closed the door and stepped away. "Tight as it gets and ready for the vault."

"Thanks, Dad." Izzie kissed his cheek. "Now, who's ready for dinner? I'm starving."

At that moment, the doorbell rang. "How about that? Millie's Diner delivery is right on time." I hurried to answer, but Tony from the diner wasn't on our doorstep. I stretched my smile ear to ear and tugged at one muscular arm to bring him inside. "Hey, handsome. Can I say how much I've missed your face?" Taking my finger, I traced the thin scar along the corner of his eye. Barely noticeable but it hinted at a story that meant something. Maybe a casualty on the job while investigating some dangerous character? No matter how often I asked, he refused to talk about it.

Hunter brought me in close for a hug. "Only my face?" His breath, soft and warm, tickled my cheek.

"Oh, and so much more." I kept my voice to a whisper and tilted my chin upward to stare at his brown eyes that seemed to deepen in color as he hugged me tighter.

"Eh em."

A voice carried from the porch step. I peeked out from under Hunter's shoulder. "Hi, Tony." I blushed and broke the embrace to move toward the doorway. "Sorry about that. How much do we owe you?"

Tony cleared his throat, avoiding the awkward moment as any teenager might do in this situation by staring at the receipt stapled to our order. "Forty-five even."

A generous tip was in order. I fished in my wallet for a second, then handed him sixty in exchange for the carryout bag. "Thanks. Tell Millie we said hi." I had to shout because Tony had already sprinted across the lawn and hopped in his car.

"Dinner!" I called out. Izzie, Mom, and Dad had disappeared, but chatter and the clinking of dishware emanated from the kitchen. "Would you like a roast beef sandwich and fries? We have plenty." I carried the bag in one hand while slipping my arm through Hunter's, then guided us toward the rear of the house. "What did you do while I was gone? Tell me everything. I'm anxious to catch up."

"Everything? Then I'm going to need two sandwiches because everything will take a while." He teased by tweaking my nose.

Since the afternoon sun warmed the autumn-like temperature, we sat on the back patio to eat while Hunter told us about a high-profile case. I chewed a large bite of my sandwich and savored the flavors of seasoned beef, onions, and pepperjack cheese. From the moment of Steele's phone call, my stomach rolled with queasiness. Sniffing at the fries and staring at the ciabatta rolls stuffed with roast beef reminded me that other than a protein bar, I hadn't eaten since we'd left New York City this morning. Suddenly, I was famished, and I forced myself to push aside all the unsettling thoughts about murder speculation and art theft.

"Like I was saying, this case is different from the usual ones that come across my desk. And no doubt, a rare event for folks in Sinclairville." Hunter gestured with a nod of his sandwich.

Sinclairville was a small village, a short distance north of Whisper Cove, and not very populated. Nothing hardly ever happened in Sinclairville, especially not crime.

"A wealthy recluse whose murder involves some rich and powerful players? One or more who may be on your suspect list? Yeah, not the norm." I took several gulps of raspberry tea.

"Pauletta Burnell. What a shame. Her family must be devastated. I imagine you're thinking this could be a burglary gone wrong. I mean, aren't lots of valuables missing?" Mom dished out another helping of avocado salad.

"Whoever they are, they have to be pros at this. No evidence left behind. Only the most valuable art was taken, paintings and sculptures that included an entire collection of Frank Lloyd Wright's work, even a Nakoma replica." Hunter shook his head.

"Nako who?" Izzie curled her brow. "I thought Wright designed homes."

"Yes, and sculptures too. Nakoma is a Native American sculpture that some country club commissioned Wright to create." Hunter shrugged. "Me sitting through hundreds of my mom's art history lectures is my excuse. I should have a degree."

I smiled. Professor Meredith Barrett taught art history at a local liberal arts college. When Hunter was a child, his mom would often take him to class when a babysitter wasn't available.

"Anyway, it's an interesting case." Hunter swirled a French fry in a puddle of ketchup.

I slurped more of my tea while thinking about the hidden painting. Could the fake Vermeer be a stolen work? Hunter's murder victim died a couple of days ago. Steele had said he was given the painting weeks before. Hardly fitting the timing of the wealthy recluse's demise and theft.

The ring of someone's phone interrupted. I glanced up as Hunter walked away from the table.

"Yeah, I'm in Whisper Cove, so I should be there within the hour." He shoved the phone in his back pocket. "Sorry, but there's a new development in the recluse case. Thanks for the meal and conversation, Abbington family. I always enjoy your company." He winked at me.

I wrapped my arms around his waist, then, on tiptoes, planted a kiss on his lips. "You're always welcome." I waved as he hurried back through the kitchen and toward the front of the house.

Izzie came alongside me. "Do you think we should've told him about the hidden painting?"

"No. At least not yet. We really don't know enough." I sucked on my tongue. "We do like you said. If you fail to get a hold of Martin by morning to tell him about it, we take the painting to the storage facility in Buffalo."

"And then?"

"And then we wait."

Chapter Three

I started at the loud bang on my bedroom door. Springing out of bed, I glanced at the clock and groaned. Ten after eight. Most mornings I woke by seven. Of course, this particular day had to be different. "Hold on!"

Izzie and I had an appointment with the storage manager in Buffalo at nine-thirty. I'd barely have time to get dressed, grab a muffin, bagel, or whatever was available, and a travel mug filled with what I hoped would be very strong coffee. Why did I feel so groggy? I wrinkled my nose. Maybe the tossing and turning most of the night was the cause.

"Well, hurry faster. We're leaving in twenty minutes," Izzie called out.

"I'm on it," I mumbled while shoving my legs into my pants. "Izzie, would you fill my mug and see if there's a muffin, bagel, even a granola bar to bring along?" I plopped on the edge of the bed and pulled on my sweater. "And why didn't you wake me earlier?"

"Eighteen minutes and counting." Her voice echoed across the hall. Footsteps pounded on the stairs as she moved from top floor to bottom.

Max popped his head out from underneath the covers. His fur stuck out in messy tufts.

I grinned. "Looks like we're both sleepyheads." I lifted him in my arms and set him on the floor.

Obviously, Izzie hadn't reached Steele this morning. The trip to deliver the canvas was still in play. My fitful sleep had a lot to do with that Vermeer imitation and guessing who the artist was and reasons why Martin was so mysterious about the whole situation. I shuddered. Nightmarish images of art thieves holding us at gunpoint flashed in my mind. Maybe after leaving the painting at the storage unit, I'd find some relief. The mere notion of it remaining even another day under our roof and in our possession unsettled my nerves. Too many details about its story had to be sorted out.

Scowling in the mirror, I worked a brush through my hair to flatten the alfalfa sprout sticking out on top. The effort was pointless. With a generous amount of hair product, I managed to hide the bedhead look. "One of us can't get away with the messy hair. You men have it so easy. No judgmental stares for you." I patted Max on his scruffy head. "Let's go get you some food. Okay?"

He woofed approval at that suggestion and scratched at my bedroom door, signaling it was time to dive into our morning routine, even though late.

"We should be back in town by noon." Izzie's voice carried from the kitchen.

I walked down the hallway with Max leading. The clank and clatter of dishes intermixed with conversation. "Morning," I greeted. Mom and Dad sat at the table while Izzie poured coffee into our travel mugs.

"Morning, shortcake." Dad smiled and gestured with a wave of one arm.

I glanced at Izzie. "I'm guessing you didn't get a hold of Martin this morning?"

"He wasn't there. His assistant, Phillip, answered. I didn't feel right telling him about the painting. Anyway, Martin has gone out of town and can't be reached." Izzie said. "He left a short message with Phillip, asking me to deliver the painting to the art storage facility as soon as possible. I prodded Phillip for more information, like where Martin has traveled to, but his lips are sealed."

"What are you thinking?" Mom sat at the table once more.

"My guess is his search has to do with finding out more about his college friend and the painting, but it's only a guess. I have no real idea. His secrecy troubles me." Izzie wrinkled her brow.

"Me too." I stood. "And the sooner we make the delivery, the better. I don't feel comfortable keeping it any longer."

"You think it's that dangerous?" Dad worked his jaw back and forth.

"Maybe you two shouldn't be the ones to deliver the painting. I could call a courier service to take care of that." He reached for his cellphone.

"No, Dad. I'm sure it's safe. No one knows we have it, other than Martin," Izzie argued and shot a disapproving glance my way.

I sighed. I might have caused our parents more worry than they already had about us. "Don't mind me. I didn't sleep well, and my nerves are on edge because of it. Izzie's right. We'll be fine."

Izzie eyed the kitchen clock. "We should leave. The traffic in Buffalo always slows down the commute."

I circled around the table to access the coffee carafe and topped off my mug. "See you this evening," I called out and waved as I followed Izzie.

"Stay out of trouble, you two," Izzie teased. "Whatever you're up to this morning."

"I think that warning should be the other way around." Mom's voice carried from the kitchen as we reached the front door.

"Maybe they have a reason to worry," I said. My mind wouldn't let go of the things that could go wrong. I cringed as I laid a hand across my stomach. Other parts of my body wouldn't let go either. I didn't understand why. Usually, I never hesitated, no matter the risk. Why should this time be different? Maybe because the crimes we dealt with had been confined to our little community. Not with international art thieves. I clenched my fists to try and calm down. My imagination ran wild and free.

"Are we back to that again?" Izzie sighed and opened the door to her Land Rover. "We drop off the painting. It's that simple. No complications involved. Okay?"

I buckled my seatbelt. "We don't know who or what or why or the answers to any other questions about the situation. Only a fake Vermeer painting that may or may not be stolen or valuable. That's what bothers me." Frustration pushed me into a corner, and I wanted out. My confidence going forward jumped all over the place. My chest heaved as I breathed deeply. I'd told Izzie I'd help Martin, and I would. "Sorry. It's probably nothing, but we'll figure things out, no matter what."

"Thank you. Again." Izzie smiled, then hummed the theme song from

Rocky as she punched the air with both fists.

The image of Rocky jogging up those stairs came to mind. I shook my head and snorted. "Goofball."

The drive to Buffalo took a little over an hour, with the view of Lake Erie all the way north. I settled back in my seat and closed my eyes. Soon, the hum of the engine lulled me to sleep. Obviously, the restless night had caught up to me.

"Hey, sleepyhead."

I slapped Izzie's hand as she tickled my nose. "I'm awake."

"This is the place." Izzie wrinkled her forehead. "Looks kind of rundown. Don't you think?"

I pried open my eyes to glance out of the window. The art storage facility could've used a coat of paint and definitely a new sign. The missing letters left a good deal of guesswork in naming the place. "Are we sure this is where Martin wanted us to store the painting? I mean…" I lifted my shoulders.

"This is the right address." She studied the directions on her phone.

"Okay. Maybe the appearance is intentional. You know, like a disguise so thieves won't realize there're valuables inside."

"Oh! Look. That must be the one we're supposed to meet." She pointed at a man waving his arm while standing in an open doorway.

We hurried out of the vehicle. Each of us took an end of the crate and carried it to the building.

"Good morning, ladies. I'm guessing you are the ones Mister Steele told us to expect?"

Izzie nodded. "Yes. I'm Izzie, and this is my sister Chloe. And you are?"

"Frank Richlen, manager of this facility. Here, allow me." He reached to take the crate out of our grasp. "Would you like to come inside? I'd be happy to show you around. It may not look like much from the outside, but we're proud to claim Buffalo Fine Art Storage has the most secure units in western New York with all the electronic bells and whistles you could imagine. We use a climate-controlled environment to assure preservation. Every detail is addressed." He puffed his chest. "As far as our security goes, no thief has ever managed to break in, though some have tried. That's a true testimony, if there ever was one."

"Sounds impressive." Izzie tapped her watch. "However, we have a business of our own to open this morning, and it's a long drive back home."

"Maybe some other time. I'll make sure the painting is properly stored and email Mister Steele all relevant information. Have a good day, ladies." He nodded and closed the door after him.

I walked slowly back to the car, contemplating. "He never asked to see our IDs. Don't you think that's strange?"

Izzie pressed her remote, and the door locks clicked open. "Not really. Martin probably sent him photos of us."

"Then why ask if we are the ones Martin said to expect?" I slouched in my seat. "I don't know. Guess I'm overthinking the situation."

"Yes. You are. Except…" Izzie fired up the engine and let the Land Rover idle for a moment. "We didn't ask for his ID either."

"Good point." I clicked open the internet on my phone. After scrolling the name, I pulled up the site. Sure enough, the familiar likeness of Frank Richlen with the title of manager captioned underneath popped up. I angled my phone for Izzie to view.

"See? No problem." Izzie turned the steering wheel to maneuver out of the parking lot.

While we waited for traffic to clear, I viewed the surroundings. Across the street, several cars parked along the curb. I frowned. One of the vehicles stood out from the others. An older model Chevy van, black in color. Fumes smoked from the exhaust pipe as the engine idled.

Once Izzie pulled out onto the street, I viewed the side mirror. Sure enough, the van did a U-turn and headed in our direction. After a few blocks, the van continued traveling behind us. On impulse, I grabbed paper and pen from my bag and jotted down the license plate. Sure, it could be a coincidence. However, if not, the driver didn't care if we noticed the tail.

"What are you writing? If it's a plan on what to do next, I'm thinking we should search all the sites about art, galleries, groups, museums, and anything else to help us find out the identity of Martin's artist friend."

I pointed the pen over my shoulder. "Actually, I wrote down the plate number of that van following us."

Izzie eyed her rearview mirror for a second before glimpsing me. "Why do you think it's following us?"

"Maybe because it sat parked across the street from the art facility with the engine on, as if the driver was waiting for us to leave. Then, the van pulled out just as we started down the road. Coincidence? I doubt it," I argued.

Izzie sniffed. "Paranoid, again? Come on, Chloe. No one is watching us. We're just two women, taking a trip to Buffalo, who stopped at Fine Art Storage to drop off a painting, which makes sense because we're artists who run a paint party business." Her voice grew edgy with an exasperated tone. "Why would anyone follow us?"

"Mysterious painting with a hidden one underneath? Martin and his secrets? The urgency to deliver the painting to a secure location? Martin said it himself. He thinks somebody or somebodies are following him." I hitched my thumb to point behind us. "Somebody like the guy in the van."

"Stop. You've made your point. I'm still not convinced some dangerous creep is tailing us." As she grew silent, her teeth bit down to catch her bottom lip. With a nod, she added, "At least, not yet, I'm not."

The ride home passed quickly. I spent the first half scrolling through my phone, searching for any information that could lead to discovering the identity of our mysterious artist. I even searched for recent art heists in case our hunch about the Vermeer lookalike being stolen was right.

Within a short amount of time, the images grew blurry, and the phone dropped onto my lap. I dozed off for almost a half an hour until Izzie nudged my shoulder. I rubbed my cheeks and eyes, still groggy and barely awake. I needed a serious caffeine jolt. "Maybe we could stop by Spill the Beans for coffee?" I lifted my chin. The café opened in the twenties and was owned by local resident, Tom Prichard. Notably, a popular place to get breakfast because of the delicious food and piping hot coffee.

"Sure thing." Izzie tapped the steering wheel. "I think I'll give Camilla a call this morning. With any luck, she can tell us more about the painting."

Camilla Huston was a friend and accomplished art dealer whose vast knowledge of art and the current culture made her the perfect one to contact.

"If her schedule isn't too busy, that is." Izzie pulled into the parking lot next to Spill the Beans.

After the coffee run, we headed to the shop. The corners of my mouth lifted with a smile. The sight of our little cottage structure—the canary yellow siding, window shutters painted robin's egg blue, and the weathered sign with the shop's name, Paint with a View, in matching blue letters—cheered my insides and banished any worries or negative thoughts.

Following Izzie inside, I turned the door sign to announce we were now open for business and flipped the light switch. "Maybe I'll call my contact at the DMV to ask about the license plate number. See what turns up. You know, just in case." I was like a dog chasing that tasty bone. I couldn't dismiss my suspicions about the van and its driver, no matter how paranoid Izzie thought I was.

"Probably worth the extra precaution." Izzie pulled the agenda binder from underneath the front counter and flipped the pages.

Wherever the switch in attitude came from or why, I took her agreement without question. Before either of us picked up our phones to dial, the hanging door chimes tinkled as someone burst inside.

"Thank goodness you're here." I turned to frown at Penny Swenson, whose chest rose and fell in rapid movements. Her platinum blonde mane was swept up in a messy bun, but several wisps of hair had escaped and were plastered to the beads of sweat covering her forehead. In her late forties, the curvy and vivacious Penny could easily pass for thirty. She held up one hand, took a final deep breath to calm herself. "Okay. I got this."

Izzie crossed her arms. "Are you sure you're feeling all right, Penny?"

Her head and messy bun on top bobbed. "Sure. Sure. I'm more than fine. Did you hear the news? Wink hired me to write the column for the Gazette. 'A Penny for Your Thoughts' debuts next Saturday." She clasps her hands together. "My dream as a reporter has finally come true."

"And the aromatherapy shop?" I dipped my chin. Penny owned The Healing Touch, situated a few doors down from our place.

"Oh, of course. Sales are doing much better, but I couldn't turn down the chance for this gig," she said.

Like all small businesses, hers had gone through a slump earlier this year. Earning some extra cash freelancing for Wink and the Gazette had been a thankful opportunity. In fact, in a way, she'd helped us with the case of Lana Easton's murder a few months ago. She'd dived in deep to find the facts for her article pitch to Wink. It had paid off for all of us.

"Congratulations. So, you gonna give us a hint what the first column will be about?" Izzie grinned.

Penny plopped in a chair. "If you figure it out, let me know because I haven't a clue. I'm nervous, ladies. I need a big idea, huge enough to wow readers and make them come back for more."

I tapped my lip, then my eyes popped. "Ooo, I know! How about the festival in Lily Dale? I bet people would find mediums and tarot card readings interesting. Of course, the annual festival was last month, but people who didn't attend could make plans for next year. What do you think?" I glanced at Izzie.

"It's a great idea, Chloe." Izzie tipped her head. "If you want another to consider, you should talk to Hunter. He's investigating the murder of some wealthy recluse whose art pieces were stolen. Maybe your column could cover how valuable art is a target for thieves."

My eyes widened. Hunter might not appreciate us blabbing about an ongoing case, especially when murder was involved. "If you go with that topic, I'd keep clear of Hunter's investigation and research other art theft cases."

"You have a point." Penny opened her phone and fingered the screen. "I'll hold off getting in touch with him, but I'm making a note to remind me. Got lots to research. Thanks for the suggestions, ladies. I'll keep your business in mind for future columns." With a wave, Penny left.

I snapped my head around to frown at Izzie.

"What? Hunter didn't say to keep quiet about the case," Izzie argued.

"You know he can be touchy. Penny is persistent, firing questions one after another. Not a wise idea."

Her fingers popped up, one at a time. "One, she can handle herself. Two, if Hunter doesn't want to talk, he won't. And three, she researches like a dog after a bone. Who knows what she'll uncover about art theft?"

I blinked. "You want to use her to help us figure out more about the hidden painting? Clever. If the painting was stolen, that is. We don't know yet." I dropped into a chair and leaned against the back.

"That's why we need to connect some dots." She picked up her phone again. "Time to call Camilla."

While she was busy finding dots to connect to give us more clues, I walked to the storage room in the back, sat down, and contemplated whether to call Hunter. Secretly, I hoped Izzie was right, and that my hunch proved to be some underlying paranoia I developed on occasion. On the upside, that affliction kept me alert and focused on my surroundings to anything problematic happening. Downside? I often ignored the warnings and dove right into trouble. The question was, would asking Hunter for help open up a dialog I wasn't ready to have. At this point, making him worry about what could be nothing and revealing too much about Martin and the mysterious paintings wasn't wise.

I opened my contacts folder and scrolled until the name Marcie Marsen filled the screen. A couple of months ago, I'd made a friend at the DMV. She loved crime shows, visited mystery room events, and was a loyal listener to the police scanner she owned. That's why she recognized my name when I renewed my license. She knew about the previous murders in Whisper Cove and how news articles had mentioned the Abbington name. Questions begging for details fired out of her mouth at such a speed that I could barely keep up. At the end of our conversation, she promised to help me in whatever way she could, if there was another murder. At the time, I prayed for that never to happen again. So far, so good.

"Hello, if she's free at the moment, may I speak to Ms. Marsen?" The muffled sound of voices, as if someone covered the phone with their hand, took a minute.

"This is Marcie Marsen. How can I help you?"

"Hi, Marcie. It's Chloe Abbington. We met a couple of months ago when I came in to—"

"Oh my!" Her rather husky voice took on a high pitch as she squealed.

Clearing her throat, she added, "I absolutely remember you, Miss Abbington."

"Do you have a second to maybe help me?"

Her voice lowered to an almost whisper. "Is this about a murder? You know I'll help you. Whatever it is. This is exciting. Me working on a murder case. Oh my word. Wait until I tell my mystery chat group. They'll be so jealous."

I closed my eyes and leaned against the wall, nearly tipping over my chair. Before Marcie could ramble on, I had to stop her from getting too enthused. "Please, Marcie. I, that is, there hasn't been a murder. I mean, you never know, but this is about a mystery. And you could help me solve it." There. Hopefully, she wouldn't be too disappointed.

"Oh. Right." Her voice deflated, but only for an instant. "Still, if it's a mystery, I'm in. What do you need?"

"Would you check on a license plate number for me? I think someone was tailing me this morning, and I want to know who. Just in case. Maybe it's nothing, but…will you help?" I held my breath.

"Of course. Maybe the driver is a criminal, you know? A dangerous criminal. Can't be too careful when you're sleuthing. Right?" She continued with the whispery voice.

My lips curled at the corners as I smiled. Maybe Marcie Marsen had chosen the wrong career path.

"Hold on. The license plate is past renewal. Looks like somebody has been a naughty driver."

My breath hitched. "Do you have a name? I'm sure the police would love to bring him or her in for questioning."

"And for breaking the law. The Department of Motor Vehicles doesn't look kindly on this sort of infraction." She tisk-tisked into the receiver. "That's weird."

"What? What's weird?"

"Evelyn Parsell is the registered owner of the vehicle, only Evelyn died a year ago. There's no record of that black van's title being transferred to another owner."

"Oh, boy." My shoulders dropped.

"If you ask me, we've found your criminal element in the mix of whatever mystery you're trying to solve."

"Yeah, you might be right. Now, if only I can figure out who that person is."

I thanked Marcie and promised to keep her in the loop. That's if Izzie and I could discover what that was. Right now, all we had is questions.

Chapter Four

"Great news. Camilla is in the area and stopping by to talk about the paintings. She got so excited when I told her about the Vermeer reproduction." Izzie walked into the storage unit. At once, she scowled. "What's wrong? You look upset. Let me guess. The news from Hunter disappointed you. See? I told you no one was tailing us."

I shook my head. "I didn't talk to Hunter, and you're wrong. It's worse than that." I explained my conversation with Marcie.

"If the driver is shady, that opens up all sorts of possibilities." Izzie nodded.

"Like was our tail after the painting?"

"Jumping to the answer you hope for won't help. We need proof."

"Yep. Now, when is Camilla getting here?" I pushed the topic of who our tail was to the back of my mind as we walked to the shop's front.

Izzie tapped her watch. "Any minute now."

As if those words were Camilla's cue, the door opened and a woman wearing a stylish print dress breezed in, her heeled pumps clicking on the hard floor. "Ladies! So, so very thrilled to see you."

I grinned. With Camilla, every exclamation of her emotions included superlatives. I leaned to take my turn for her air kisses to the cheeks. "Nice of you to drop by. I'm sure your schedule is booked solid."

"Chloe's right. We read about you all the time. You're in high demand to speak at all those art functions," Izzie added.

Camilla waved her arm. "It's part of the job. Some days I wish I hadn't written the art history series and just focused on research." She took a seat next to me. "Now, let's see those photos. I'm so very curious."

I pressed the photo app on my phone to open the gallery. "I wish these were as good as viewing the paintings in person." I handed the phone to Camilla.

Izzie and I remained quiet, giving our art expert time to study the photos. Murmured words about how beautiful the seascape was, the dedication to tiny details, the chosen colors were all she said.

After what seemed like hours, she glanced up and smiled. "Well, ladies, I do have news for you. The seascape is one of maybe three paintings by this artist. At least as far as I've heard. I visited the gallery where his works are displayed and spoke with the gallerist. Anyway, it's a sad story, an absolute tragedy." She settled back in her chair. "He was from a wealthy family. Living on a huge estate just outside of Buffalo. He held such promise as an artist. Unfortunately, he died a short time ago in a car accident. Unfair, isn't it? How fate wields such cruel acts. I remember the headlines. 'Art collector turned artist meets an untimely death.' His family was devastated and have withdrawn from the public eye, which is a great loss to the art community. They have done so many philanthropic events, donations, anything to promote art."

I blinked. This story matched what Martin had told us, except his version ended with murder, not an accident. I glanced at Izzie, whose eyes widened.

Camilla tipped her chin. "By the puzzled expressions, I'm guessing you don't know. I'm surprised since the news was in all the papers and on television. Clive Whitmore is your mystery artist." Her voice lowered. "I've heard rumors that his parents insisted their son was depressed for a while and that his death was most likely a suicide. At their request, though, the final police report determined it was an accident with the slippery roads causing him to lose control." She shrugged. "Guess we'll never know the truth."

My mind took another direction, and I reasoned aloud. "What about the truth coming from people who knew him? Other than his parents, some might know more about Clive and his emotions before his death. Did he have a girlfriend or a wife? A close connection to some in the art circle?" I stood and paced the room.

"He does have a sister, I believe." Camilla snapped her fingers. "Arthur Storing. He wrote a biography on the Whitmore family. I met him once at some event. The man bragged about knowing the family better than anyone. All their secrets, likes and dislikes, he even hinted at some unscrupulous behavior they'd carefully kept hidden."

Izzie raised her brows. "Really? Does he live close by?"

I swallowed, recognizing the gleam in Izzie's eyes. We might have within our reach the first clue, or possibility of a clue, that could make sense of the hidden painting and why Clive Whitmore had involved Martin in whatever drama went on in the artist's life, right before his untimely death. I felt it too. That tingling of excitement surged through me. I gave my arms a vigorous rub. "We should speak with him, even if it's only by phone."

"Actually, he lives in Buffalo. At least, the last I heard, which was only this past January. Let me see." She rummaged through her oversized leather bag and pulled out a card. "Yes, here it is. The man was bold enough to offer a handsome sum if I wanted to hire him to write my biography."

Izzie nodded. "Thanks, Camilla. Do you have any thoughts about the Vermeer imitation?"

"Oh yes. We call that one a pastiche. Any work of art that imitates the style of another artist. It's quite good, actually. Those brush strokes, along with the contrast of light and dark. Whoever painted this captured much of Vermeer's qualities. The added touch of a jeweled crown is interesting, though odd. Perhaps the artist wanted to keep some originality. Or the crown could be a message."

"I had the same idea. Have you come across any artists who paint in the style of Vermeer? From the baroque period, wasn't he?" I pushed for more answers.

"I'm afraid I haven't. Not even on my trips to the Netherlands, where he's from," she said.

"We're wondering if it could have been stolen, and the thief planned to sell it." Izzie glanced my way.

"Even if we could identify who painted it, without a provenance to authenticate, no buyer would be interested. Sorry, I can't help you there, either."

"We can at least speak with Storing. Who knows? Clive Whitmore may have told him more. Thanks again, Camilla. You've been a huge help." Izzie shook her hand.

Camilla shouldered the strap of her bag. "Anytime. I love a juicy mystery when it involves art." She pointed at my phone. "Hold on to the seascape, if you have it. It will be worth a lot in a few years. The story of Whitmore's tragic life should add six figures to its value. Trust me."

After she left, I turned to Izzie and whistled. "Now, that's something I never expected to hear."

"You bet. Think about it. In a matter of less than twenty-four hours, we've learned about a possible murder, a wealthy family with rumored unscrupulous behavior, and, of course, our Vermeer that's correctly referred to as a pastiche. Looks like we're in the middle of another mystery, possibly a murder mystery. Trouble seems to follow us like a virus that can't be cured." She moaned. "I'd be more enthused if Martin wasn't involved somehow."

"Is he, though?" I pointed. "Sure, he suspects Clive was murdered, but beyond that, what does he know? He won't say. Isn't that why he's looking for answers?"

Izzie slumped in her chair. "You might be right. I'm projecting without any evidence, but that's why we're paying Arthur Storing a visit, as soon as possible."

"Agreed." I smacked the chair. "Tomorrow is another day. Right now, I'm thinking about Mom's turkey tetrazzini. I'm starving."

"Hold on. We have a crate or two to unpack, and I want to call Willow." Izzie glanced up at the clock. "It's what? About noon in California. She should be at home with her brother."

Willow Stone was our talented employee. A true natural and without any formal education in art. Izzie had hired her instantly after her interview. Willow was inspiring, creative, and had a strong mind. I suspected Izzie would ask her if she knew about the Whitmores. After all, she came from a wealthy family, too. Not that you'd know it. Humble and totally without prejudice. In fact, she'd emancipated herself, severing family ties both physically and financially. It was a brave act and hopefully one she wouldn't regret later on. During the past couple of weeks, she'd gone to visit her younger brother in California to help out since his wife was seven months pregnant and confined to bed rest. He was the only family member she liked.

By the time I finished unpacking the crates and stocking the shelves with supplies, Izzie wrapped up her call to Willow. "Well? How are things with her sister-in-law?" I wiped the sweat off my brow.

Izzie sat and nibbled on her nail. "Willow wasn't home, but I spoke to Zeke. Solena is doing well. The doctor thinks she might deliver early."

"I frowned. "What's wrong? Is she okay?"

"He sounded worried. Even though the bed rest is helping, the little guy must be anxious to make his debut." Izzie nodded.

"Oh boy. Let's hope Solena can hang on another couple of weeks. That way, she'll be closer to the nine-month mark." After wiping my face, I dropped the wet towel into the laundry bag.

"That's what the doctor said. He ordered Solena not to get upset or move from the bed, which makes her daily routine a challenge. Anyway, I told Zeke to have Willow give us a call." She brightened. "I did get an answer we needed. Turns out the Stones are close friends of the Whitmores."

"Wow. How about that? Did he give any details about Clive?"

"Only that he'd met him once or twice. And like Camilla mentioned, there's a sister. No other family besides the parents. Oh, and how they hosted lots of parties to raise money for the children's art centers and schools." Izzie grabbed her laptop and bag off the front counter.

"They sound like good people, which puzzles me. Why would Arthur Storing claim otherwise?"

"Lots of people have secrets, Chloe. And some are very good at hiding them." Her eyes narrowed.

"Still, whatever Storing tells us might not be totally the truth. We don't know him or his character."

"We don't know the Whitmores, either."

"In other words, we take what Storing says with a bit of skepticism, and then prove whether he's right."

"Or wrong." Izzie flipped the light switch. "Let's close up. We've done enough for one day."

The ride home was quiet with each of us buried in our own thoughts. Mine perused all the details of the past two days. We didn't have a chance to share the highlights of our trip over the weekend. Upon finding the painting from Martin, the conversation about our travels had been hastily put aside. It was quite the homecoming. I had a hunch that hearing Martin's claim about Clive Whitmore being murdered and then having someone with a shady background, who more than likely tailed us this morning, were only the start of what was to come. After all, wasn't that the way things went in our lives? Whether we stumbled onto the messy details or intentionally put ourselves there, it didn't matter.

I powered down the window and stuck my head out to take a deep breath. A cool, refreshing breeze carried from the lake. The scene of Chautauqua offered me a sense of peace. I smiled at the mallards nibbling at the aquatic plant life, their heads dipping below the surface. In the background, boaters were fishing or taking a relaxing cruise, barely causing a ripple on the glassy water.

Izzie pulled the vehicle into the drive and killed the engine. "Home, at last." She opened the door and stepped out, stretching her arms in a yawn. "After dinner, I might go straight to bed. That's how exhausted I am."

"I hear you. I'm thinking the same thing." I followed her up the porch steps and into the house. A loud moan escaped me as I sniffed the aromas of turkey tetrazzini and freshly-baked ciabatta rolls.

Since Mom and Dad had eaten early and gone next door to play cards with our neighbors, the Bixbys, Izzie and I opted for a casual meal, sitting in front of the television while we gorged on casserole and ciabatta. We kept the conversation light, which made me happy. A reprieve from mystery and mayhem, even if only for an evening, replaced by sharing fun memories of our past, was just the prescription to rejuvenate the brain cells, as Granddad Abbington used to say.

Izzie waved her hand. "Hey. Turn up the volume. They're giving the local news."

I clicked the volume on the remote and studied the images on the screen. A reporter stood on the street. Behind him was a gated brick wall, and at a far distance, you could see a large house, more like those mini mansions found in pricier neighborhoods. Next to the reporter, a brick pillar etched with the name Whitmore in the center was clearly visible.

"Authorities will be investigating the victim's death, but from all the reports given by our sources, the conversation coming from inside the precinct is that this is a homicide. Hold on." The reporter placed a finger to her earpiece and nodded.

I nearly choked on a bite of tetrazzini. The name Whitmore couldn't be a coincidence. And the brick mini mansion with turrets anchored at either end looked sort of familiar. I'd seen photos in the society section of the Buffalo newspaper, hadn't I?

"Holy wow. Chloe, it can't be." Izzie gasped and dropped her fork on her plate.

I put a finger to my lips. "Listen."

"For those of our viewers just joining us, Erin Whitmore, age thirty-three, was found dead early this morning from a fatal gunshot wound. Police are not yet releasing any more details, but foul play is a strong possibility. Those living in the Buffalo area know the family is well-respected in the business community, having invested and developed enterprises that keep building our economy. Stay tuned to our news station for any updates as they develop."

I muted the remote. "Izzie, this is…" I couldn't find the words.

"Scary? Disturbing? How about dangerous?" She set her tray aside and scooted forward in her seat. "Chloe, what has Martin gotten us into?"

"Possibly murder." I stiffened. "And maybe more than one."

Chapter Five

Early this morning, I'd attempted to contact Hunter, but got his voicemail. I left the message to call me back. With this many details to explain about Martin's painting, as well as our involvement and suspicions of being tailed, a voicemail wouldn't work. There'd be questions from his end. Lots of questions. I needed to speak with him directly. After the news about Erin Whitmore's death, aka Clive's sister, the same Clive who painted the seascape and had hidden another painting underneath, I was overwhelmed and panicked and worried. Izzie and I were out of our depth on this one.

I had a hunch that with a prominent and powerful family like the Whitmores involved, Alan Whitmore would pressure the BPD to summon all the help they could get, including outside authorities like the Chautauqua County homicide division, which meant Detective Hunter Barrett, for one. If Erin's death was a murder. What if the incident was an accidental shooting? I scrunched my nose and pointed at my reflection in the bathroom mirror. "Why do you always assume foul play? Oh, that's right. Maybe because in the past year and some months you've found yourself smack in the middle of murder cases. More than a couple, in fact."

I washed my face and dried off. For the moment, I needed to take a step back and wait for those updates. Running a brush through my hair, I then hurried downstairs. Before opening the shop, Izzie and I were following Camilla's advice, making that trip to Buffalo and visiting with Arthur Storing. When Izzie called him last evening to explain we were interested in Clive Whitmore's art and life story, he was enthused to meet and promised to be at home until noon today, giving us plenty of time to chat. With any luck, we'd learn something relevant to fill in details of the story behind the painting, and help out Martin in the process.

By nine a.m., Izzie pulled to the curb in front of Storing's apartment building. The structure showed signs of neglect with its splintered window frames and overgrown weeds in the flower garden. Yet, there was something quaint about the structure. The gabled roof with its triangular frame, a trellis attached to the front, woven intricately with devil's ivy, and several dormer windows with dark green trim to match the color scheme gave the building a definition and character that stood out from all the other homes on the block. A little TLC was all it needed.

Arthur answered his door in seconds. He welcomed us with a wide smile and hearty handshake. His slender frame, black-rimmed glasses, and pencil stuck behind one ear portrayed the perfect image of an author. In my mind, I pictured him sitting behind his laptop, pounding away on the keyboard, gulping copious amounts of coffee, and snacking on some salty or sugary treat. Once inside, I glanced around his apartment. My eyes popped. Clutter was everywhere. Books were stacked in unsteady piles, and numerous dirty dishes next to them drew the attention of a furry feline. A huge whiteboard situated to one side was covered in illegible scribbles. Today's newspaper lay on the table. The front page headline, one in bold letters, made me shudder. *Erin Whitmore Found Dead.* I had guessed the outcome, but a huge part of me prayed I'd be wrong.

Arthur waved an arm as he cleared the sofa for us to sit. "I apologize for the unsightly mess. I rarely get visitors. Besides, my current project demands—oh, never mind. That's not what you came to hear." He waved again. "Please, have a seat. Would you like something cold to drink? I'm sure it's been a long drive from…" He frowned. "Where did you say you live?" Giving his head a vigorous shake, he added. "It's not important. Would you like a drink? I asked you that, didn't I?"

I blinked. My hopes for something productive coming out of this meeting were taking a nosedive off that proverbial cliff. Watching Storing as he scrambled for clean glassware and a pitcher of iced tea, I wondered how scatterbrained he might be. Or nervous. That thought gave me pause.

He handed each of us a glass, sat in a comfy recliner, and sipped his own beverage. He cleared his throat and nodded at the newspaper. "Such an awful demise. Erin could fill the room with her enthusiasm and good humor. We spoke often, you see." He swiped the corners of his eyes.

Izzie set her glass on the floor, the only clear place to do so. "I'm sure it's a shock to family and friends. Do you have any idea what happened? I mean, we've heard about your Whitmore biography. You must be close to the family."

I pursed my lips. Nothing like getting to the point of our visit. I hoped Izzie didn't scare Storing and end the conversation.

Storing adjusted his glasses and frowned. "I know more about them than they know about themselves. Every tiny detail I could glean from their private lives, every accolade they've received, high moments, low moments, the most intimate snippets, found their way into my work. No one, and I do mean no author, could've accomplished what I've managed." He sighed. "Not one, but three biographies, over ten years of research, and yet none so lucrative. My profession has not been as profitable as I'd hoped. Still…" He glanced at the stack of books next to him. "This project will make a difference. Big money involved. I could finally move out of this dilapidated living quarters, even purchase a decent car. Do you know how embarrassing it is to ask your brother to borrow one of his vehicles because you can't afford the repairs on your own?" He threw up his arms.

"I'm so very sorry you're dealing with those problems, but maybe talking about the family will help? Sharing all your knowledge with us, I mean." Izzie's gaze dropped to her lap. She lifted her glass off the floor and took several gulps.

I shifted in my seat. The transformation from spacey and confused to lucid and sharp happened in an instant. It seemed Arthur Storing had many layers to his personality. I was both amazed and perplexed.

"Would you listen to me sounding like someone having a mental break-down?" He chuckled with a headshake. "I apologize. Whatever questions you have, I'm sure I can answer."

"Great." Izzie's tone lifted. "How about we start with Clive, Erin's brother, who died in a car accident. What can you share about his life, especially his artwork?"

"I can tell you this. His death was not an accident. I believe Clive, the dear soul, was murdered." The narrowing eyes and stern voice punctuated his words.

"How? Why are you so sure it was murder?" I asked, leaning forward.

"Erin was so convincing. She came to visit last week. Frustrated. Frightened. I worried about her that day." He adjusted his glasses. "She claimed Clive wasn't depressed, contrary to what their father told the press. In fact, he was excited about an art piece he'd acquired and planned to sell to some prominent buyer who was willing to pay a significant amount. The conversation Erin had with her brother had been only a few days before his death." He shrugged. "Why would someone that excited for his future kill himself? I agree with Erin. This was no accident."

My mind reeled. What if the hidden painting was the item Erin spoke of? I knew Izzie wouldn't want to tell Storing about our discovery, not until she talked to Martin. "So, did Erin tell you details about Clive's valuable piece?"

Storing shook his head. "I'd asked, but she refused to say more, claiming she needed more proof, first."

"I don't get it." Izzie leaned back against the sofa. "Why was he so thrilled about making money from the piece? Isn't the family wealthy? He has all the money he needs at his fingertips."

Storing wagged his finger. "That's where you have the wrong assumption. Clive didn't get along well with his parents. In fact, Alan Whitmore threatened to cut him out of the will if Clive didn't join the family business."

"What sort of business?" I asked.

"Where do I start? There are so many. Most of them in the art community. Their gallery on Main Street. It's quite successful. Their charity business raises millions, and all that money is doled out at events. Everything from children's art schools to grants awarded to emerging artists are just some of those. Oh, and the Whitmores have heavily invested in local businesses, and their stock options are substantially profitable. Clive told me his father wanted him to take over the charity functions as CEO. Because of his interest and involvement in art acquisitions, Alan figured it would be a perfect fit. Clive wanted nothing to do with it. He was determined to make a name for himself, outside the Whitmore legacy."

"That seems admirable." I thought of Willow and her severed ties with the Stone family wealth. Sharing the same blood didn't always mean you shared the same ideas. Or in her family's case, lack of a moral code. Willow couldn't accept that.

"I told him it was foolish. Stepping into the role his father offered would give Clive's future the security that people seldom have." Storing sighed. "He despised his father. Any olive branch would always be rejected. Such a sad affair."

I rolled my tongue across my cheek. An unpleasant theory took over my thoughts. What if the tension between father and son had led to a heated quarrel? Hurt and angry, Clive could've driven his car so recklessly that it crashed and ended his life. Maybe an accident, but the guilt Alan Whitmore would be carrying around was unimaginable.

Storing's voice grew raspy. "I can't help thinking about Erin's search for answers about Clive's death. What if that led to Erin's own demise? There are many unsavory people in the world, and art collectors are among the most ruthless when it comes to possessing what they most desire. They don't care how it's done. Trust me. They'd do everything to keep their secrets. Possibly with all the noise Erin created, announcing to anyone who'd listen that her brother was murdered, someone wanted to silence her permanently." His eyes narrowed. "Even her parents demanded she stop spreading that story."

Izzie shifted in her seat. "You certainly are a writer, Mister Storing. Your ideas about what could've happened are kind of disturbing."

"Maybe so." He tapped his head. "Writers are the ultimate observers of the world around them. I'd think as an artist, you'd understand."

Izzie stood and grabbed her bag. "Thank you for your time. You've given us a lot to think about."

"It was a pleasure," he said.

As we walked to the door, Storing called out.

"You might try contacting Martin Steele. Clive often spoke of their days in college and years after graduation as they collaborated sometimes in art acquisitions. Steele could have a theory or two about Clive's death." He paused. "Come to think of it, during our last visit, Clive mentioned he planned to gift one of his paintings to Steele. A seascape of the northeast coast with a lighthouse in the background. Quite impressive."

I lifted my brow. "You've seen it?" This was as close to the topic as I'd want to get. For the moment, I'd keep a skeptic's eye on Arthur Storing. He could be filling us with lies, rolling them out as quickly as his author imagination was able.

"No, but Clive showed me photos," he explained.

"We'll be sure to follow up on that. Thanks." Izzie tugged my arm to get out of the apartment.

"Do you think his mention of the painting was intentional? Trying to get our reaction? I really don't trust the man," I said as we stepped outside and headed for the Land Rover.

"Coincidence? A pretty big one, if that's the case." Izzie clicked the remote and hopped into the driver's seat. "My suspicions spiked when he suggested the parents or some shady art collector as the possible cause of both Clive's and Erin's deaths. I mean, talk about being obvious. Storing has accumulated plenty of knowledge about the Whitmores, but that doesn't qualify him as an expert detective who solves crimes. As if that's likely." She snorted out a laugh.

I blinked. "You mean like we aren't detectives who solve crimes?"

"Oh. Yeah, but that's different." She fired up the engine and traveled across town.

"How? We are artists who run a paint party business. We snoop and somehow manage to find clues that lead us to discovering the bad guys. We aren't wearing badges or police uniforms. We're just amateurs sticking our noses into trouble." That admission sounded worse when I said it aloud.

Izzie stopped for the red light, drumming her fingers on the steering wheel in an irregular beat without comment.

"I think we should keep an open mind. You know, like Detective Winsell said this past summer when he solved Lana's murder. 'Everyone associated with the victim is a suspect until you prove otherwise.'"

"Fine. We consider Storing's suggestion." She turned, eyes widened. "In that case, Storing is a suspect, too. From the sound of it, he spent plenty of time with Clive, as well as with Erin."

"What about motive?" I pointed at the light, which turned green.

"I need to think on it. I'm sure one of us will come up with something." She punched on the gas pedal, and we sped out of Buffalo and into the outlying suburbs.

"You missed the exit." I looked over my shoulder.

"I want to drive by the Whitmore estate and see what's happening."

"Happening? Now? The murder was yesterday morning."

"And the investigation is just getting started. I'm sure of it. Besides, maybe we'll spot Hunter. You must be wondering if he's part of the case, right?" Izzie tipped her chin.

Of course, I wondered. Selfish as it seemed, Hunter being involved would give us an advantage. Without a word, I studied the navigation screen on the dashboard. "Turn right at the next road. We should reach the Whitmore estate within a half a mile."

"Chloe, do you think Martin knows about the hidden painting? What if he's involved with one of those shady people Storing talked about?" Izzie's voice strained.

I clenched my jaw, not wanting to admit how I suspected as much. "I think Martin must have convincing reasons for not telling us the whole story. We should trust him and give him the benefit of the doubt." I waved an arm. "There. Oh wow. It's huge."

I took in the sight of the estate, which, by the looks of it, included several wooded acres. The brick façade, situated at the front of the property, had a porch covering the entire front with columns of pillars like those seen in southern plantations of the Old South. A balcony on the second floor appeared to lead out from what could be a master suite. The French doors were ornate with wrought iron framing the sides. A half-circle drive and a flower garden with a fountain in the middle decorated the entrance.

Almost at once, I spotted Hunter's car. Off to the left and near the front door, several men stood by. One of them, tall and fit with light brown hair, brought a smile to my face. Quickly, though, my expression sobered as I reminded myself of what brought us here. Hunter had been summoned to help solve Erin Whitmore's death. A queasiness rumbled through my stomach as I thought of all the people who could be involved, whether guilty or innocent. And Izzie's close friend, Martin Steele, was somehow right in the middle.

Chapter Six

On the drive home, my phone dinged with a message reminder. "Great. I forgot about Max's vet appointment this morning. Sorry." I winced at Izzie.

"No problem. Brody and I are stopping at Bob's Barbecue for some sandwiches and Fizzy Orange drinks before heading to the shop, which will probably be around noon. Besides, we have most everything ready for the children's paint party tomorrow evening. I can use the time to clean the shop. It gives me the perfect opportunity to think about all we've learned and maybe come up with some ideas on how to move forward." Izzie turned into the drive.

"Thanks. You're the best. Oh, and can you buy me a bottle of Fizzy Orange drink? I'm dying for one of those." Bob's place was the best for barbecue sandwiches and curly fries, but his family recipe for Fizzy Orange was famously known throughout Chautauqua County. We stopped there for lunch or late-night snacks at least twice a week.

"Sure thing. Tell Max I said good luck and to relax. You know how stressed he gets with those appointments."

"Relax? That will never happen." I snorted. "Hey, maybe he should enroll in your yoga class. Give him some tips on how to let go and decompress."

"Ha! I'm sure the instructor would have something to say about that."

"I bet." I opened the car door. "See you in a couple of hours."

Ten minutes later, with Max leashed, I stepped outside. The weather being so pleasant and the vet's office close by, I decided to walk instead of drive. Reaching the end of our street, I aimed our steps north on Whisper Cove

Boulevard. With only a brief stop at Spill the Beans for coffee, we reached the office of Dr. VanCamp on time.

Max pulled on the leash in the opposite direction.

"Eh, eh. Not a chance, buddy. This is your yearly checkup. Besides, if I remember correctly, you're only due for two of the…" I didn't finish my comment. Max had an extensive vocabulary list stored in his brain. The words shot and vaccine triggered his anxiety. "How about a treat? I have peanut butter biscuits in my bag." Many words on his list prompted happy responses, too.

After a short, half-hour visit and a healthy canine report in hand, we headed home. Max tugged at his leash, as if anxious to distance himself from the vet's office. Deciding we could use the exercise, we moved at a jogger's pace and made record time. As we hit the front porch, I bent over to touch my knees and took several breaths. "Hold on a minute, would you?" I sat on the porch swing while Max spread out on the cement floor, panting.

My phone jingled in my pocket. Pulling it out to glance at the screen, I smiled. "Hey, Ross. How's married life? Hope you're giving that bride of yours some attention. Lawyering isn't everything." Ours was a complicated relationship. We were a couple, then we weren't, and after a failed attempt to win me back, he found someone who was willing to accept his time-sucking career as an attorney in a prominent New York law firm. I just couldn't be that person. I needed someone to put me first sometimes. Not always, but at least remember to show up for our dates, spend romantic evenings with me instead of using what little free time he had playing poker with his buddies. Maybe I asked for too much, but that's the way I felt. It was important to me. Still, after all we'd been through, we kept our friendship, spoke now and again, shared our problems, our celebrations. We were comfortable with each other, flaws and all.

"Funny. Miranda and I are doing great, like two lovebirds, all cozy and affectionate. How's that for a picture-perfect life?"

"I can't tell if you're sincere or sarcastic." I reached down to scratch the top of Max's head, then handed him another treat.

"Totally sincere. She's my soulmate."

"Ah, rub it in, Ross Thompson." I laughed.

"Speaking of soulmates, how is yours?"

"Hunter is great. In fact, he's working a murder case right now. That's why I'm glad you called. I want to pick your brain."

"Should have known. You always ask for my legal expertise," he chided.

"Because you are the best, most successful attorney in all of New York. Right?" I couldn't help teasing him. Bragging about all his wins was a favorite topic of conversation with him.

"Enough. You're making me blush."

"As if. Do you remember one of your cases a few years back when you defended that client who was charged with art theft?"

"Of course, I remember every case I win. Charlie Pickling. Common petty thief who got caught in the wrong place at the wrong time. I shut down the prosecution so fast, it made their lead attorney embarrassed. What a show."

I ignored the boast and moved on. "And the real thieves were never caught?"

"That's right. Plus, the painting was never recovered. I have to admit, the authorities did everything they could to solve the heist. Not an easy case. In fact, did you know only ten percent of stolen art is recovered? Too many greedy collectors out there who are willing to pay a huge sum for art. They don't care if it's stolen. Why are you asking? Does this case involve art theft?"

"Not exactly. At least I don't think so." I explained the details of Erin's death, the painting behind the painting, and the untimely demise of the artist who also happened to be a Whitmore.

"Whew." Ross let out a breathy whistle. "That's quite a bit of tragedy for one family in such a short amount of time. Do you and Izzie think the hidden painting is from a heist? Chloe, you need to be careful. People in that world are ruthless and dangerous."

"So I've been told. Have you heard anything about stolen art recently? If the hidden painting was part of a heist, maybe it was a local incident. Or maybe someone was arrested for buying collectibles illegally? I'm planning to search through newspapers online but haven't had the chance to yet. I was hoping you might put me on the fast track." I recalled Hunter's case about the wealthy recluse's murder and her stolen art collection, which gave me hope.

Max hopped up on the swing, placing his head on my lap. I reached in my bag for the water bottle and collapsible dish I always carry on dog walks and poured him some.

"None that I've heard about, but I'll check with guys in our firm. One or two handle this kind of crime case exclusively. If I find anything worth sharing, I'll get back to you."

"Great. Thanks. I need to get ready for work at the shop. You take care and give Miranda my best."

I dropped my phone in my bag and gathered the bottle and dish, then led Max inside. I hadn't much hope that Ross would offer any leads, but I had to try. In my estimation, if the hidden painting was stolen, and assuming Clive did business with dealers and clients all over the world, the theft could have happened in another country, any country. However, the buyer could be local. And of course, this was all supposition. No evidence, only a painting purposefully hidden for reasons we didn't know yet. I groaned as I hung my bag on the hall rack and unhooked Max from his leash.

"Chloe? Is that you?" Mom called from the den.

I walked into the room where she sat behind the desk. Her eyeglasses rested on the opened ledger that contained the family financials. Dad insisted on keeping records the old-fashioned way. No computers involved. It drove our accountant crazy with frustration. Obviously, he loved computer technology.

"Having fun?" I teased. Taking a seat in one the leather chairs, I squirmed to get comfortable.

She scowled. "Doing the monthly finances is not what I'd call fun. I wanted to give your dad a break from it all, this time around. You know how he gets."

"You mean when Aunt Constance decides to redecorate her entire house or take one of those guided tours of Europe and spends a huge chunk of her inheritance? Yeah, I do know."

Mom sighed. "It is her money. As your uncle David's widow, she rightfully inherited his share of the family's wealth. Joe can't argue with that. Not legally, anyway."

David, Dad's only sibling, died a couple of years ago and left Aunt Constance depressed and alone. She filled the void by spending money in amounts that nearly caused Dad to have a mental breakdown. He tried reasoning with her on occasion, warning the money wouldn't last forever at the rate she spent it. We all thought that warning fell on deaf ears.

"How was your walk? Did Max hold it together at the vet's?" She relaxed in her chair and sipped from her glass of iced tea.

"The walk was pleasant, at least. As for Max, you'd never imagine a dog his size could yelp so loudly." I laughed and relayed in detail how the visit went, and also a brief overview of my conversation with Ross. I had a hunch she needed a moment's distraction.

"I've heard Max when the neighbor's dog chases him into the backyard. The noise is enough to make me reach for earplugs." She chuckled.

"Yep." I pointed to the newspaper lying next to the ledger. "Did you read about that tragedy? Erin Whitmore was so young. It's such a pity."

"It certainly is. I called the Whitmores this morning to give them our condolences. I feel so badly for them. I mean, losing two children? It's not the natural order of things, is it?" Mom kneaded her temples with her thumb pads.

I straightened. "You know them?" I'd never heard her or Dad mention the Whitmore name, or maybe I just didn't listen when they did.

"I'm surprised you ask. They're in the patrons of the arts group we belong to. Monthly meetings give us plenty of time to air our personal problems as well as talk about art projects. Alan and Faith Whitmore are well known and respected for their support in the art community, but they have their share of troubles just as anyone else."

I suspected her comments were somewhat of a defense or argument to squash any rumors I would bring up that put the Whitmore family, especially Alan, in a negative light. She should know me better. "We spoke to someone who knows the entire family very well. He thinks Alan is lying about Clive's death and insists that father and son didn't get along."

"I don't know anything about that. What I've witnessed was a mother and father who love their children, who, by the way, could be difficult. Erin used to come to the meetings. She was extremely critical, often baiting Alan and Faith into an argument in front of all the members. Not respectful at all." Mom shook her head.

I shrugged, then stood. I didn't have any proof about Alan Whitmore or any of the Whitmores. "It's just a rumor. I should change and get to work. Izzie will be expecting me." I rubbed Max's furry head. "Give this little guy some TLC. He could use it after this morning's appointment."

Kate laughed. "I'd be glad to. Tell you what, Max. As soon as I'm finished here, we'll go out to my work shed. You can be the subject of my next masterpiece."

I took a quick shower and pulled on pants and a sweater before leaving for work. My mind raced over Mom's comments. She and Dad were friends with the Whitmores. Somehow, that made any search Izzie and I attempted, and where it took us, awkward. Our parents were part of the equation. In investigating Erin's murder, Hunter would take a look at those close to her, which included family. Alan and Faith Whitmore would be at the top of the list. He'd follow up on every aspect of their lives, including their involvement with the patrons of the arts group. Unfortunately, that would mean questioning Mom and Dad. Not that they had anything to hide.

I squinted at the sunlight streaming through my windshield as I drove across town. Shifting the Mazda into park, I killed the engine. After a few deep breaths to slow my heartbeat, I exited the vehicle and jogged over to our shop entrance. I stopped short when I spotted a familiar face. Brody was shutting the front door as he stepped out.

"Hi, Brody. You and your girlfriend have a nice brunch date?" I smiled as Brody blushed. He always blushed when someone called Izzie his girlfriend. I thought it was cute. And so were his looks. Blonde hair, ocean blue eyes, and a smile that would grab anyone's attention. But looks aside, he was kind and generous, always willing to help people. Izzie fell for him after one date.

He brushed a hand through his hair. "Hey. Good to see you, Chloe. Izzie told me about what you two have been up to or maybe into." His face grew stern. "Be careful. I don't want anyone harming two of my favorite ladies."

I pointed to my chest. "Me? Izzie? Never. And what about your mom? Isn't she one of your favorites?" I teased.

"Funny. Of course she is." He checked his watch. "Look, love the conversation, but I'll be late for work if I don't leave now." He jogged backward to his car. "Take care. And don't forget what I said."

"I absolutely won't forget," I shouted after him, then turned to go inside.

"Hey, there you are. I started to worry. Is Max okay?" Izzie shoved her laptop aside, handed me my bottle of Fizzy Orange, then rested both arms on the counter.

"Absolutely fine. Well, maybe a little irked at me for taking him to get those vaccines, but he'll get over it." I chugged some of my drink, then explained running into Brody and stopping for a quick conversation.

"Okay, what's wrong? I can hear something off in your voice." She straightened.

"Not getting anything past you, am I?" I plopped in one of the chairs. "Did you know about the Whitmores being in that art group Mom and Dad belong to?"

Izzie shook her head. "I might've heard them talk about the group, but don't remember them dropping any names. Why? What did they tell you?"

I explained the conversation I'd had with Mom and my concerns. "I'm sure Hunter will question their relationship with the Whitmores, and that worries me."

Izzie came from behind the counter and sat next to me. "But why? Questioning people who know a potential suspect is something Hunter would do. Heck, we've even done it. Somebody looks guilty, and you figure the people that person hangs out with might have useful information that helps solve the case. Not a reason to worry. I think you're overreacting."

"I guess, but Mom seemed defensive, like she's totally on the Whitmores' side. What if we find dirt on the family? I know people say not to kill the messenger, but that's exactly the reaction you get." I wrinkled my nose. "I don't like this. Maybe we should step back and let Hunter and the BPD handle things."

"Are you kidding? If we do nothing and Martin ends up being charged with art theft or something even worse, like murdering Clive or maybe Erin, I won't forgive myself."

I snorted. "Now, who's overreacting?"

Izzie squeezed my hand. "I am, aren't I? Let's take a breather from talking about murder and art theft. Okay? I've got some news to share that'll lift your spirits." She sprang out of the chair. "Our shop is going to be featured in *America's Arts and Crafts* magazine next spring. Can you believe it?"

I blinked, my jaw worked to find a way to speak.

"I know, right? Paint with a View in a popular magazine. Doesn't get too much better than that."

"Wait. Our shop. Our little business in *America's Arts and Crafts* for people all over the country to read about? What's the catch?" My eyes narrowed.

"No catch. Artisan Alley and its craft shops have been noticed. Some reporter visited here the summer before last and pitched the idea to his senior editor." Izzie avoided my stare and grabbed a handful of bookmarks to hang on the rack.

"Uh, huh. Not just our shop. Still, it's great exposure," I said. In fact it was a great boost for all the shop owners.

"Anyway, I got the call from Paul Wayne this morning. He's the reporter. You remember him. He was the one who bumped into one of our easels and made all the others topple over like dominoes. Not a shining moment, but he laughed anyway."

"Oh, that's right. You were gushing and blushing all over him. Poor Brody. He didn't even know he had competition." I giggled.

"Hey! I wasn't that bad. Besides, I hadn't met Brody yet." She lifted her chin.

"I'm sorry. My mistake." I jabbed her in the side. "But you were flirting. Maybe that's why he's coming back. And he called you personally to deliver the news. My, my, my." I tisk-tisked with a head shake.

"Oh, stop. You've had your fun. Let's get to the finishing touches on the children's party event." She peeked out the window. "I see some customers heading this way. I'll deal with them while you grab supplies from the back."

"On it."

The shop remained busy until closing. Lots of customers searching for creative gifts or signing up for the future events streamed inside and out like a revolving door. By the time I flipped the sign to announce we were closed for the day, I was more than ready to call it quits and head home.

Leftovers were warming in the oven with a note on the kitchen counter. Mom and Dad were attending their pottery class in a neighboring town this evening. I smiled. No one could claim our parents lived a boring life. They were always doing something or going somewhere.

"I'm taking a shower first. You don't mind eating alone, do you?" Izzie waited at the bottom of the stairs.

"Nope. I'm gonna grab a plate of leftovers and plop on the sofa to watch some comedy movie. I need a good laugh." I slipped out of my shoes and waved as I walked down the hall.

I practically drooled at the sight of Dad's homemade chicken pot pie. After today's events, comfort food, no matter the carb overload, was the recipe for relieving my stress. That and watching a romcom. Bonus points if the leading man was Ryan Reynolds or maybe Chris Pratt.

I snuggled in my comfy spot on the sofa and clicked the remote. Before I could mute my phone, a familiar ring made me sigh. Tired as I was, I needed to speak with him. "Hunter. I'm glad you called."

"Sorry it took so long. Too much on my caseload barely gives me time to sleep or eat."

I set my plate on the end table. "I figured you were busy. Speaking of cases, have you heard about Erin Whitmore's shooting?" Why admit I already knew? Questions about how would lead to the details of visiting Andrew Storing and driving past the Whitmore estate. Time for that later, I decided.

"Not only have I heard, I'm a part of the investigation." He paused to yawn. "Like I said, too many cases. I'm fine, though. My duties are limited to questioning anyone associated with the victim."

"Oh?" My heart skipped a beat as I thought of Mom and Dad. "I bet that will uncover plenty of family drama."

He sighed. "Already has. According to Alan Whitmore, Erin's father, there's plenty. He highly suspects a family acquaintance by the name of Martin Steele is our perp."

I gripped the phone. This was not the turn I expected things to take. "Why is that?"

"For one, Erin accused Steele of involving Clive in a shady art deal. Alan also confirmed that Steele visited the estate to see Erin that evening. That's damning evidence since the coroner estimates she died six to eight hours before Alan found her the next morning."

I shifted in my seat, attempting to process what Hunter told me. If Alan claimed Martin visited Erin at the estate that night, how did he know? Did he see Martin? Or did someone else tell Alan about the visit? I straightened. "If Alan or someone else saw Martin Steele at the estate, why would Steele murder Erin there and then? Sounds kind of reckless and unlikely to me."

"I'm not finished. Alan also told us that he'd had a conversation a few weeks ago with Clive, that's the son, who seemed despondent and anxious at the time. When Alan asked him why, Clive said he was having trouble with a business deal, but asking a college friend for help. And guess who that college friend is? Martin Steele. That's a lot of coincidence not to mean something worth investigating. Now, if only I could get a hold of Steele. He's hard to track down. His assistant has been uncooperative, to say the least."

I struggled. Inside my head, the battle of how much to tell him or not tell him was fierce. "Alan could be lying about Martin Steele to make him look guilty. I'd also take that into consideration."

"All right." He drew out the words. "What gives? You seem to be defending a man you don't even know. You don't, do you? Chloe?"

"Fine. I do know Martin Steele. He's a friend of Izzie's. Close friend, actually." I recapped the story of Clive's painting, Martin's request, and everything else that had transpired in the past few days, including the visit with Arthur Storing and the person driving the black van, who I suspected tailed us. "So, you see? Storing's description of Clive's mood is the total opposite of Alan Whitmore's. What about that?"

The silence put my nerves on edge. I braced myself for whatever Hunter would say, and he would say a lot.

"Let me understand. You and Izzie found a hidden painting that may or may not be stolen. Instead of contacting the authorities, you took it to a storage facility when you were tailed by someone unknown, then proceeded to question a potential witness rather than contact the authorities, which you know is tampering with a murder investigation. How am I doing so far? Is there anything else you want to add?"

I winced. He was upset. Of course he'd be. I would be, too, if I were officially part of the investigation, which I wasn't. "No. Nothing else." My voice had grown raspy. "Look, he's Izzie's friend, and you know how loyal she can be. Always wanting to help the people she loves. That's Izzie."

"I don't want to argue. We've been down this road too many times. I'll just say you should be careful. If you find yourself in a dangerous situation, and you usually do, stay clear and call me." His voice had grown calm.

"You got it."

"Text me Storing's address since you have it."

"Yep. Doing that right now."

"And let Izzie know I want to speak with her about Steele."

I gulped. Izzie would be furious with me. "Sure. She's probably in bed, but I'll tell her. Maybe wait until later tomorrow? She's not so much of a morning person." What I really needed was time to explain what I'd done and apologize to her beforehand.

"I guess I should say thanks. You've given me some leads, but—"

"I know. Don't worry. We'll do our best to avoid stepping on your investigative toes and mucking up things." He and I both knew that promise wouldn't last. The sigh he made told me he was thinking the same.

"Goodnight, Chloe."

"Night." I dropped the phone in my lap and massaged my neck. On one hand, I felt relieved. I hated keeping secrets, and Hunter deserved to know what we'd been up to. I stared at the plate of pot pie and clenched my stomach. On the downside, telling him wasn't as easy as I'd hoped for.

I picked up the plate, meal untouched, and carried it to the kitchen. Max's nails clicked on the hall floor as he kept pace with me. Telling Izzie what

I'd done wouldn't be any easier. "We can deal with that tomorrow. Right, Max?"

"Deal with what?" Izzie shuffled along behind me.

I nearly dropped my plate. The time for a conversation about Hunter had just moved to now.

Chapter Seven

She hadn't taken it well and went to bed, totally peeved at me. Apparently, I was disappointing and couldn't keep a promise. How was I supposed to choose? My boyfriend or my sister, one of them, was bound to get hurt. Somehow, I'd managed to upset both. I'd reasoned with Izzie. Hunter would've found out another way, and that was worse. Honesty was the best approach. My argument was weak and failed to hit home.

I tossed shirts out of the drawer, searching for the one to match my capris. I mulled over our conversation, or maybe I should say argument, taking place a few hours ago. Even the warmth of sunlight bathing my bedroom hadn't cheered me up.

I set Max on the floor and we made our way downstairs and to the kitchen. Conversation buzzed. I recognized the voices of Dad and Izzie. She was laughing at something Dad had said. That was a good sign. The scowl on her face as I entered the room wasn't. "Morning. Looks like a day full of sunshine and hope." Sort of cheesy, but I tried out the cliché of positivity anyway.

Izzie turned up her chin. "Guess we'll see."

Dad frowned. He stood and wrapped one hand around his coffee mug, and the other clutched his newspaper. "I'll give you two girls the room. Seems you need to work something out."

Wise man, I thought. He knew when to avoid female drama. I waited until the patio door shut. "Come on, Izzie. Staying mad at me isn't productive. Besides, we have too much to do at the shop. Giving up time to have a gripe session won't help, either."

She dropped into a chair. "You're right. I'm just—frustrated as I can possibly be. I tried calling Martin's cell this morning, thinking maybe Phillip had it wrong and there would be reception available wherever the heck Martin is." She buried her head between folded arms.

"Straight to voicemail?"

"Yep. I can't even guess what he's thinking or doing. What am I supposed to tell Hunter when he asks?" She lifted her head with a worried expression mirrored in her eyes.

I took her hand. "You tell him the truth. Tell him about Martin's request, how he believes Clive was murdered, that someone is following him, and he's scared enough to go in search of answers. Tell him that."

Izzie pulled her hand out of my grasp. "Thanks, Chloe. You always manage to talk me down."

"Great. Now, let's get to work." I crooked my arm through hers and led us to the front door. "I have some fantastic ideas for the fall schedule to share." I reasoned taking her mind off Hunter and Martin by talking business would work.

"Oh! The cornucopia theme? Yes. And how about Halloween? The jack-o-lantern event we did last year earned all kinds of praise." Izzie's eyes brightened.

"Sounds like we have a plan for two events. Let's brainstorm more when we get to the shop. Okay?" Satisfied, I hummed a tune as I drove the Mazda across town.

The morning hours moved into afternoon without us noticing. We kept busy, stocking shelves, rearranging the wall of canvases, and putting a new display in the picture window. I suggested one task after another to fill the day until Hunter showed up. By three o'clock, I worried he wouldn't come. If my anxiety was building, I couldn't imagine how Izzie was feeling. Turned out, I read the situation totally wrong.

The chimes rang to announce a visitor. I turned as Hunter stepped inside. "Good afternoon, ladies."

A shorter figure stepped from behind him. My breath caught. I should be accustomed to meetings with Detective Winsell, especially after this past spring when he took over the case involving a dear friend of mine. We'd certainly gotten to know each other, but I was just as uncomfortable. Why had he come along with Hunter, I wondered.

"Chloe." Hunter leaned in for a peck on the cheek. He turned and smiled at Izzie. "How are you, Izzie?"

"I'm great. Thanks for asking." Izzie's tone oozed with confidence.

I frowned. She appeared calm, even happy. If this was an act, she'd win an Oscar. "Detective Winsell. I'm surprised to see you," I said, facing him.

He raked fingers through his messy mop of hair and adjusted his rumpled coat. "You and me both, Miss Abbington."

"Winsell has been working on the case I told you about. The one with the murdered wealthy recluse?"

"Right." I waved them to the closest seats, then moved to flip the sign on our door and close the window blinds. There was no point in arousing customers' curiosity.

"Why? Are Erin's death and that one related?" Izzie's eyes widened. "Are you suggesting both were murdered?"

"Izzie, please. Let them finish. I'm sure that's not the case." I sank into my chair and gripped my knees, fighting the urge to let Izzie's overactive imagination get to me.

"I'm more focused on the art theft, actually. That's why I plan to keep informed about Erin's case. I've heard Clive Whitmore's painting might somehow be involved." Winsell scooted forward in his chair, gazing at Izzie. "Tell us about Martin Steele."

Izzie blinked. "He's my friend and business partner. We've known each other for a little over two years, but mostly on a professional basis. The truth is, he doesn't talk about his personal life, like family or friends. He asked me to paint a reproduction of a famous painting he owns. That's when we became acquainted." She squirmed in her seat and stared at the floor for a second. "During that time, we talked often. I told him about my plan to open this business. He offered to become a silent partner." She shrugged.

"Izzie, what Detective Winsell means is, what can you tell us about the painting he gave you?" Hunter said.

She looked miserable. I couldn't help but jump into the conversation. "It's like I already told you on the phone last night. Martin sent the painting to our house with a note asking Izzie to deliver it to an art storage facility in Buffalo. Izzie spoke to him later when he called. He explained that someone was following him and didn't want to take a chance of the painting being stolen."

"So, he asked me to do it, figuring no one would suspect and follow me, too," Izzie continued.

"He never mentioned anything about the hidden painting," I said.

"Really, he might not even know. I haven't been able to speak with him since we found it." She wrung her hands.

"We only discovered it because Max scratched the seascape on top and revealed the hidden one. A Vermeer pastiche." I nodded.

Winsell's forehead wrinkled. "Remind me, who's Max?"

"My dog."

"Yes, and pastiche? That's…"

"A painting done in the style of another artist. In this case, Vermeer," I explained.

"I see. And do you have any idea where Mister Steele is at present?" Winsell asked, his gaze volleying from me to Izzie.

"We only know that he left on a trip to search for answers. That's what Phillip told us," Izzie said.

"Phillip, his assistant." Winsell tapped his pencil.

"You also said on the phone when we talked earlier that Steele believes Clive Whitmore was murdered. Did he say why he thinks that's the case?" Hunter asked.

"No, he didn't say." Izzie squeezed her eyes shut for a moment, rubbing the back of her neck. "Look, I'm frustrated and worried. Martin has always been honest with me. Whenever he thought I was making a bad business decision, he would tell me. Whether it hurt my feelings or not, he believed in telling the truth." She opened her eyes.

"If he's certain Clive was murdered and that he is being followed, then I believe him. And don't think for one second that Martin is capable of taking someone's life. Not Erin's or anyone else's. That's all I have to say." Izzie stood.

As if that was her cued gesture for them to leave, Hunter and Detective Winsell got up and walked to the door, but not before Winsell issued a warning that if Steele contacted either one of us, we should let Hunter or him know at once.

Hunter paused and turned to face me, leaving Winsell to walk on ahead. "I can't tell you the details of Erin's death, but please don't let your guard down or trust anyone who may be involved. No point trying to stop you and Izzie from doing what you always seem to do—" He shook his head. "Just text me the photos you took of the paintings. Okay?"

"Sure. I'll do that." I held open the door as he cleared the walkway. My hands were shaking. "Call me if you learn anything."

Hunter nodded and picked up his pace to catch up to Winsell, who'd already reached the road.

"Glad to get that over with." Izzie pulled a bottle of water out of the mini fridge and guzzled the contents.

"I'm surprised Winsell came along. Do you think there's more to Erin's death than what they've told us?"

"Of course, there has to be more. I have a hunch this all centers around stolen art. That's what the two cases have in common." Izzie tossed the empty bottle in the trash.

"Agreed." I pointed. "And that hidden pastiche also connects Clive to the situation."

"What puzzles me is Alan Whitmore. He's so adamant that Martin killed Erin. It's like he's pushing the narrative to make the police focus on Martin."

"On Martin and not on Alan. Clever move."

"Yep. If only we could get closer to the Whitmores. Their estate is definitely off limits. I'm sure the BPD has officers guarding the place, day and night." Izzie snapped her fingers. "We need to speak with Storing again."

"Why?"

"Because he might know what Alan and Faith do away from home, how they spend their time, where and when."

"Places they go and friends they might visit. Yeah, that just might work." I rubbed my chin.

"Then maybe we run into the Whitmores and have a conversation, do a little investigative interview of our own."

The satisfied gleam in her eyes told me she'd recovered after the visit from Hunter and Winsell. Not much could keep her down for long. I had to admire the amount of courage that took.

I peered out the front window, following a flock of geese as they swooped down to the sandy shore. "I think we're forgetting the easiest path to meeting the Whitmores."

Izzie tilted her head. "Oh?"

"The art group Mom and Dad belong to? They've been asking us to attend one of those meetings. I say we should go the next time."

"Absolutely should. Meanwhile, we talk to Storing. First thing tomorrow." Izzie checked her watch. "Almost showtime for the kiddos. Got your earplugs ready?"

I laughed and turned the sign on the door once again and pulled the blinds open.

* * *

"I think every nerve in my body is fried. How do parents do it? Every day, all day and night. It's exhausting." I stretched my body side to side and yawned.

"They do it by attending events like this one, or maybe they drop off the kids at the grandparents' house for the weekend. No doubt, those breaks save them." Izzie closed her laptop. "Ready? It's getting late."

The clock ticked and inched toward nine. For obvious reasons, clean up after the children's event took longer than usual. I'd used up a whole roll of paper towels and several rags, along with a half bottle of spray cleaner. "Ready." I grabbed my bag and jacket and followed her out the door.

Chapter Eight

I skirted around the several bags of clothes cluttering the front hall. Once or twice a year, Mom insisted we all clean out our closets and dresser drawers to find usable items for charity. It was a worthy cause, so I didn't mind taking the time to complete the task. Izzie, on the other hand, got quite emotional. Parting with anything in her wardrobe was like saying goodbye to old friends. Silly to me, but just one more example of our different personalities. For every ten pairs of shoes she owned, I had maybe two. Utility was my main focus. That and comfort. Put me in a fancy dress and you'd find colorful sneakers on my feet to throw the ensemble off. But hey, if I didn't have to worry about my feet suffering, I was satisfied.

Once in the kitchen, I filled Max's bowl with kibble, poured coffee and creamer into my travel mug, and snatched a bagel off the plate before heading out to the screened-in porch to find Izzie. Mom and Dad had left the house to sail around the lake before putting their boat into storage.

"Morning!" I muffled the greeting while chewing on a bite of bagel.

"It's about time," Izzie said. She raised her mug and sipped.

"I'm ready when you are." I held up my coffee mug and bagged what was left of my bagel. I avoided letting on the real reason I'd come downstairs later than usual.

Izzie stood. "We should be at Storing's door by nine. He told me that he has a busy schedule but can spare an hour to speak with us."

"Did you tell him why? He could've answered our questions over the phone, you know." I admitted the long trips were becoming tiresome.

"If he has suggestions on where to find Alan or Faith Whitmore, I want to follow up quickly while we're in Buffalo. Two birds with one stone, Chloe." She climbed into the Land Rover. "Besides, seeing his reaction to our questions might hint at whether he's telling us the truth or maybe holding something back."

"Why would he do that? He doesn't seem the type to hide anything," I argued.

She shifted her gaze to me for a second. "Are you kidding? If he's writing another book on the Whitmores? And I'd bet my last nickel he's planning on a true crime spin, especially after Erin's murder. You know as well as I do that authors are notorious for guarding any details about their writing before it's published."

"Huh." I leaned back in my seat. "Why didn't I think of that?" I turned. "Here's a thought. While we're at his apartment, we should search for clues as to what he's writing."

"Yes! You make an excuse to use the bathroom, sneak into his office or whatever room he might store his research in, and see what you can find."

"From what I was able to see, his living room is his office with those stacks of books and reams of papers all spread out on the tables and furniture." I scowled.

"Maybe he keeps the valuable research tucked away in the back. Never know." Izzie nodded.

"Nope. That's going too far. There's a huge risk of getting caught. Besides, it seems intrusive to go through someone's bedroom. Let's keep the search to the living room."

"Fine." Izzie sighed.

With very little traffic to slow us down, we turned onto Storing's street a little before nine. A trail of cars lined both sides for a couple of blocks. A sign posted at the corner announced a yard sale. Plenty of tables filled empty spaces on front lawns and driveways. Fortunately, Izzie managed to squeeze into an empty spot a few hundred feet from the apartment building.

"Okay, let's get to it." Izzie marched on with determined steps to reach Storing's building with me close behind.

Storing answered within seconds of ringing his doorbell and ushered us inside with a wide swipe of his arm. "Ladies, it's so nice to see you again."

Was it my imagination, or did he emphasize the word *again*? I managed a stiff smile. "I hope we're not imposing too much. Izzie and I have some questions about the Whitmore family, and you are such an expert. We thought you'd be the perfect choice to give us answers." There. Buttering up his ego might get better results. "You mind?" I gestured at the sofa to sit.

"Please do. I don't mean to sound impatient, but I have an important meeting to get to by ten-thirty."

Izzie sat across the room in a chair next to the end table filled with a stack of books, spines and titles facing her way. "Oh, we won't take much of your time, Mister Storing. Promise."

"We have a confession to make." I proceeded to explain our association with Martin Steele and how we wanted to help him. "Sorry we weren't totally honest with you the other day. We needed to discuss the matter first."

Izzie leaned forward. "You see, Martin and I are very good friends. I know him to be honest and very loyal. His concerns about Clive's death and other matters involving the Whitmores are worth pursuing."

Storing glanced at his watch. "Do you know where Martin is? Perhaps I can speak with him."

"We don't know." Izzie spoke up first. "In fact, my worry is that he's gone in search of answers, and it might be dangerous wherever that's taken him."

"I see. Well, what can I do to help?"

"Can you make any suggestions as to where we can go to speak with Alan or Faith Whitmore? It's obvious we can't visit their home. Security detail by the authorities would turn us away," Izzie said.

"You're right about that. Let's see." Storing tapped his lip. After a few seconds, he picked up a notepad resting on the floor next to his chair. Flipping through several pages, he then nodded. "The horse stables. Fuller's ranch. It's only a couple of miles outside of town. Faith goes there to ride her horse every Tuesday and Friday morning. So, looks like this is your lucky day. She should be…" He glanced at his watch. "Arriving a half hour from now. I'd say if you hurry, you can catch her before she saddles her horse. A pretty mare whose name escapes me at the moment." He stood. "Anyway, she'd be easier to talk to. Alan is a stiff bore who seldom engages in small talk and never about business or personal issues, unless it's with one of his employees, accountant, or attorney. I know because I've tried."

"Are there any other places she frequents? Like a hairdresser or fashion shop or something?" Izzie asked.

"Hmm. I can't help you there. The stables are your best bet."

"Really? I'd think there are other places she's talked about. Visiting with friends, maybe at a country club? Places like that." Izzie pressed.

Storing shook his head and led us to the door. "None with a set schedule. Look. I'm sorry to rush you, but I need to get ready for that meeting."

"Thank you, Mister Storing. Good luck with your meeting." I waved as we hurried down the stairs.

I powered down the passenger window as we headed out of town. "Why did you keep pushing?"

"What do you mean?" Izzie flipped the turn signal.

"Is there a reason you don't want to visit the horse stables?"

"All right." She smacked the console. "I'm afraid of horses. Okay?"

"Since when?" I tossed around thoughts of the past and memories of our childhood. Did we ever ride horses together? Sure, plenty of water activities filled our days. Most kids living along the lake did that. "When did you ride horses? I don't remember you going with me."

"A couple of years ago. I dated this guy who owned a horse ranch. He loved those animals and coaxed me to come riding with him." She shuddered. "Never again. And don't you dare ask me to tell you what happened. It's too scary to repeat."

I held my breath to keep from laughing. "So, who says we're riding? This will be a short conversation with Faith. If it makes you feel better, I can talk to her while you stay in the car. You won't have to look at a single four-legged creature while we're there. Okay?"

Izzie grunted her reply and drove to the stables in silence.

I tallied a mental list of questions to ask Faith Whitmore. Chances were she'd know any secrets her daughter had been keeping. Daughters confided in their mothers about romance and boyfriends. If Erin had a relationship with a man or woman, that could be a lead.

As we pulled onto the dirt drive leading up to the ranch, I peered out the window to see around the dust kicked up by the Land Rover's tires.

A tall, rather lean woman stood by the barn and alongside a gold-colored mare. She threw a saddle over the horse's back and tightened the straps underneath. A man dressed in jeans and a cowboy hat appeared from inside the barn and stepped toward the woman. They were engaged in conversation as we stopped a few feet away.

Izzie powered off the engine. "It's showtime. Good luck." She patted my arm.

"Thanks." I hopped out of my seat in the Land Rover and approached the person I immediately recognized from newspaper photos as Faith Whitmore. Composed demeanor in her eyes as well as her posture. The man next to her had to be maybe twenty years younger than her. Closer to my age, I guessed. I plastered on a grin. "Good morning. Looks like a great day for a ride."

Almost at once, I felt uneasy as her apparent judgey gaze slid from my head and down to my worn sneakers with mud on them. Boy, was I stereotyping the wealthy, or what? I shifted my stance and cleared my throat. "Yes, well, I'm not here to rent a horse. My name's Chloe and—"

"Are you a reporter or with the police? I've told you people I have nothing to say." Faith turned her back on me to climb on her horse.

"No! I'm not either one. Missus Whitmore, please. Will you give me a few minutes?" I scrambled to think of how to persuade her. "My parents are Kate and Joe Abbington. They belong to the same group, the patrons of the arts, as you and your husband. Right?"

Her face warmed, and a genuine smile erased the sour expression she'd had only a moment ago.

"Of course. I should've recognized you. Your mother shows me photos of you and your sister all the time. She's quite proud of you. Tells me stories of—" She dismissed continuing her comments with a wave of one gloved hand. "I'm sorry for being rude. The press has been relentless. They can't get past the security detail stationed at our estate, but that won't stop the phone calls. I've unplugged the landline, yet somehow they know my cell number. If I could escape, go on a trip far away, I would." Her eyes glazed over for a moment as she stared out across the field next to the barn.

I cleared my throat again.

"Would you listen to me?" She sniffed. "My problems sound petty, I'm sure. With all the horrible things going on in the world, it's selfish of me to complain. Now, what would you like to ask me?"

Her horse snorted and nudged Faith's arm with its nose.

"I have an idea." She stroked the animal's neck. "You'll ride with me. That is, if you ride? That way, Sunny can get her morning exercise, and I can answer your questions without losing my time with her."

"Great! I do ride, but is there a horse in the barn that's maybe more easygoing than Sunny?" It had been five years since I last sat in a saddle, but Izzie and I needed some answers.

"Samuel, would you bring out Lucky Lou?" Faith suggested.

Once we were on the well-worn trail, I eased into Lucky Lou's pace and relaxed. The canopy of tree branches hanging over our path shaded us from the sunlight and chilled the air. Thank goodness I'd worn my jacket. Refocusing my thoughts, I shuffled through the mental question list I'd prepared to decide on where to start.

Faith slowed Sunny's gate to let me catch up and ride alongside her. "I suppose you've watched the news and learned as much about our daughter's death as we have. I'm not sure I can be of any help. If answers are what you're looking for?" She turned her head to study me. Her brows inched closer together for an instant before she relaxed with a sigh. "My husband can be abrupt. If you caught the interview where he insisted Martin Steele murdered Erin, you most likely agree with me. He's angry. More often nowadays, I'm afraid. Too much pressure in the family businesses makes him tense. But this…" She reached forward to stroke Sunny's mane. "We've lost both our children, now."

My heart sank. Guilt washed through me in remembering the reason why Izzie and I wanted to speak with Faith. This woman was hurting, and I came here to fish for clues when I should be consoling her. "I'm so sorry, Missus Whitmore. Maybe we don't talk about what happened and enjoy our ride instead? It is really a beautiful morning for it." I attempted to smile.

"No. No, I have something on my mind, and you might be the perfect one to share my thoughts with. First, tell me why you came to talk to me. Did you know Erin?"

I hesitated. Admitting I knew Martin might anger her and get me kicked off the property. After all, what if she agreed with her husband about Steele being the killer? On the other hand, if I told her about Clive's painting, I'd have to explain where it came from. I slumped in my saddle. I was at a loss.

"Of course." She lit up with a smile. "Your parents must have told you about her and how close we'd all become, especially after so many years being in our patrons of the arts group. I'll never forget how your parents treated Erin. Kind and understanding, even when she'd blow up or complain how those who had everything didn't give enough to those who had next to nothing. I bet they asked you to help us, didn't they? It makes perfect sense."

My jaw dropped for an instant before I snapped my mouth shut. The temptation to spill the truth lingered, but what she suggested could have happened in time. Mom and Dad would want justice and to help their friends, the Whitmores, wouldn't they? And with Izzie and I deep in the middle of other murders, snooping on the sly to solve them, we'd offer to help. That made perfect sense, too. I straightened and lifted my chin. "I'm glad you understand. Thank you. Now, can you think of anyone in Erin's life who gave her trouble or wanted to harm her? I confide in my mom all the time. It's what mothers and daughters do. Right?"

"We do." Her eyes teared, and she blinked them away. "Or did. I'm sorry. This is still so emotional for me. Let me just…" She reached inside her jacket pocket and pulled out a tissue to wipe her face. "Carry some with me everywhere. I can't seem to stop turning into a blubbering fool."

I was close enough to extend my arm and touch hers. I squeezed. "Don't apologize. I'd think you weren't human if you didn't cry."

"Thank you," she sniffed. "Now, as to who would harm Erin, I can think of one person. Her boyfriend, Peter Fanning. I never trusted him. He's the perfect example of a gold digger. I warned Erin, but she wouldn't listen. I suspected him from the moment Erin introduced us. He only used Erin to get access to our inner circle of friends, parties, and events that are by invitation only. I watched him. He worked the crowd like a pro."

"What do you mean? Worked them how?"

"For business. He needs investments to open his own restaurant. Or so that's what I've heard from some of our friends. He's a chef, you see. A very talented and dedicated one. I'll give him credit for that, at least." She tugged the reins to pull Sunny to a stop. I did as well. "Erin and Peter fought constantly. That was a bad sign, too. Then, finally, she had a change of heart. I'm not sure what exactly happened, but a few weeks ago she came to me. Crying so hard, she barely got the words out. She told me her plan was to break up with Peter. She couldn't trust him any longer. I got no more out of her."

Faith snapped the reins, and Sunny resumed her steps. "When the time was right, she said. That's when she'd break it off. I can't help but worry. Maybe he got angry and…"

She didn't finish, but I knew what was implied. I shuddered. "Did Fanning have a bad temper?" It seemed reasonable to ask.

"Erin claimed he did. He started most of their arguments and said some awful things to her. I don't understand why she stayed with him for so long. Now, it doesn't matter."

"I guess sometimes couples stay together for the wrong reasons. Maybe Erin loved him so much, she believed their relationship could eventually work." I thought of Ross and all we'd gone through. The long hours at his office, not giving us enough personal time together, and thinking all was fine. Until it wasn't.

"Life teaches us that love can be truly blind. Then, one day, you wake up to find it's too late to change things." She turned to stare at a hawk as it swooped down to catch its prey.

I swallowed, unsure if she was still talking about Erin. "Is there anything else you found odd about her behavior in the weeks before she died?"

"Well, I caught her going into Alan's study once or twice. When I asked if she needed help finding something, she seemed defensive and dismissed the incident by walking away without any explanation."

"Was her behavior odd, though? Is that what you mean?" We approached the end of the trail that had looped around the property. The barn was in sight, and I was running out of time to talk.

"Nothing emotionally wrong, but going into the study was definitely odd. You see, Alan insists that's his space and says it's off limits. We should never trespass. That's the word he uses. Trespass. Silly, really, but Alan is very territorial and possessive. So, it makes sense for him to behave in that way."

I dismounted from Lucky Lou, and Samuel took the reins from my hands. "Do you have any idea why Erin would trespass, as he puts it, in your husband's study?"

"Not a clue." She took off her riding cap and gloves. "I don't believe there's anything else to say, and I'm parched. Would you like to come inside the gatehouse for a beverage?"

"Sorry." I hitched my thumb over my shoulder. "Izzie's waiting. Thank you, though. I don't suppose you can tell me where to find Peter Fanning? I'd love to ask him a few questions."

"He works as the head chef at The Bistro in Buffalo. You'll find him there from morning to night. Like I said, dedicated to his job." She turned toward the gatehouse. "Have a good day, Chloe. Tell your parents I said hello." She paused briefly, not taking a step away. "Be careful. I'm not sure what happened to end our daughter's life, or why. What I am sure of is that digging into the matter could be dangerous for you. Stay safe."

I waited, watching her until she disappeared through the gatehouse doorway. Pivoting on my heel, I hurried to the Land Rover and pulled open the passenger door.

Izzie bit down on her lip. "Well? Did she help? Please tell me she gave you something to go on."

I nodded as I buckled my seatbelt. "We need to make a visit to The Bistro and have a conversation with Peter Fanning. Faith seems to think he had reason to murder Erin."

Chapter Nine

I unboxed the fish replicas we'd ordered for the gyotaku painting event scheduled for tomorrow evening. Izzie discovered a Florida local using the Japanese art form on a trip she'd taken to the Keys. Her suggestion to take the guests fishing and use our catch for the paint event caused me to wrinkle my nose and gag. I couldn't imagine smelling up the shop with the stinky odor that would probably linger for days. Customers wouldn't like it either. We'd lose business, I'd argued. Fortunately, that logic worked on Izzie.

Izzie examined the rice paper sheets as she removed them from the shipping package. "These should hold up without tearing. We can't afford to use up extra supplies because of mishaps."

Always about saving a dollar, or in this case, every cent. That's the way Izzie's mind worked. Of course, she was right. Owning a business meant accounting for every dollar spent or earned. Our accountant loved her meticulous behavior.

I waved the silicon fish in my hand. The rubberlike replica flapped back and forth. "Would you look at this? I swear, at first glance, you'd think they were real but without the smell."

Izzie tapped her forehead. "I'm doing it again, aren't I? Complaining about money issues."

I laughed and reached out to squeeze her hand. "Wouldn't be you, if you didn't worry about keeping us afloat, maintaining a budget, things like that."

"Speaking of maintaining, while you stepped out to get us lunch from Bob's Barbecue Pit, I did a bit of research online. Peter Fanning isn't exactly a fan of social media."

"Oh?"

"No accounts like Facebook or Instagram, but The Bistro has a website. He's listed as head chef, just as Faith told you. I only found one home address. It's in North Tonawanda, which is only a half-hour commute to Buffalo. So, he probably still lives there. I couldn't pull up any previous places of employment. Without having that software the police use, my search ended there." She huffed while stacking the box of rice papers and shelving the bottles of sumi ink that she'd found a good deal on. "I also checked and found Erin's Facebook profile. She doesn't post anything, though. At least not in this past year."

"Society page of the newspaper?"

"Photos of him and Erin at charity functions. Lots of photos but no leads. He's good-looking. I can see why Erin had been initially attracted to him."

I slid the unopened box of brayer sponge brushes across the counter. "Then we make a visit to the restaurant and speak with Fanning to find out more."

"Can't tomorrow. We're too busy."

"What about Sunday? We're closed that day for some housekeeping and bookkeeping. We can finish up by noon and head to the restaurant. What do you think?" I finished counting the number of fish replicas.

"Agreed." She drummed her fingers on the counter. "I keep coming back to Clive's painting, or I should say paintings."

"How so?

"Why hide the Vermeer lookalike? Where did he get it? Did he steal it? Buy it on the black market? Are one of those reasons why he didn't sell it?" She drummed her fingers harder. "And why, for heaven's sake, give it to Martin? I mean, if it's a hot item, sending it to Martin was so very wrong. It's put him in danger, like with those criminal types who'd do anything to—"

"Izzie, stop." I laid my hand over hers to silence the movement. "Martin can take care of himself. I'm sure he's dealt with shady players in the art business and knows how to handle them. Besides, carrying on like this won't help him."

"You're right. Absolutely right." She heaved her chest to inhale, then breathed, slow and easy, to steady herself. Walking to the storage room, she added, "I'm going to try calling him again. If anyone knows Clive's comings and goings, where he did business, and the clients he had, Martin would."

I slumped in a chair as she disappeared beyond the doorway. Even though I did what I could to diffuse her worry, secretly, I felt the same as Izzie. Clive had a strong reason for hiding the painting, then putting it in Martin's hands. Valuable? Most likely. Sought after by criminal types? I'd bet my career on it.

I lifted my head to gaze at Izzie as she returned from the back. I didn't need to ask the obvious. Her discouraged look with those downturned lips and the slow, labored pace as she walked over to me said it all. Martin hadn't answered.

"Here's another idea." I sprang out of my chair. "You know I'm having dinner this evening with Hunter and his mom. I'll show Meredith the photos. She could have something important to say that would help us." Hunter always bragged that his mom had an encyclopedic knowledge of art, from prehistoric rock art to post-modern contemporary. Even Hunter picked up on a few facts while growing up. I was both impressed and surprised. A detective who knew his art. What could be a better match for me?

"Thanks, Chloe. I know I sound like a whiner and talk like the glass-is-half-empty kind of person, but I do appreciate everything you're doing to help. Honestly." Izzie sat on the stool and rested her elbows on the counter. "How about we take a look at those photos you took of Clive's painting? There's something about it that puzzles me."

I swiped through my photo app until the image of the seascape showed, then handed the device to Izzie. "What are you thinking?"

"The lighthouse." She pointed. "You know how artists choose an object to be the focal point of their paintings? We do it all the time. Remember that art class we took together in high school? The pastoral scene with the barn?"

"Right. The barn became the focal point by using bright red color."

"While the sky and background colors used were neutral and somewhat drab."

I squinted. "The lighthouse is dark and drab, while the ocean water and sky are painted with vivid colors. Yeah, so?"

She tapped the screen. "So maybe Clive wanted the lighthouse to be some sort of clue. Or maybe to distract from other objects in the painting. Like that ship. Or the seashells on the beach. Or how about the rocks along the side?"

I sucked on my tongue. "But a clue to what? Really, Izzie. I think that's a stretch. The painting is a lovely seascape. That's all. It served its purpose to hide the Vermeer pastiche, which is the one we should be concentrating on."

Izzie slid the phone back to me. With her arms crossed, she rested her chin on them. "Just a thought, and kind of crazy because I'm desperate. All I can say is your boyfriend's mom better come up with something. Otherwise, we've got little to go on."

I checked my watch. "I should go home to change." I grabbed my bag and jacket before stepping toward the door. I hated being a downer and dismissing her interpretation. I turned the knob, but paused to look back at her. "I'll bring up your focal point theory and see what Meredith thinks. Who knows? She may agree with you."

Three hours later, I slid inside Hunter's car, ready for the drive to Meredith's home just north of Fredonia. I'd loaded the photos on my laptop and carried the device with me. Of all the possible reactions I could have, the notion of meeting Hunter's mom overloaded my insecurity.

As Hunter concentrated on the road, I withdrew inside my head, replaying every conversation my mind created, praying I'd choose one that worked and didn't make me sound like a babbling idiot. I couldn't handle embarrassing Hunter in front of his mom. He'd forgive me, even if I didn't. A well-respected art history professor, someone who'd been praised in newspapers, academic journals, and been given awards? Who wouldn't be intimidated?

Hunter nudged my shoulder. "Why so quiet? You've barely said a word since we left your house."

I lifted my shoulders and frowned. "I'm figuring out how to address your mom. Do I call her Professor Barrett? Missus Barrett? Or would using her first name be rude and presumptuous?" I twisted in my seat to face him.

"And what if I say something stupid or ignorant?"

Hunter chuckled. "Call her Meredith. I've spoken of you so often that she feels like you two are already best friends."

"Really? You're messing with me, aren't you?" I narrowed my eyes.

"Nope. Those were her exact words. Oh, and she asked what are your favorite foods. Be expecting a feast. I told her you had a voracious appetite."

"Hunter Barrett." I gasped, and heat warmed my face. "You said what? That makes me sound like a glutton."

"Would you stop. I was kidding." He sighed with a headshake. "You need to relax. My mom is the most easygoing person and loves everyone she meets. Her students adore her. *I* adore her, and you will too."

"If you say so." I slouched in my seat.

"I do. Now, look over there. Do you see that building to the far right? That's where Mom has her classes. The campus is beautiful. Have you ever visited there?"

The State University of Fredonia had been one of my choices to attend college. Instead, I'd gone to NYU on a scholarship. "I toured the campus during my senior year of high school. If NYU hadn't offered a full ride, I might've ended up here."

We traveled out of town and drove through miles of countryside until reaching Dunkirk. Hunter's mother lived in a spacious ranch home surrounded by acres of land. He'd told me how after long hours of lecturing and listening to the constant chatter of students, she loved coming home to the peace and quiet.

I stood alongside Hunter in the large foyer, clutching my bag with both hands to keep from fidgeting. I held my breath as, within seconds, Meredith appeared from the rear of the house.

She took long, confident strides across the hall to greet us. A smile brightened her eyes. Unlike Hunter's, hers were a shade of blue, almost violet. A mass of brown curls framed her face and trailed down to her shoulders. She swiped a loose tendril from her forehead before reaching out with both arms to embrace me. "Chloe Abbington. It's wonderful to finally meet. My son's had such wonderful things to say about you." She gave an extra squeeze before letting go.

"I'm so happy to be here. Thank you for inviting me, Meredith." Her name stumbled out of my mouth in an awkward manner. I took a deep breath. "Hunter can't say enough about you. He's very proud."

"He better be." She kissed his cheek. "I brought my son up to be respectful and appreciative."

"Okay, Mom. We get it." Hunter rubbed his palms together. "Now, what can we do to help with dinner? I'm starving."

Meredith laughed. "When aren't you? Come." She clasped my hand. "While Hunter sets the table, you and I can talk, artist to artist. I was excited to hear about your career, spending a year in Paris, then in Manhattan, and now running a business with your sister. Quite a busy lady."

I followed along to the kitchen. "I have to give my parents some credit. They're artists too."

"Talent is partly innate. Don't dismiss that," she said. "Hunter, bring out the good china and crystal goblets, would you?"

Dinner passed without me stumbling in conversation and blurting out something stupid. The meal was delicious. Chicken and spinach pasta covered in a cream sauce made with goat cheese, asparagus, and a chocolate soufflé for dessert. I was totally stuffed. Sitting in the cozy den, surrounded by ceiling-to-floor bookshelves that covered two of the walls, I sipped on coffee doused with a heavy pour of Bailey's. My eyelids grew heavy, but I managed to keep awake somehow. I hadn't shown Meredith the photos yet.

"Hunter tells me you have a friend who might be in some serious trouble. And he says you think I might be able to help." She leaned forward. Her eyes twinkled. "I'd be thrilled to try."

I set my coffee cup on the table next to me. "I have some photos of a painting, two actually." I pulled the laptop out of my bag. Hitting the power button, the screen lit up. I opened the photo folder. "This is a painting by Clive Whitmore. You may have heard about the family?"

She nodded. "The Whitmores are always in the news. They like to hold charity events and donate to anything that involves the promotion of art. It's sad to hear they've lost both of their children. But why do you have photos of Clive's painting?"

I stood and carried the laptop to the desk near where Meredith sat. "It's a long story, but the short version is Clive gave the painting, a seascape, to Martin Steele as a gift. In turn, Martin sent it to us. By accident, we discovered another painting hidden underneath Clive's. We all fear Martin is in danger." I glimpsed Hunter for a second. "And he could be involved in Erin Whitmore's death. You see, Martin is my sister's close friend and our business investor. She wants to help him in whatever way she can. Figuring out more about these paintings could benefit our search for answers." I waited while Meredith leaned closer to view the first photo.

"It's a lovely seascape. Simplistic in style, but the innocence of it is what draws you in." She pulled open a drawer from the desk and removed a magnifier. "Intriguing that Clive hid a painting underneath. There are only two explanations I can think of. One, it's stolen. Or two, someone had threatened or tried to steal it. Of course, I can't say for certain. Only Clive knew, and he can't answer, can he?"

I shivered. Her words were blunt but truthful.

She viewed the painting through the magnifier, covering corner to corner, top to bottom. Finally, she stood and turned to face me. "You can't see it without using the magnifier, but the ship far off in the distance has a date painted on it. March eighteenth, from what I'm able to make out.

"The lighthouse fascinates me. Did you notice the dull colors, and there's no beacon of light like we'd usually see? In contrast, the water, sky, and beach are bold and bright. The lighthouse as a focal point makes me wonder if it means something. Something more." She tapped the handle of the magnifier against her chin.

I muttered Izzie's name under my breath. "My sister mentioned the same thing about a focal point. She wonders if the lighthouse is meant to be a clue or distract from another part of the painting." I touched the image of the ship. "Like the date on this?"

"Possibly. Like I said. The only one who could've explained it is the artist."

I clicked to pull up the image of the Vermeer lookalike. "This is the hidden painting."

"Ah, yes. Someone has a good knowledge of paintings by the masters. I believe this one's a pastiche, made to imitate one of Vermeer's tronies. Impressive. The artist is very talented. Unfortunately, there's more money to be made by imitating the masters and selling them as originals. Despicable business, but it's very common. Has been for centuries." She stepped away.

Hunter cleared his throat. "It's getting late. We should be going. Thank you, Mom, for a delicious meal. I can't get enough of your chicken and noodle dish."

"You don't fool me for a second." Meredith poked a finger at his chest. "I've already boxed leftovers for you to take home."

We walked out of the den and toward the front door. "Thank you, Meredith. For both dinner and your help with the paintings."

"I'll make a suggestion. I have a friend, Benson Brown. He runs the Alan W Art Gallery in Buffalo. And yes, Alan W stands for Alan Whitmore. The family owns the gallery. If Clive painted any other work, I'm sure it would be displayed there, and Benson could have information to share that may help you in your search." She opened the door, then handed Hunter the food containers she'd placed on the foyer table. "If you like, I'll give Benson a call to let him know you'll be contacting him soon."

"That would be great. Thank you." I extended my arm to shake her hand, but she pulled me into her arms for a hug.

"Absolutely. Come around to visit, often, Chloe. I've enjoyed your company." She smiled.

"You two seem to get along well." Hunter opened the passenger door of his car for me. "Which I had no doubt would happen, despite all your worries."

"You were right. I'm not sure why I got so anxious. This was fun. I love your mom. Can we visit again, soon?"

"Okay by me. She cooks, and I'm always up for a free home-cooked meal."

"Men. Always about their appetites." I chuckled, but that quickly turned into a yawn. "Now, get me home, please. I'm exhausted."

"Yes, ma'am."

I mulled over the conversation I'd had with Meredith about the paintings. Secret messages, clues in focal points, and images of dangerous players danced and tumbled in my head until I eventually dozed off on the ride home.

Chapter Ten

"How about that? A famous art history professor and I think the same way." Izzie nudged me.

"Go on. You can say it." Closing my eyes, I kneaded my forehead with the pads of my thumbs to alleviate the throbbing. I'd woken with a painful headache this morning, most definitely due to the three glasses of wine I'd had at dinner the evening before. Against my better judgment, I'd pushed myself to come to work. We had an important event this evening, and I couldn't wait to share Meredith's comments with Izzie. Reaching for my water bottle, I popped a couple of pain reliever capsules in my mouth.

"Nah. With that headache, you've taken the fun out of an I-told-you-so moment." She handed me a cool gel pack. "This should help."

I thanked her and pressed the pack to my forehead. "If you both are right, then we need to consider Clive was hiding more than the Vermeer lookalike."

"When I talk to Martin, that will be one of my first questions. Oh, and how about Storing? If Clive spoke with him about the painting, he may have explained what it meant. Remember, Storing knew about Clive giving Martin the seascape."

"Something was off about his comment. We hadn't mentioned knowing Martin, and yet he asked us if we knew about the seascape Clive gifted him." I leaned back in my chair. The cool pack was doing its job.

"Yes! Like he'd already found out we know Martin, maybe even about the seascape. But why not tell us?"

"You said it yourself. He wants to protect his book proposal. Authors can be possessive when it comes to that sort of thing, suspicious that another author or publisher will steal their idea."

"That's only if his project is about one or all of the Whitmores. We don't know for sure." Izzie popped a mint in her mouth. "We need to dig deep into Clive's life in the months leading up to the accident. His comings and goings, who he spent time with, friends, business associates, family. One of them could help answer some of our questions."

"How about vacations?" I stood. Lifting the cool pack off my forehead, I set it on the chair. "A beach vacation to a place that has a lighthouse."

"That could take a lot of time, but yeah, it's a thought."

"So's talking to everyone Clive knew. Obviously, a tall order, but I'm sure we can do it." I grew more confident. We had plenty of ground to cover, which felt better than having no plan of action. Take one step at a time, gather the evidence without speculating, and come to a viable conclusion. That's what Hunter and Winsell would tell me.

Without speaking, Izzie sipped her coffee and studied the painting photos on my phone. After a minute or two, she looked up. "Meredith said the date on the ship is March Eighteenth, the day after Saint Patrick's Day. I wonder if the holiday is significant?"

"I have no idea what it could mean." I sighed. Aiming with your eyes closed was what this felt like. Not certain whether you'd even hit the target. "If we're going to learn more about Clive, we should start with those closest to him." I snapped my fingers. "Yes! Of course. I almost forgot. We'll talk to Mom and Dad about attending their next patrons of the arts meeting. With any luck, the Whitmores will be there so we can speak with them."

Izzie scrunched her nose. "They will wonder why we want to go now. After all, we've be telling them no for the past several years."

"We tell them the truth. When is the next meeting? The sooner the better."

"It happens to be this Monday, only two days away. Here's a snag in our plan, though. What if the Whitmores don't show up? They've just lost their daughter, and we know from Storing that they have been avoiding the public eye," Izzie said.

"In that case, we speak with the other members. Their art group started like what? Eight years ago? They must have learned plenty about the Whitmores.

Remember my talk with Mom? During the meetings, Erin often got into arguments with her parents, criticizing them for wealth and entitlement. Sounds like art wasn't the only topic on the agenda. Personal stuff found its way into their conversations."

"Yeah, kind of like book clubs where people drink wine and talk about everything but the book." She chuckled.

"Exactly. I'm sure we can learn plenty from the members." As if our plans helped, my head was no longer throbbing with pain. "You know, I'm feeling better and full of energy. Why don't we finish setting up for the gyotaku event, then close the shop for maybe a half hour or so and take a walk? We can follow the path along the lake and stop at home to speak with Mom and Dad about the art group meeting, maybe grab a quick lunch."

"Moving forward feels great, doesn't it? You finish setting out materials for the guests. I'll add any details needed on the step-by-step canvases with our instructions and paint process." She tapped her lip. "Times like these, I really miss Willow."

Willow came up with the idea of displaying two or three canvases around the room with illustrated images of our current paint theme from start to finish, along with sticky notes attached. Sort of like cheat sheets, providing guests a way to check on what to do next if we all were too busy to help in the moment.

"Oh, and I'll double-check the roster to see if any guests have canceled. We do have two people on the waitlist. They both told me to notify them if there's an opening, even if it's last minute," Izzie said. "I know I was skeptical when you suggested we call the event Gone Fishing."

Corny, pun-filled, but it worked. People snatched up the available seats within a day. I put on a smirky grin. "Apology accepted. Let's get this finished so we can go for that walk."

* * *

I shook sand out of my shoe and hopped on one foot to slip it back on. The choppy lake water pushed waves further into shore to wet the sand in our path. Up ahead, kids jumped and splashed each other, laughing and squealing in their moves. The last thrills of summer as days wound down the month of September.

I turned to face Izzie, who stopped to pluck wildflowers and make a bouquet. "You know, I'm thinking I'd like to skip having a birthday party this year." I held up a hand as she opened her mouth. "Hear me out. I want to do something different. Something more intimate." I worked out details in my head before continuing. "How about we, and I mean Mom, Dad, you, and me, take a trip to the rock and have a picnic? Just the four of us like we used to do with Granddad."

"The rock? Oh wow. I haven't thought about that place in years," Izzie said.

The rock was a tiny sliver of land on Chautauqua Lake and not really a rock. As I recalled, when Izzie was about three or four, she would ask to go to the rock, so the name had stuck. We only had to swim or boat a couple hundred feet from shore to reach the land. Granddad discovered it after moving to Whisper Cove, and he loved going there for our picnics during the nice weather months. Having one in September was intended as our tributary goodbye to summer fun. Since my birthday was around that time, we'd combine the picnic and my party to celebrate. After Granddad passed away, we stopped going. Maybe it hurt to visit. Or maybe continuing the tradition without him didn't seem right. I couldn't remember for certain why, since I was only ten or so when he passed.

Izzie squeezed my arm. "I think that's a wonderful idea, Chloe."

As we approached our house, I crossed the road, and Izzie followed close on my heels. Cutting through the front lawn, I patted the tangerine swan that now stood next to the wrought iron trellis. Mom couldn't seem to make up her mind where she wanted it to be.

Passing through the doorway, I shouted to Mom and Dad. They answered almost in unison to come to the back patio. I stepped outside with Izzie close behind me. The smoke wafting from the fire pit stung the eyes, but the delicious scent of steak cooking on the grill teased my appetite. I rubbed my stomach. "You guys. Grilling in the middle of the day? What's the occasion?"

"No occasion. It's a nice day. Summer's almost over. Why not grill while we can?" Mom smiled and set a basket of fries on the table.

"Yeah, why not?" I popped one of the fries in my mouth and gave Mom a hug. Family time warmed my heart. That was the special occasion, if you asked me.

After a delicious meal, fun conversation, and a moment to relax in the sunshine, we returned to open the shop and set out items for our event. The afternoon streamed by until the hour came. Guests filed in to grab plastic cups for their wine and chat until Izzie and I gave the sign for the event to start.

"Good evening, everyone. We're happy to see such an enthusiastic group. I know Chloe and I are excited. This is our first event using gyotaku. I learned about the ancient Japanese art form while visiting the Florida Keys a couple of years ago." Izzie held up one of the silicone fish replicas. "Fortunately for you, we'll be using these rubber fish instead of real ones like the ancient method calls for."

Several people chuckled and nodded.

"On your table setting, you'll find sponge brushes, a bowl for your sumi ink, rice paper, and of course your fish replica. The last step will be to mount the rice paper image of your fish on a canvas. We'll bring those out later," I said, holding up each item.

"You can frame your prints, preferably behind glass, to preserve them. I've known artists to mount them on canvas, too. If you need any suggestions to do either of those, stop by. We're always here to help," Izzie said.

The tinkling chimes brought my attention toward the front door. Penny tiptoed inside with a wave. She sat on one of the counter bar stools and pulled a notepad out of her pocket. She'd asked if we'd allow her to stop in this evening to take some notes for her next column about craft shops on Artisan Alley. No doubt, the column would serve double duty for Penny by giving her own business a boost.

The hour flew by, and everyone was satisfied with the results. "Another total success." I tapped Izzie's shoulder and nodded at the guests as they staggered out of the shop, carrying their finished products on canvas and chatting with excitement. In the far corner, next to the doorway, Penny caught two or three people before they left to engage in a conversation. No doubt, she was asking what they thought of the event to get a couple of quotes for her article.

"Absolutely was." Izzie eyed the scene, her chest filled with pride. "I think gyotaku will be trending on social media by tomorrow."

"Yeah, you might be right." I gathered supplies and placed them in boxes to sort later. Brushes were tossed into the tub for washing.

As we cleared the last of the tables, Penny approached. I set down the box I was carrying. "So, what did you think? What did the guests you talked to have to say?" I held my breath.

Penny flapped her notepad at us. "You can mark this one as your best effort, or at least it ties with those events to paint your pet. Folks can't get enough of those. Anyway, I have lots to write about, and it's all positive. So, you can relax, Izzie." She wiggled her fingers at her face. "Frowning like that causes permanent wrinkles."

Izzie rubbed away the concern and took a breath. "Sorry. You know how I get, sometimes. Thank you for coming and for featuring us in your column."

Penny shook her head. "It's my pleasure. I'm amazed by what you two do. I'm proud of my knowledge of aromatherapy, but your art is impressive. Who knew fish could be a theme?" She laughed, shoving her notepad in her back pocket.

"It's something different. Izzie is always coming up with new projects," I said.

"Yes, and people keep signing up." Penny glanced at her watch. "Well, I should get going. Need to finish up the column article by morning. Besides that, Wink is paying me a bonus to do some footwork and gather info on the Whitmore shooting. You've heard about that poor woman, haven't you? Such an awful tragedy."

I blinked and glanced sideways at Izzie. "Yeah, it's been on all the news channels. Those poor parents losing both their children. I can't imagine." Hunter wouldn't like it if we spilled all we knew about his case.

"Fortunately, to represent the Gazette, Wink got me an invitation to the memorial being held at the Whitmore estate this coming Tuesday. Rumor is the Whitmores are planning to make an important announcement, so they wanted the media to attend. Sounds in poor taste to me. I mean, a memorial for their daughter coupled with some media announcement? My guess is it's about a business project. Anyway, I have two tickets, but no one wants to tag along with me. Too bad. I hear there's going to be a scrumptious spread."

"I'll go," I spouted. The opportunity was too good to pass up. Getting inside the Whitmore home was something Izzie and I thought would be impossible.

Penny pulled back her head in surprise. "You would? Then I guess it's a date. I'll give you a call on Tuesday to discuss final details. Thanks, Chloe."

I waited until Penny closed the door behind her, then shifted to face Izzie. "Now, before you say anything, think of—"

"You did great. It's the perfect opportunity to find out more about Clive and Erin." Izzie grinned.

"Yeah, well, don't get your hopes up too high. The Whitmores may not be approachable, and I don't know if I'll have a free moment to snoop around the place."

"It's worth a try. That's what we need."

I let my thoughts wander. The excitement I'd had initially about gaining access to the Whitmore estate dampened a bit. I needed to be extremely careful. Alan Whitmore could be too smart to work around and possibly a dangerous adversary. However, like Izzie said, it was worth a try.

Chapter Eleven

It was Sunday, and our shop was closed for inventory. Being in no hurry to leave, we lingered at home and sat at the kitchen table. I spread cream cheese on my second bagel. Claire's bakery, For Sweet's Sake, was my favorite place to buy breakfast. Mom and Dad had left earlier to do some shopping in town. With no word yet from Martin, I decided to call Benson Brown at the Buffalo art gallery to set up an appointment. He could know more about Clive and his work, details that might explain if the seascape has some significant meaning, as Meredith suggested.

I scrolled through my phone to find the contact information Meredith had given me for the gallery and Benson's cell, in case he wasn't at work. Most likely, the gallery would be closed, unless a client had made an appointment. I tried his cell number.

Izzie attempted to do work on her laptop, but she didn't fool me. Every few seconds, her gaze lifted from the screen as she glanced my way. I knew she was anxious, grasping at every tidbit of information we could get to help our search. Hunter implied the authorities were taking a close look at Martin. After Alan Whitmore's claim, of course, they'd want to speak with him to hear his story about that night and his visit with Erin. I was sure the Whitmores had the kind of power needed to influence the investigation.

"Hello, this is Benson Brown."

I cleared my throat and sat up straight. At once, I hit the speaker button. "Hi, Mister Brown. This is Chloe Abbington. I'm a friend of Meredith Barrett. I believe you two have met on occasion?"

"Yes! How is Meredith? I haven't seen her since the spring art festival at the university."

"She's well and sends her best. She also suggested we speak to you about a certain matter." I waved my arm to silence Izzie, who mouthed for me to hurry the conversation along.

"Oh? Of course, if Meredith thinks I could be of assistance, I'd be glad to help."

I shifted in my seat. "My sister and I would like to come by the gallery and see Clive Whitmore's paintings, if that's okay."

"Is that all? Here, I worried your request would involve a lot more work." He chuckled.

"Nope. That's it." Up to this point, outside of people we knew and trusted, Izzie and I were reluctant to share information about the hidden painting. We didn't know Storing or Brown. Too many people having knowledge about it didn't seem like a wise move.

"I tell you what. Why don't you and your sister drop by Tuesday morning, say around nine? The gallery opens at ten. An hour should give us plenty of time to chat. Does that work for you?"

"Perfect. Thank you, Mister Benson. We'll see you on Tuesday." I set down my phone and turned to Izzie. "We've got that issue covered. Let's hope he can tell us something that explains the seascape."

"Or better yet, something that could clear Martin's name from Hunter's suspect list," Izzie added. She closed the lid of the laptop. "We should probably head to the shop if we're going to get the inventory done, and don't forget our plan to clean." She sighed. "We haven't done a thorough cleaning since this past spring."

I slid my chair back from the table. "Maybe if we get done early enough, we can make that trip to The Bistro and speak with Peter Fanning. I'm curious to see what he's like."

"Sounds like we have a full day ahead of us."

I grabbed two more bagels out of the box and a container of cream cheese. Turning on my heel, I caught Izzie's eyeroll. "What? With such a busy day, we'll work up an appetite."

"You mean, *you* will." She grabbed her bag off the counter. The upturned corners of her mouth couldn't hide the smile.

"Yeah, wait until you get hungry and ask for one."

"I won't."

"You will." I teased in a sing-song voice, following close behind her.

We rode in my car to the shop. I turned up the stereo as "Cruel Summer" by Taylor Swift came on. "I'm both excited and nervous about the Swiftie Sweet Sixteen party event we're hosting this Friday."

"Why?" Izzie turned. "It's only been a few years since we were that age. I think we're hip and know all the current music."

I lifted my brow. "Seriously? You're the one who sets the station to classics from the nineties. Name one artist trending. I bet you can't."

"Hmm, give me a second." She slid her phone to the side and glanced down.

"Hey, no cheating. You can't mention one, can you?" I laughed.

She poked my shoulder. "Well, at least you're kind of hip, even if you are almost twenty-eight going on thirty."

"Ooo. That one will cost you. Just wait." After I pulled the car into a parking spot, I poked her back.

Izzie let go of a deep belly laugh as she got out. "Taylor Swift. She's trending, isn't she?"

I locked the doors and hurried to catch up to her. "Obvious choice. Now, what do we tackle first? Cleaning or inventory?"

Izzie pushed open the door and made her way back to the storage room. A squishy sound caused her to gasp. "I'd say cleaning will be the only thing we get to do."

I peeked around her shoulder, and my eyes grew wide at the disaster in front of us. Water puddled on the floor from front to back, covering the entire room. "What the…?"

Izzie squeaked across the room to peer underneath the sink. "There's a crack or something in the pipe." Her voice was shaky. She turned to me, tears welled in her eyes. "We need to call the plumber."

I tilted my head, drew back my shoulders, and mustered confidence. "It'll be fine, Izzie. Gabe Thursby is always available. He can fix it in a jiff." Gabe owned the only plumbing service in Whisper Cove and the surrounding area. He and his wife were also close friends of our family.

I stepped toward Izzie and took charge. "We use the wet vac to suck up most of the water, then mop the floor dry. Meanwhile, I'll grab that huge bucket to stick under the sink and start moving boxes."

"Sure. We can do this. Not a problem." Voice quivering, she sniffed and managed a weak smile.

I gave her a quick hug before moving past her. She took setbacks to heart, and in the moment, found it difficult to believe we could find a way to fix this one. The upside? She always bounced back to become her lively, positive self. I paused to view the mess and those boxes on the floor, darkened with soggy bottoms. I prayed none of them contained paper products or canvases, but that was wishful thinking at best.

"I'm calling the plumber, now," Izzie announced.

"Great. I'll be in here, taking care of all this." I clenched my jaw. After setting the bucket in place, I lifted boxes off the floor and set them on any available flat space. Tables, shelves, even setting some outside in the back of the shop.

Izzie returned, and without comment, pulled the wet vac from its box to power on. A sucking noise drowned out any possible conversation, not that we were in the mood to talk. I certainly wasn't. The only conversation happening was in my head. The leak must've started during the night. I hadn't noticed any dripping water when we had closed up shop after the event. Then again, I'd been distracted by Penny's news. The opportunity to see the inside of the Whitmore estate and the possibility of speaking with Alan or Faith were a huge step forward.

Feeling a gentle tap on my shoulder, I jumped and nearly dropped the box I carried out to the back. Turning, I smiled. "Hi, Megan."

"Sorry. I didn't mean to startle you. The front door was locked, so we came around back." She frowned. "Why are all those boxes sitting out here?"

"We?" I peeked over her shoulder. A man with dark, curly hair and the most vivid blue eyes stood at the privacy fence opening.

"Hey, there." He waved.

"Chloe, I'd like you to meet one of our newest craft merchants on Artisan Alley. He owns a metal art shop called Metallica. Remy Bouchere, this is Chloe Abbington. Like I told you, she and her sister Izzie are artists and host painting events." Megan shifted her gaze. "Where is Izzie, by the way?"

"Well, we sort of have a problem." I winced and pointed at the shop. Izzie's back faced us while she moved the wet vac around the room.

Megan peered around the doorway. "Oh, that's not good." She lifted the flap of a soggy cardboard container filled with paper plates. "Not good at all."

I raked fingers through my hair. "A cracked pipe under the sink. Must've happened after we left last night. As you can see, water puddled all over the storage room, and I'm afraid those soaked boxes on the floor will cost us in supplies. Izzie talked to Gabe Thursby, who I hope will be here soon."

"I guess you could use a helping hand or two, then," Remy spoke up. His southern drawl was pronounced.

"That would be…I mean, thank you." I pushed down the slight tremble in my voice. Remy was a stranger, yet he offered to help. I had a hunch we would become good friends.

Once inside, we all got to work and spent the next hour mopping, reorganizing boxes, and dumping buckets of water outside until Gabe showed up. Introductions were made, then the four of us walked outside to sit by the lake while the plumbing was being fixed.

Izzie sucked on a blade of sweetgrass. "So, Remy. That accent has me curious. What part of the South do you come from? And why move way up here? The winters can be brutal and hard to get used to."

"I'm from a small town along the coast of Louisiana. My family has lived in that area for generations. In fact, one of my ancestors, Renaut Bouchere, settled there when the land was occupied by the French," Remy explained. He leaned against an oak tree, arms crossed over his chest.

I couldn't help notice that Megan glued her attention on his every move and blushed whenever he spoke directly to her. "Like Izzie, I'm curious to know why you moved to Whisper Cove."

"Hurricanes, for one. And heat so strong it suffocates you. I'd rather have your brutal winter weather."

"Yeah, we'll see what you have to say come January." Izzie winked. "Metallica is a clever name for your shop."

"Clever, yes, and also my favorite band. Metal art is something my granddad used to do. He taught me and my brother when we were kids. I've loved crafting metal ever since." He sat cross-legged on the ground next to Izzie. "And what about you and Chloe? Are your parents artists as well?"

"You guessed it. Chloe and I doodled and drew on everything we could when we were kids."

"Except the walls of our bedrooms. Dad swore he'd make us paint over them without any help, if we did." I chuckled.

Megan smacked her thighs and stood. "We should go and let you two get back to the shop. I promised to show Remy around town. He wants to visit the tobacco shop to buy cigars, and they close soon." She scrunched her nose when she said cigars.

"It's nice meeting you, Remy." Izzie held out a hand to shake. "And thank you both for helping out. I'm sure Chloe and I would still be inside mopping up the mess if you hadn't come by."

Megan and Remy walked toward town while Izzie and I remained seated on the grass. "Nice guy. You think Megan likes him more than a little?"

"How about likes him a bunch?" She waved an arm. "Here comes Gabe. Keep fingers and toes crossed this won't cost us too much."

Within a couple of hours, Gabe had fixed the pipe and offered to make a trade. His charge for the work in exchange for a paint party. His wife had her fiftieth birthday coming up in November, and he wanted to do something special.

"She dabbles a bit in painting pictures of the lake, birds, and other creatures, even our backyard. I was thinking you could come up with an idea that she'd enjoy. I plan to invite her friends and sisters. Not her brothers. They'd hate it. No offense. My guess is around twenty people? What do you say?"

Izzie clasped her palms together and bounced on tiptoes. "I'd say you have a deal, Gabe Thursby. Thank you so much. I have a feeling we're getting the better end of the deal. Very kind and generous of you." With no warning, she wrapped arms around him for a tight hug.

Gabe blushed three shades of red and stammered. "Yeah, well, I'm glad you're, ah, glad." He shook both our hands. "You ladies have a great day. I'll be in touch." He waved as he hurried to his truck. "Tell Kate and Joe me and Louise said hi."

"See? I told you everything would turn out okay." I patted her shoulder.

Izzie eased the tension in her body and sighed. "Fate sure has a way of balancing things out, doesn't it? At least for us, it has. Thank goodness. We barely made it out of the red when I balanced the books last month. Someday, maybe." Another sigh released, only louder.

"We'll get there. Wait until August's tally. Remember that full month of events and the festival in Jamestown? We scored big with the sale of our pastels. Sure glad I suggested we paint some during our downtime. Did you forget?"

"No. I didn't. And you're right. I'll stop complaining and worrying, and how about you? All positive vibes. I'm impressed."

Grasping her hand, I pulled her toward the shop. "Get on board the Chloe train. We're headed for positivity and sunny days ahead." I whistled a tune.

Izzie giggled. "Chloe train? You are the ultimate goofball."

"I consider that a compliment," I quipped. The buzz in my pocket made me take a pause to answer my phone. "Hey, you. How's the detective business? Solve many crimes lately?" I snickered under my breath, feeling considerably cheery despite our setback this morning and all the muscle it took to turn the problem around.

"I'm good, especially hearing your voice. I needed that pick-me-up."

I frowned and waved Izzie on ahead of me. "Why? What's wrong? I recognize that tone, all serious and down."

"It's Martin Steele. He's returned, and one of our men just brought him in for questioning. Chloe, you better warn Izzie. The evidence against him is getting stronger. I'm positive there will be an arrest any minute now."

I sat on the front step. "Are you serious? He couldn't have murdered Erin. I mean, Clive was one of his best friends. Why would Martin want to harm his sister? I'm sure he must have an alibi. What did he say?"

"That's the problem. He's said very little. Only that he'd gone out of town on business, right after visiting with Erin. And that she was alive when he left. Gave us no names to confirm where he traveled to. Said nothing about the painting, not even why he thinks Clive sent it to him, and after my conversation with Arthur Storing yesterday, I'm convinced that painting is a crucial part of this case. I tell you, the Captain doesn't like Steele's attitude much. He's pretty angry with him. My guess is he'll keep him behind bars as long as possible."

I gnawed on the pad of my thumb. How was I supposed to tell Izzie? A flooded shop was nothing compared to what Hunter was saying. "Okay. Thanks, Hunter. I'll let Izzie know, but don't be surprised if she storms into your office to protest. I know my sister's loyalty runs deep. She won't settle for Martin being arrested."

"Just the same. The evidence is pretty damning."

"I remember everything Alan claimed about Martin and his visit to the estate that night, and Erin's accusation about him involving Clive in a shady art deal. Still, isn't that his word against Martin's? Where's Alan's proof?" I stood.

"I know what you're suggesting. This is one more example of powerful people manipulating the system. Chloe, I can promise you, if Steele is innocent, I'll prove it. No prejudice or manipulating on my end."

"Thanks, Hunter. I'll let Izzie know that, too." I ended the call and dragged myself inside. This wouldn't be a pleasant conversation, but I had to tell her. My head hurt. This certainly had been a day, and we were only halfway through it.

Chapter Twelve

Izzie rang the doorbell. Her foot tapped the porch floor with deliberate impatience or anger or maybe both. We'd learned this morning that Martin had been arrested, after all. Since he hadn't cooperated when questioned, the Captain had done exactly as Hunter suggested. Even so, within a couple of hours, Martin posted bail. Hunter told me his lawyer presented an impressive speech to get the judge to agree.

Right now, I knew what most likely had Izzie fuming. Martin wouldn't answer her calls, and there were many yesterday and again this morning. That brought us here, standing on his doorstep. Izzie refused to give up. She wanted answers, and some part of her needed to see with her own eyes that he was okay.

"Miss Abbington. We weren't expecting you." Phillip answered the door. His towering six feet and so many inches was enough to intimidate the bravest of people. Add the stoic face and cold manner of his presence, and you had a force to reckon with. Martin had chosen his assistant wisely.

"Well, we're here and coming inside." Izzie pushed past Phillip, undaunted by his demeanor. "Where is he? I need to speak with him." She zigzagged down the hallway, left and right, peeking into each room.

"I'm here, Izzie. You don't have to carry on so." Martin stepped down from the spiral stairs that led to the second floor.

I studied the man dressed in casual attire. Even though Martin was attractive and fit, the dark shading underneath his eyes hinted at the fatigue and maybe stress he'd endured. Izzie had told me he was in his early forties.

"It's a pleasure to finally meet you, Chloe." Martin's eyes sparkled as he cupped my hand in his.

He totally ignored Izzie and her mood, which I found amusing. "I wish it were under better circumstances. Izzie compliments you all the time, except maybe yesterday when we found out you'd been arrested."

"Let's call it priorities. Getting out of jail as soon as possible was my number one concern." He finally shifted to put his attention on Izzie. "Trust me, you've been on my mind. Every minute since I left last week, I worried what you must be thinking of me or about me." He pulled her into a warm embrace before letting go.

"Don't you ever do that again. No word for several days, not answering my calls, making me worry? None of that is okay. Understand?" She sniffed.

"Point taken, and I promise to always answer your calls from now on."

"Thank you. Now, what the heck is going on with you? Where did you disappear to? What does the police have on you? It can't be based on Alan Whitmore's testimony." Izzie stepped back and heaved her chest.

Martin motioned us into his library room, where we sat. "Nothing that would keep me behind bars. The judge weighed in and scolded Captain Morris for acting rashly. I was surprised. As for where I disappeared to, as you put it, I won't discuss it right now. I need more time to figure things out."

"But what did you say when they questioned you? Hunter claims you weren't cooperative and told them very little," I said.

Phillip walked in carrying a tray with refreshments. Without a word, he set the tray on the table and left.

"I understand his frustration. I told him I'd visited Erin because she asked me to. She wanted to know about Clive's and our relationship in business. I told Detective Barrett and the other one who sat in—rumpled man with dark, curly hair and keeps a pencil stuck behind his ear." He paused to sip his beverage.

"That would be Detective Winsell. He's investigating a break-in involving the Bernell murder and art theft." True to his word, Winsell kept his nose in the investigation. I had a hunch he believed the art theft and Clive's hidden painting were connected somehow.

"Anyway, I told them I arrived around nine and left the Whitmore estate around ten, then came home to pack since I needed to catch my flight."

"Hunter also said you had no alibi," I added.

"You mean to account for my time during the hours when Erin was murdered? I do have an alibi and the person who can confirm it, but she can't be reached at the moment. She's away on a business trip. Of course, that didn't satisfy Captain Morris."

"Martin, there is more to your visit with Erin, isn't there? Something you didn't share with the police?" Izzie leaned forward, hands folded and resting in her lap.

He remained quiet, as if deciding what to say. "Erin seemed anxious, almost agitated. She suspected Clive's death wasn't an accident. I agreed with her. What really worried me, though, was her concern that someone wanted to stop her search. She had a theory, and it involved one of Clive's art pieces. She worried whoever he planned to sell the piece to may have murdered him."

"Theory? You mean about the seascape?" Izzie said. "Did she know he'd hidden the Vermeer reproduction behind it?"

"I won't explain her theory because the less you know, the safer it is for you. In fact, until Erin's killer is caught, I don't think you should stop by to see me again. Remember? I told you I'd been followed. I don't want to put you in any further danger." He stood and pulled open his desk drawer.

Izzie hurried to explain our visit with Arthur Storing, how he had similar ideas about Clive's death, and figured that someone would've wanted Erin dead. He knew she'd been asking questions and telling anyone who'd listen that her brother was murdered.

Martin nodded. "I'm familiar with the man. He's rather obsessed with the Whitmore family but has extensive knowledge of them. I may have to pay the man a visit and chat." He stepped closer.

"As for the hidden painting, I swear I knew nothing about it. Your detective showed me the photos, asking if I recognized or knew anything about the hidden painting. A pastiche of a Vermeer tronie. I'd say that's rare." He handed a paper to Izzie. "I imagine this is a clue. Clive was always very cryptic, enjoying his puzzle games and making us guess. He included this with the painting."

Izzie studied the paper and read aloud. "Thanks for being such a good friend and astute judge of art. Enjoy this gift. Despite my naïve attempts, it's a nice likeness, isn't it? Remember our days in the wild. Love Clive."

"Days in the wild? What does he mean?" I asked.

Martin shrugged. "I'm guessing maybe our college days? We were young and impulsive, which often got us into trouble. The word likeness, however, puzzles me even more."

Izzie tapped her chin. "How about the date, March eighteenth? Did you two ever go to the beach around that time of year? Maybe it's supposed to be a scene from one of your vacations."

"Possibly. I don't know yet. What I do know is I overheard someone at the precinct say they've issued a warrant to search the storage facility and confiscate the painting as evidence in the case."

"At least there's that." I walked alongside Izzie as Martin led the way to the front door.

"Yes, but it also means I won't have any opportunity to take the painting home and get a closer look." Martin rubbed his face. "I'm exhausted and need time to decide on my next move."

"We want to help, Martin. Please," Izzie said. "Let us do something."

He shook his head. "Right now, I want you to go home and take care of yourselves. Get back to your lives. This is my problem to solve. I never would've involved you in the first place, if I'd known then how serious things would become. I apologize for that."

"But," Izzie started.

Martin gave us a gentle push through the doorway. "Go home. Stay safe." With that, he closed the door.

"Stubborn man." Izzie groaned.

"He only wants to protect us. Maybe we should listen to him?" I linked my arm through hers and guided us across the lawn to reach the car.

"What if they charge him with murder? It's his word against Alan Whitmore's. Who do you think the police will listen to?" Izzie climbed into the passenger seat.

"Hunter won't take Whitmore's word over Martin's, not without solid proof. I told you that. Besides, Alan and Faith Whitmore, Peter Fanning, Arthur Storing, and anyone else who'd been in close contact with Erin before her death are suspected. Remember that, too." I steered out of the drive and headed for home. With no more ideas of how to convince her, I remained quiet. Despite all I'd said, I knew what Izzie claimed had merit. Right time, right place. Those elements covered opportunity. But what would Martin's motive be to murder Erin? Without that crucial piece, I was confident Hunter and Captain Morris wouldn't make the move to charge Martin with murder. At least, Hunter wouldn't. He'd gather the evidence, stay clear of speculation or assumptions, and then decide who the killer was. A clean and thorough investigation. Meanwhile, we needed to focus on other potential suspects. Like the Whitmores, who might be at the art group meeting this evening. I crossed my fingers and wished for a lucky break.

* * *

After dinner and a relaxing soak in the tub, I was ready to put on my sleuthing cap. This evening, the art group held their meeting at the historical society building in a nearby town. I learned that in order to be fair to all of the members and how far they traveled, the group rotated locations between here and north of Buffalo, every month.

We entered and found Mom and Dad standing next to a table set up for coffee and several bottles of water. A tray of cookies sat to the side, along with plates and napkins. I scanned the room and counted ten members. With us, that made twelve, but I was sure stragglers would come to join us by the time the meeting officially started. I'd been right about how many members we'd know by name. The couple who ran the art supply store in Jamestown, Janice and Tom Nellim, and the curator from the art museum in Erie, William Shaffer, were the only recognizable faces to me.

Mom was engaged in conversation with the Nellims. I waited until they walked away and then approached. "Hey. Do you know the man standing over by the punch bowl? Dark hair, tall, good-looking." I tipped my head in that direction.

"Ah, yes, that's Tito Alma. He's an art dealer who lives in Rochester, I believe. He's not officially a member, and this is only the second or maybe third time I've seen him at a meeting. Traveling constantly throughout the United States and to other countries for his clients often takes him away from home. From what I hear, his wife doesn't like the traveling, either."

"Is that her, talking to him? She looks enthused about whatever the conversation is about."

"No, that's another member. She moved here recently from Paraguay. Probably happy to find a fellow Latino in our group."

"Oh? Tito is from Paraguay, too?"

"He's lived in Brooklyn most of his adult life, but comes from Paraguay, where his family still lives, and as you'd guess, he speaks fluent Spanish."

I tapped my lip. "Yes, I've read about him. Wasn't he the one who managed to close a multi-million dollar deal last year? It involved an Incan artifact from Peru."

"That makes sense. Most of his business in acquiring art for clients sends him to countries in South America. Your Dad has an opinion about the man, but I'll let him tell you." Kate turned to pour coffee into a Styrofoam cup and stir in creamer. "Oh, there's Carli Descente. You have to meet her. She's around your age, paints, and owns a craft shop. You have lots in common."

Mom took hold of my bag strap and used it to pull me along with her across the room. I grabbed a bottle of water as we passed by the table. At the far corner, past several poofy leather chairs and beyond the rustic shelves with their displays of photos, mementos, and such, a woman with red hair cut in some crazy new style that must require a whole can of spray product to maintain stood drinking from her cup. She dressed in black casual slacks and high-heeled pointy-toed boots and looked totally bored. The only detail I cared about, though, was whether she could tell me anything about Erin, Clive, or their parents that might help Martin.

"Carli, I'd like you to meet one of my daughters. Chloe, this is Carli Descente. She owns a craft shop in Lily Dale."

"Not crafts. Tarot cards. I do readings. If you'd like, I could do yours. I always keep a set in my bag." Carli lifted her chin.

Her voice had that deep, husky sound. She eyed every inch of me, as if she could do a reading without any help from the cards. I shivered slightly but managed a smile. "Nice to meet you. Maybe a tarot reading some other time."

"Okay, I'll leave you two to talk. Izzie looks like she needs some introductions." Mom retraced her steps.

"Izzie?" Carli finished off her drink and set the cup on one of the shelves, next to a worn leather copy of a Charles Dickens book.

"My sister."

"Right. Your mom and dad mentioned her a few times. I tend to forget people's names. Not faces, though."

She was studying mine again. I crossed my arms. "So, have you been coming to these meetings for long?" I walked to sit in the closest chair, hoping she'd follow.

Carli gestured with one arm. "How about we sit out there. It's much more private."

Out there looked to be a type of atrium. From this angle, I could see several hanging pots with trailing plants like Devil's Ivy and a stained glass window.

Before Carli gave me a chance to answer, she headed toward that room.

If I was going to learn anything, this might be the best opportunity. By being away from the other members, Carli would be more inclined to talk about them, including the Whitmores. I quickly caught up to her.

The atrium was warm and cozy. Several Tiffany lamps glowed to brighten the area. I chose a wicker chair topped with a thick cushiony cover and sat. "This is nice. Have there been very many meetings hosted in the building?" I kept pushing. If Carli was new, I doubted she'd know anything about the Whitmores that would help.

"Once or twice. I've only been a member of the group for a couple of years. Joined after I moved to the area from a small town in New Hampshire. Do you smoke?" She pulled out a cigarette and lighter.

I shook my head. "All smoke tends to give me a migraine, and maybe you're not allowed to in here?"

Carli shrugged, then pocketed both cigarette and lighter. As if looking for something to replace the habit, she smacked the palms of her hands on the chair arms in a rhythmic beat for several seconds. At once, she sprang out of the chair and paced the room, stopping to check out each hanging pot and giving an affirmative grunt to all.

I blinked but kept quiet.

"So." She came to an abrupt stop and plopped down in her chair once more. "I suppose you want to know if I can tell you about the Whitmores. Isn't that why you came to the meeting?"

My jaw dropped, my words stuck to my tongue. I gulped water from the bottle until I felt confident to talk. Tarot Lady might just be for real. "The fact is, my sister and I are trying to help a friend."

"Martin Steele." She nodded.

I blinked again. "Ah, yes. Him. You see…or maybe you already know this." My brow creased. "He's a suspect in Erin's shooting. You probably decided she was murdered, even though the police haven't officially announced that." My voice trailed off. She rubbed a spot on her pant leg, ignoring or seemingly ignoring me.

Her head snapped up. "Yes, I am aware of all that. I can tell you this much. Erin most definitely was murdered. I haven't figured out who killed her, yet. However, I will, and probably before you or that detective friend of yours can. What's his name?" She glanced up at the ceiling for a second, then snapped her fingers. "Hunter. Detective Hunter Barrett is on the case. Nice." She nodded and grinned at me. Her lips spread, becoming pencil thin.

I dismissed her bizarre behavior, tarot card reading, and all, and became curious. "Can you or would you tell me about Erin? Or her parents? I was told they come to meetings, though I noticed they aren't here this evening."

"You wouldn't believe the drama between Erin and them when all three would attend. Erin didn't care much for her parents, the family businesses, or their self-entitled attitude. She called them the bougie rich, totally out of touch with the real world and unsympathetic with the working man's struggle. I'm paraphrasing her words." Carli chuckled. "As if Erin could manage without them. She wouldn't know how to survive. I'll give her this. The woman had guts."

"Did she argue about anything else?" After hearing what Storing had to say about the family dynamics, especially Clive and Alan, I wondered if that issue had come up.

"I guess what bothered her most near the end was how Mom and Dad treated her boyfriend. What's his name?" She tapped her chin.

"Peter Fanning." I leaned back in my chair.

"Yes. That's him. She accused them of treating Peter like he was nothing but a gold digger."

"I heard she finally realized they were right, and that she planned to break off their relationship because she couldn't trust him. That would've been a few weeks before her murder. Did she say anything to you about that?"

Carli folded her hands and laid them in her lap. The creases in her face deepened. "She confided in me that her world was falling apart. The relationship with Peter and something else."

"What? Can you tell me what else bothered her?" I didn't want to put words in Carli's mouth by suggesting what I'd been thinking.

"Clive. She was obsessed with proving he'd been murdered. It became a mission. She told me there wasn't a waking moment without Clive in her thoughts."

I tensed. This was similar to what both Arthur Storing and Martin had described to us. "Did she give you her reasons for believing he was murdered?"

Carli shook her head. "A week before she died, after our monthly meeting, Erin and I decided to go to a local bar for drinks. Some of the members go out on occasion, but this time it was only us two. She was scared, frightened someone was after her. I thought she was being paranoid. Turns out I was wrong."

My thoughts went to what Storing had said about the painting. "Did she ever mention a painting Clive had done?"

"Yes!" Carli's eyes brightened. "She talked about it several times. Something about how it might be a clue to Clive's death, or murder as she always insisted we call it, though I don't believe for one second he was murdered. She wanted to find the painting, which she believed was missing. She planned to speak with Clive's close friend and business associate to find out what he knew."

"Martin." We echoed his name together. "One more question. Do you have a theory as to who would want to kill Erin?"

"Theory or premonition?" She winked. "In truth, I'm not clairvoyant, just very observant. And from what I've seen here at the meetings, I'd say there's not a chance Alan or Faith Whitmore killed their daughter. Despite the arguments and outbursts, they always showed her understanding and compassion. I'll admit, I'm jealous. I don't have parents. I was raised by a cold and distant grandfather. I would give anything to have what Erin and her parents had. Tragic that they don't have that any longer."

She seemed sincere. I wondered if we'd been wrong to point fingers at Alan and Faith. Storing too. He talked about the Whitmore parents with anger in his voice. Maybe his view was biased because he'd only heard Clive's and Erin's words. Not the parents' side of things.

I straightened. "Any other guesses? Could someone in this group have wished Erin harm?"

"Terence Ashe," she said.

"Who's he?" I glanced around me to make sure no one lingered by the doorway, possibly to eavesdrop.

"He is a member and not a fan of the Whitmores. In fact, I think Terence hates everyone who comes from money. Maybe he's a socialist."

That was blunt, I thought. "Why do you think that?"

"It's total speculation on my part, but I overheard Erin and Terence arguing at the bar after one of our meetings. I think five or six of us went out that time to Sammy's. It's a pub down the street from the place we meet in Buffalo. Anyway, Erin left to visit the ladies' room. When she didn't come back after twenty minutes, I got worried and went to look for her."

Carli fidgeted with the hem of her shirt. "When I got closer to the hallway leading to the bathrooms, I spotted Erin and Terence, nose to nose, shouting at each other. Of course, I hurried back to our table. I didn't want to get in the middle of whatever it was."

I leaned forward. "Did she say anything when she returned? Was she upset?"

"Oh, she was upset, all right." Carli snorted. "She grabbed her coat and bag and announced she was leaving. I had to go along because, well, I worried Terence would follow her and do something more harmful than slinging word garbage."

Carli certainly knew how to draw out a story, and I could see from the corner of my eye that people were starting to leave. "What did she tell you about the argument?"

"She wouldn't say, other than how Terence was a despicable person. I just don't trust the guy. Never talks business, yet he owns one. Or about family. No personal details, which is why I'm suspicious. Like I said, my opinion, take it or leave it." Carli rose from her chair. "Well, meeting's over, so I'm gonna head over to the closest bar. You and your sister are welcome to join me. We can chat some more. Maybe about something other than Terence."

"Thanks, but Izzie and I have an early morning at the shop. You have a good evening, Carli. I appreciate you talking to me." I held out my hand, and she gripped mine to shake.

Hurrying back into the main room, I spotted Izzie, alone. No sign of Mom or Dad. "Hey, sorry. I was talking to one of the members." I hitched a thumb over my shoulder. "We were in the atrium."

"Thank goodness. I was worried. Who is that woman, all dressed in black and with the interesting hairdo?"

"I'll tell you all about her and what she had to say, on our way home." I tugged at her sleeve, and we made quick steps outside to the car.

Before I could power on the engine, my phone rang. "Hold up. It's Hunter." I clicked to open. "Hey, you. What's going on? I thought you were busy on a stakeout this evening."

"Something came up. You wouldn't happen to be at home, would you?"

The tightness in his voice caught my attention. "No, Izzie and I are on our way there, though. We attended one of Mom and Dad's art group meetings. Why?" I turned to shrug at Izzie with one palm facing up.

"Boring and uneventful trip home, I hope. How was the meeting? Learn anything interesting?"

The edgy clip to his voice lingered, and now mine was about to match it. "Enough. You're upset about something. I can hear it. So, spill. Now, please."

"Well, I told you about the search warrant we were waiting for from the judge. We received it late this afternoon. Problem is, when we got to the Buffalo art storage facility, we discovered Clive's painting had been stolen, and the night guard had been knocked out cold on the entryway floor. Chloe, the people who wanted the painting so badly and willing to harm someone to get it are dangerous, and I'm worried about you being involved in this mess."

"Yes, but—"

"No buts. I want you to listen carefully. Anyone who interferes with that painting or goes looking for answers about Clive, like Erin did, is putting themselves in danger, maybe even taking the risk of being killed."

I kept quiet. I had no argument, no reason to think he was wrong. Maybe a tad dramatic about it, but not totally wrong. I figured this wasn't the best time to mention Carli and her suspicions of the group member, Terence Ashe, or suggest he look into Peter Fanning, Erin's boyfriend. Nope. I'd wait for an opportunity later, when he wasn't so upset. Right now, I considered his warning carefully. Maybe Izzie and I should back away from the case. I took a breath and held it while looking at Izzie. The question was, would she agree?

Chapter Thirteen

Brody dropped off Rex at our home last night. He had an unexpected business trip and no time to make other arrangements. Without a doubt, the whole family enjoyed having Rex stay over, especially Max. I watched the two of them romp in the yard while Izzie and I discussed our next move.

Of course, Hunter's warning had been pointless to share with her. She insisted he was being extremely dramatic, and he worried about us as if we were children who didn't know how to be careful. I raised a brow at that comment. Sometimes, careful didn't play into our actions. I'd proven that once or twice. Still, paying a visit to the gallery in Buffalo and having a chat with Benson Brown sounded totally safe. That stayed on our agenda.

"First, we ask to see Clive's other paintings, then ease into questions about Benson's knowledge of the Whitmore family." Izzie tossed the Frisbee to Rex, who jumped to catch it while Max ran in circles around him.

"Speaking of asking him questions reminds me. We've been so focused on money as the motive for murder, but what about a crime of passion? Let's say the victim had an affair and cheated on their partner, who then found out and killed the victim in a jealous rage."

"You mean Benson and Erin having an affair?" Izzie shook her head. "I don't know. That sounds—"

"What? No! I mean Erin and someone else. Good grief. No, not Benson."

"Oh yeah, that makes a lot more sense." She let out a breath before her eyes widened. "You mean Peter Fanning could be the killer."

"Um, hmm. That's where my mind went." I reached down to scratch the top of Max's head.

He licked my hand and lay down in the grass, panting from his workout.

"We have to go to that restaurant and have a talk with him as soon as he returns home," I added. After our botched plans on Sunday, I'd called The Bistro in the morning, only to learn Fanning had gone out of town due to some kind of emergency. He wouldn't return until late Wednesday evening.

"Meanwhile, we stick to the money motive and see if Benson knows anything that would help." Izzie whistled for Rex.

I settled back in my chair, feet tucked under my legs, and sipped my coffee. If Benson did know something relevant, we could follow up on that bit of information. If not, Peter Fanning was the next in line for questioning. My impatience picked at my nerves. Sooner or later, something had to break open this case. I prayed for sooner.

* * *

"Wow. Now that's an impressive showcase." Izzie pulled the Land Rover into an open space along the curb and conveniently in front of the building.

The name, Alan W Art Gallery, was displayed in glossy gold letters above the door. Several paintings framed in gold and mounted on tripod stands sat in the showcase window. An announcement in the same glossy gold lettering placed front and center informed anyone curious enough to stop and see that a gallery event by this artist would take place next week.

I felt a twinge of jealousy and quickly dismissed it. When the time was right, I told myself. Reaching for the handle, I pulled to open the door and stepped inside. A subdued bell tone announced our arrival.

A short man with silver hair, looking to be in his sixties or so, stepped from behind the front desk. He adjusted his glasses by sliding them up the bridge of his nose with one fingertip.

"Mister Brown?" I held out a hand. "I'm Chloe. We spoke on the phone this past Sunday."

Izzie stepped forward. "We appreciate you agreeing to meet us. I'm Izzie Abbington, Chloe's sister."

112

"I was surprised to get your phone call. It's been several weeks since I've talked about Clive. His family was devastated by his death. And now their daughter is gone." Benson shook his head. "No parent should suffer the loss of a child, let alone two." He heaved his chest with a sigh, then pulled his shoulders straight. "So, how can I help?"

When he motioned for us to take a seat, Izzie and I situated ourselves next to a table covered with stacks of program brochures and business cards. "We were hoping to speak with you about Clive's paintings," I started.

"Professor Barrett mentioned you have two hanging in the gallery," Izzie added.

"Oh, yes. Of course. Mister and Missus Whitmore asked me to showcase them. They own the gallery, you know." Benson held up a carafe filled with water and poured it into three glasses. He handed one to each of us. "They are extremely generous people, always doing something charitable, especially for the art community."

"Tell us more about Clive. Did you know him well?" Izzie asked.

I bit down on my lip. She'd gotten straight to the point. I hoped it paid off.

"Actually, it took some time, but we became somewhat friendly and comfortable with each other. Clive was quite shy, not given to small talk or any talk. At least, not with me. His paintings, though, speak massively. Each one tells a story with underlying messages so cleverly done, I can stare at them for hours. How unfortunate that he only managed two before his death." Benson set down his glass and rested both palms on his legs. "Would you like to see them? Of course, you would." He chuckled and stood, motioning us farther into the gallery.

His steps kept a hurried pace along with his conversation. I had to pick up my normal speed to follow.

"I admit to some selfishness when I heard of his death. I had told Clive that as soon as he finished two or three more paintings, I planned to schedule a showing of his work. He was that talented." Benson waved an arm above his head. "Fate had other plans."

I waited for Izzie to say something about the third painting. She wanted to hold off until Benson offered something of interest. "Your gallery has quite a collection. Tell me about those paintings in your showcase. I'm not familiar with Edmund Taylor. Is he local?" I stopped to adjust my shoe, then skipped to catch up.

"Yes, he's fairly new to the area. He loves gilding in his art. The man's obsessed with that method. He applies the gold leaf to almost every painting he does. I'm sure you noticed from the display." Benson came to a halt and beamed as he stared at the wall. "Here we are. Clive Whitmore's masterpieces."

I chewed the inside of my cheek while studying the images. One was a water scene, similar to Monet's water lily paintings. The other was a portrait of a young woman cradling a baby. In truth, neither one impressed me as what Benson called masterpieces. Then again, appreciation of art was subjective to some degree.

"He certainly had a style of his own," Izzie said.

And that was as close to the truth as Izzie would allow.

"He was one of a kind. And underappreciated. His sister felt the same. She came into the gallery many times, especially after Clive's death. I understood when she explained how seeing these made her feel closer to her brother." Benson sniffed. "Such a tragedy. We'd spoken the day before her death. She planned to make another visit to the gallery but then…I don't think I'll ever get over the loss. Such wonderful people."

I puzzled over his comment. Had Benson been that close to the siblings? "How long had you known Clive and Erin?"

"Would you believe since they could walk? Missus Whitmore used to bring them to the gallery whenever an artist she admired was being showcased. The children loved seeing the artwork almost as much as she did."

"You've worked here that long?" Izzie asked.

"Over forty-five years. The Whitmores are very loyal, and I've gained their respect over time." With an upward tip of his chin, he straightened his shoulders.

Izzie cleared her throat. "Did you ever hear Clive talk about another painting he was working on? A seascape?"

Benson frowned. "No, I don't recall. His parents never mentioned another work. Why? Is there one? That would be a tremendous addition to his collection." His eyes brightened.

Izzie explained how Clive had gifted the seascape to Martin. "Did Clive or Erin ever talk about Martin Steele?"

"I don't remember hearing the name. Now, about the painting." Benson stepped closer. "Do you know where it is? Maybe I could persuade Mister Steele to loan it to our gallery."

Izzie glimpsed me for an instant. "Actually, Martin has put it in storage. And we're not sure when he plans to release it."

"That's a shame. Well, if you speak to him, would you please pass along my name and number? I'd love to chat with him." Benson placed a business card into her hand.

"Sure. Thank you for your time. We should be going. Lots on our agenda today." Izzie waved and rushed out of the gallery, and I followed.

"You think he already knew about the seascape?" I hustled to open the car door and slide into my seat. "He might be keeping secrets of his own." Even more secrets than having knowledge of the seascape.

"Possibly, but what really caught my interest was his comment about a conversation with Erin only a day before she was murdered. What if Benson is one of a handful of people who last saw Erin alive? Tracking his whereabouts around that time could be worth it." She gasped. "And what if he was the last one to see Clive before his accident? We need to find a way to retrace Clive's steps that day. Places he visited. People he spoke with."

"Woah. One thing at a time. I agree Benson could be a person of interest, as the police say, but that's only based on the fact he was close to the Whitmore family. We can't be sure of anything else." I had to reason with her and keep us on a sensible path.

"You're right. While you attend that memorial at the Whitmore estate with Penny, I'll start digging for details about Benson Brown, maybe make a few phone calls. Oh! Do you think Hunter would be willing to share the file on Erin? That information could be extremely helpful." Izzie drummed her fingers on the steering wheel, then pulled out onto the road.

I whistled. "How about limit this to a little online research first? Besides,

I highly doubt Hunter would let us look at a file of an ongoing case." Not exactly true. He'd shared details with me, more than Izzie knew.

"Right, right." She snapped her fingers while sitting at a red light. "How about the reporter who covered Clive's accident? I could call the Buffalo News and ask who did. Or Google videos from when it was in the news. That should show me who covered it."

I sighed as her excitement elevated. "We'll regroup tomorrow morning and go over anything we find." I touched her arm. "We'll get this done. Don't worry."

* * *

I rested my shoulder against the back wall of the expansive gathering room while Alan Whitmore engaged in his lengthy monologue, covering the history of the family, the building of the estate, and now, stories about Erin. Penny had left me to mingle with guests, hoping to get some info for her article. Done on the sly, it wouldn't look so distasteful, she'd told me.

Since the beginning of Alan's speech, twenty minutes ago, I'd been waiting for the opportunity to break away from the crowd and explore. In other words, the moment when I could sneak into other rooms to find anything that revealed information about the family that hadn't been in the news and was not public information.

As one of the hired staff passed by, I tapped her shoulder. "Excuse me. Could you please direct me to the closest bathroom?"

The woman, grey-haired with a pointy chin, stared me down from tip to toe, while remaining silent. I kept my hands from fidgeting and attempted to look calm. No doubt, she was assessing whether I could be trusted.

Her stern face broke into a smile. She pointed to the hallway on my right. "Three doors down on the left." In the next second, she vanished into the crowd of visitors.

"Didn't even ask my name or check my guest pass. I don't know whether to be proud or insulted." I grumbled on my way past the three doors and the bathroom, continuing to the rear of the house. I'd already found a website on the Whitmore estate that provided plenty of images, including a diagram of the inside layout. I knew exactly where Alan's study was located. With any luck, I'd find the door open because the skill of picking locks wasn't in my bag of tricks.

I sniffed the odor of tobacco as I neared the study. With my backside hugging the wall, I paused to listen for any sounds, voices, or otherwise, which would stop me from going any further with my plan. Deep voices echoed, growing louder, that hinted to me someone or someones were in the room. Taking quick, light steps on tiptoe, I hurried to the closest door. I breathed easily as it opened. Stepping just inside and out of sight, I peeked around the frame and spotted a man exiting the study with a phone pressed against his ear as he chattered in an excited tone. I didn't recognize him, but relief flooded over me as he walked in the opposite direction and disappeared around the corner. Taking a quick glance at each end of the hallway, I stepped out of the room.

Once inside the study, I eased the door closed and collapsed against it, counting my breaths as my heartbeat pulsated. Trespassing or sneaking into places where I shouldn't be never got easier. I steadied myself and moved into the room, making a path to the desk, a massive walnut fixture that covered a sizable area. Three of the walls were covered in ceiling-to-floor bookshelves. A glance at a few of the titles told me Alan was a fan of classics such as works by Dickens and Thoreau. Even what appeared to be, with its worn edges and cracked leather, a first edition of a Voltaire play. The man was well-educated, even if a bit boastful. I ran my fingertips along the spines of several volumes, searching for anything that might seem off or suspicious. Next to the classics was an entire section of books devoted to the arts. Of course, those would be in his collection. The perfect tie-in with the Whitmores' devotion to all artistic endeavors. Volumes covered each movement, individual artists like da Vinci and Picasso, and Vermeer. I puzzled over the five books devoted to that artist. A fascination with the baroque artist could be a coincidence, but the nagging voice in the back of my mind would argue the point.

I checked my watch and moved on. Time was precious, and several minutes to peruse through those books wasn't smart. I scanned the items resting on the desk. A planner lay open to the current date. A couple of entries marked this evening's memorial and an early meeting with someone whose name I didn't recognize. I flipped through pages to the day Erin was murdered. The date was missing. Eying the center seam, I could barely detect the frayed edge of where the page had been torn away. Had Hunter and other team members noticed the missing agenda? I couldn't ask him without confessing I'd been trespassing. Turning back to the days before Clive's death revealed nothing. At least to my mind, they didn't. Numerous appointments with charity organizers, a bank manager or two, and social functions appeared totally innocent.

I shifted to glance at the trash can sitting next to the desk. Crumbled paper and some torn pieces covered the bottom. I doubted the BPD team would've left anything behind. This trash had to be thrown away very recently. Hunter had informed me that the crime team finished collecting evidence and examining the study only yesterday.

Footsteps resounded in the hallway and grew louder, along with the voices of two people. One sounding deep and the other high-pitched. I hurriedly stuffed all the trash in my pockets and searched for a place to hide.

"I'm sorry, Mister James. She asked to use the restroom. I checked the facility a few minutes after and it was empty. Then, I searched the guests but failed to spot her. Maybe she left the estate?"

I recognized the voice of the staff member who'd helped me.

"Hopefully, she left and only used the restroom, Miss Long. We don't want any news about trespassers to upset Mister Whitmore."

I took hurried, light steps to the closet and wedged myself between two tall stacks of boxes, then eased the door shut. My guess was these people were both staff employees, coming to check the rooms to make sure no one was hiding. Like me. I huddled further behind the towering boxes to wait.

"See? No one is in here," Miss Long said.

"What about the closet?" The man spoke, and steps sounded.

I held my breath, ready for a confrontation, and I scrambled for any possible excuse I could give Mister James, whom I pictured as Lurch from

The Addams Family, ominous with a threatening face and sour demeanor. Besides, there was no believable excuse for someone hiding in a closet.

"We don't have time for that. Mister Whitmore is expecting us to serve guests after his speech, which should be any minute now," Miss Long argued.

"Then let's hurry to the kitchen. Mind you, there's no need to mention this to Mister Whitmore," he said.

"Agreed."

I heard the door close and leaned closer to one stack of boxes. They teetered sideways. I yelped, grabbing what I could, but one fell to the floor. The lid popped off and the contents spilled out. An object clattered onto the planks of hardwood and twirled like a spinning top. My eyes circled to follow until it came to rest.

"Well, that's an interesting development." Using my shirt to cover my fingers, I grasped the handle and examined the pistol that had been hidden in the box. Why was the weapon here, of all places, and not stored away in a gun cabinet or locked drawer? Could it have something to do with Erin's death? I held it for a few seconds longer, then tucked it back inside the box. On impulse, I snapped a photo before replacing the lid. Once I tidied up the closet, putting everything back the way I found it, I inched the closet door open and peeked around. Taking lengthy steps, I sprinted across the study and out into the hall. Moving fast, I ended back among the crowd of guests who now stood in line, picking through the various appetizers and finger foods, while waiting for the main course to be served.

"There you are. I've been looking everywhere for you. The buffet selection looks unappetizing. So, if it's all the same to you, I'd like to cut out now."

Thank goodness, Penny eyed the front door rather than my face, which probably showed frustration, panic, and relief, all rolled into one mix of emotions. I gazed with care at the room, searching for Miss Long and her fellow employee. Three other staff members stood at the lengthy buffet table, ready to serve guests. No sign of the grey-haired lady who'd helped direct me to the bathroom.

"Sure thing." I followed Penny out into the parking area and hopped in her vehicle, a vintage Mustang painted bright red. I let Penny do the talking.

"I can't wait to write about this. I got nothing to go on about Erin and her murder, but here's the big news. The Whitmores will be making sizable donations to Chautauqua County small businesses that deal in arts and crafts. Who knows? Maybe yours and mine will be two of them. Isn't that exciting?"

"Um, hmm. Yeah, it would be." I half-listened to her chatter because I had a conversation of my own going on in my head. Fingering the bits of trash in my pockets, I couldn't help but wonder how many secrets Alan Whitmore was hiding because my gut told me there were quite a few and several of them about Erin.

Chapter Fourteen

I forked a couple of potato pancakes from the stack. Dad's special recipe, using seasonings he kept a secret, were too delicious to resist, despite the calories. Sitting back in my chair at the table, I chewed a bite contentedly.

"I don't understand why you take such chances," Mom said with a pointed stare at me.

"You mean like the chance you suggested we take to sneak into the men's locker room at the fitness center and check out a certain someone's shoe size? That kind of chance?" Izzie teased with a wink.

I smiled. This past spring, we did just that but never got caught. Fortunately, the risk paid off, and Mom never spoke of it again.

"That was different," she sniffed. "The Whitmores are not the kind of people you mess around with."

"Wait a minute. I thought you liked the Whitmores. You told me they are respected for their generosity in the community and showed great love for their children," I said.

"Well, they are all that, but they also are very powerful people who tend to get their own way. You could've been caught, arrested, and put in jail." Mom's brow creased with worry. "We can't have that happen."

"Look. Everything turned out all right. So, can we leave it at that? In any case, I'll pass along my news to Hunter, and he'll take it from there. No more lurking about in places we shouldn't." I felt a twinge of agitation. At least Izzie was excited by my news. The pistol was a huge discovery. If Erin's death was murder, I might have found the weapon used to shoot her. As for the trash I'd lifted from the Whitmore study, I kept them a secret. I needed to decide if any of it was important first, and I hadn't yet had the opportunity. Late to bed and early to rise was my excuse. What I had noticed were some tiny bits and pieces that looked to be part of a photo.

"Props for finding out the reporter who covered Clive's story. That's huge." I used the comment to shift the conversation away from my risky actions.

"Maybe. Time will tell. I tried getting in touch with him, but he's out of town on assignment until next week. At least I found out Benson Brown was nowhere near Buffalo in the days before or after Clive died," Izzie said.

"How'd you find out that?" I eyed another potato pancake but dished out several chunks of fruit from the serving bowl instead. Making healthy choices was hard.

"I called in a favor." Izzie grinned.

"Ah." I nodded. Her friend who worked at La Guardia. Becky had access to flight lists that would cover any travelers flying out of New York. Chances were, if Benson had left Buffalo by plane, Becky would find out.

"It was a stretch, I know. To think he'd gone anywhere, especially flying, were against all odds. Still, I was willing to cover all options. This one just happened to pay off." Izzie dabbed her lips.

"What about the day Erin died?" We already knew Benson had spoken to her the day before.

Izzie shook her head. "I couldn't find out more than what we already have."

"Okay, then. I think that's enough talk about the case. How about this evening's event at the amphitheater? You still plan to go with us?" Dad asked as he gathered dishes from the table.

"Absolutely. Max is ready too. Aren't you, buddy?" I laughed.

Max stood on hind legs and pawed the air with a bark.

"I'll take that as a yes. Izzie, what about Brody and Rex?" I turned.

"Yep. They'll meet us at the park by seven-thirty." She stood and finished the last dregs of coffee from her cup before rinsing it off at the sink.

The last movie of the season, *The Secret Life of Pets*, was showing at the amphitheater. Because of that, we'd made sure to keep the evening free from our schedule of events. All dogs contained on leashes were invited. Cats, too, if brought in carriers. Pet owners appreciated the gesture to include their fur friends. Time would tell if such an event worked smoothly. I had my fingers crossed.

After helping with the dishes, Izzie and I headed upstairs.

"Are you still meeting Hunter for lunch?" Izzie asked as she stopped at her bedroom door.

"Yep. I called him first thing this morning to see if he was free. I'm hoping we'll have news to swap." Though not always, Hunter could be accommodating and share important details about a case I was in some ways connected to. On other occasions, his lips were sealed tight as a steel trap.

I pampered myself with a bath instead of a shower, giving myself plenty of time to mull over what we'd accomplished. After the news Izzie shared about Benson Brown, I was tempted to take him off our people-to-watch list. Sure, he was friends with the Whitmores and knew quite a lot about them. That wasn't enough to pin a bullseye on him as the killer. Talking with Erin the day before seemed coincidental, an incident that had no implications. That left the parents, Alan and Faith Whitmore, Arthur Storing, Peter Fanning, and Terence Ashe. We really didn't know much about Fanning or Ashe, only hearsay. Faith was almost completely convinced that Fanning, Erin's boyfriend, did the deed. I wanted a lot more evidence, and we'd have a chance to acquire that when Izzie and I visited him at The Bistro, as soon as he returned from his trip. As for Ashe, Carli Descente's opinion was questionable. For one thing, I wasn't sure I trusted her. She'd acted bizarre, flighty, and what about the fortune teller mumbo jumbo? I didn't buy into tarot card readings and all that occult or spiritual stuff. Still, her information could be valid, and I wouldn't dismiss any potential suspect until that suspect was found in the clear.

I stepped out of the tub and dried off. Once I dressed and fixed my hair, I made a path for downstairs to feed Max. With that many suspects, Izzie and I had lots of work to do. Starting tomorrow. But for today, I'd have some relaxing fun this evening going to the park to watch *The Secret Life of Pets*, chat with friends, cuddle with one special guy, or make that two special guys, and enjoy the moment. But first up, lunch with Hunter. Despite my anxiety in confessing my faux pas at the Whitmore Estate, that was, snooping where I shouldn't have been, I was curious to know more about the weapon I'd found in the closet. I felt confident the pistol was used to murder Erin. At least ninety percent sure. I shrugged my shoulders. Maybe more like seventy percent.

After dishing out kibble for Max, I hurried out of the house to meet Hunter. Once I pulled to the curb in front of Millie's, I spotted Hunter through the front window, already seated in a booth. Taking a few breaths to calm my nerves, I entered the diner.

Hunter stood and wrapped his arms around my waist. "I love how seeing you warms my heart." He whispered in my ear.

I felt the heat rise in my cheeks. "I hope you feel that way after what I'm about to tell you." Might as well rip off the Band-Aid, I figured.

His jaw tightened before his shoulders slumped in a gesture of defeat. "Then let's have a bite to eat and something cold to drink first. Okay?"

I nodded without a word. As always, he knew how to take it slow, especially when he guessed troubling news was about to come out.

Once the orders were in and our server disappeared, we managed small talk—when we'd meet this evening at the park, the latest news about the Whisper Cove Ferry being closed until late spring for some repairs, and the cooler weather prediction for next week.

I finished the last bite on my plate, then drained my second glass of tea. Leaning back against the booth, I sighed. Postponing the inevitable didn't help ease my nerves.

Hunter wiped his mouth with a napkin, then crumbled it up. "Okay, let's have it. What did you do, and how much is it going to upset me?"

I blinked and treaded water by starting out with the good parts. "I think I found the weapon used in Erin Whitmore's case."

His jaw dropped. "What? How could you—?"

I quickly opened the photo on my phone and slid the device across the table before he could finish. "That's it. You see? A pistol I found hidden in a packing box and tucked away in a closet. Do you think it could be the weapon you're looking for?"

He pulled the phone closer and narrowed his eyes. "Whose closet?" When I didn't answer, he glanced up. The intense scowl puckered his forehead.

I splayed fingers on the table. "Look, it's more important that this could be the weapon used to shoot her, right?"

"Chloe." My name was drawn out as he said it, giving me a warning not to fool around.

"Fine. The closet is in the Whitmores' study. I admit it wasn't my best move, but it paid off."

"You could've been in so much trouble if someone caught you. You know that." He shook his head, but kept an eye on the photo. "The thing is, we don't have that many leads to figuring out this case. What surprises me is how the crime team missed it. Sloppy work."

"Or it was placed in the closet afterward," I suggested. After taking a second to think about it, I decided now was that opportunity I'd been waiting for. "Hunter, there may be some other people you'd want to consider investigating. To help with those leads you're looking for?"

His tongue made a sucking sound. "And who might those people be?"

I spilled the story of meeting Carli and her comments about Terence Ashe. "At their group meetings, Ashe made plenty of comments that implied he despised the Whitmores. He even got into a huge argument with Erin."

"Okay." He typed the name on his phone, then lifted his gaze. "Who else?"

"Peter Fanning. He is or was Erin's boyfriend. Faith Whitmore is convinced he could've killed Erin. She knew they'd been having problems. Now, I see that look. You're thinking both those are based on opinion and not evidence." I threw up my arms. "But, come on. Don't many potential suspects start out as possibilities without evidence? Look at Martin. He knew Erin, and based on Alan's story, he visited her that evening."

"Opportunity." Hunter held up one finger, then added another. "And motive. Remember? I told you about Clive having a business deal with a college friend, meaning Steele, that was not going well. We know from searching through Erin's emails how she was investigating her brother's death. Plus, Steele visited the estate the night Erin was shot. The housekeeper confirmed Alan Whitmore's story. If Erin confronted Steele and accused him of causing Clive's death, silencing her would be Steele's motive. You have to see where I'm coming from."

"But you don't have proof Erin felt that way about Steele. Now, you're speculating," I argued. "For all you know, Steele had no more reason than Fanning or Ashe or Storing to murder her. Even her parents were upset with how she kept blabbing to anyone who'd listen, telling them Clive was murdered. I'm not going so far as to say Alan would harm his own daughter, but hey, people do some insane things."

He sighed with a slight headshake. "Point taken."

Relieved, I leaned back in my seat. "Have you spoken to Storing yet?" I risked the chance of pushing him too far. He had plenty of cases to work on besides solving Erin's.

"I did. He's a bit eccentric, isn't he? From what I can tell, he's obsessed with the Whitmore family, but does that make him a killer?"

"Too obsessed, if you ask me. And you should know that he's aware of the seascape Clive gave to Martin. Even Benson Brown, who runs the gallery, didn't know about it. I doubt more than a few were aware Clive had painted the seascape." The thoughts kept reeling in my head. I waved to the server and asked for a refill on my drink.

"As for Storing, he and Clive had numerous conversations, right up to Clive's death. Nothing suspicious there." He pushed a few buttons, then handed the phone back to me. "I sent myself a copy of your photo, but this is becoming a complicated death."

"Why? What do you mean, complicated? Erin was shot in the study. The pistol was hidden in the study. Makes sense to me." I hugged both arms tightly across my chest.

"I can send someone from the team out to the estate this afternoon to confiscate the gun. We'll tell the Whitmores there's been a development and we need to do another search of the crime scene." He drummed his fingertips on the table. "Ballistics can handle the rest."

I fiddled with the salt shaker, twisting it back and forth, before sliding it back in position, next to the pepper. "There's something you're hiding. I know your tell, Hunter Barrett. Tugging at your left ear. It's the thing you do. Now, spill."

"This stays between you and me. Not even Izzie can know. Got it?" His voice lowered.

I crossed my chest. "What is it?"

"A partial report from the coroner came through last night. "

"What do you mean?"

"The coroner found powder burns on Erin's hand and on her clothes."

"Which tells you what?" My heartbeat thumped against my chest.

"She was shot at close range. I see two possible scenarios. Either she fought with her killer or she committed suicide." The grim expression surfaced.

"Suicide? That can't be." I shook my head in denial.

"The coroner hasn't finished, so we'll see what he decides."

After her brother's horrible death, would Erin have been depressed enough to take her own life? Her relationship problems with both Fanning and her parents certainly didn't help her disposition. But suicide? She'd been determined to find out why Clive died, to prove it was murder. She'd even called Martin to ask for help. It didn't make sense, and I refused to accept Erin killing herself was a possibility. I settled back in my seat and kept quiet. The coroner was going to have to come up with some serious evidence to change my mind.

* * *

"Scoot over. I can't see the stage over this guy's head," Izzie whispered in my ear.

I shimmied to the left a few feet with Max on my lap. The evening was refreshingly cool, and only a slight breeze came off the lake. We'd laid a thick comforter on the ground to avoid any dampness and carted a cooler filled with beverages and sandwiches. Bob's Barbecue Pit was closed for the evening so Bob could enjoy the movie with his furry friend, Picasso. I warmed to the idea that someone was able to coax the free-spirited feline into domestic living. Until recently, Picasso—the name I'd aptly given him—

wandered from house to house where he'd appreciatively consume the milk and food people would set out for him, but was never willing to accept anyone as his adopted family. I had a feeling the scent of barbecue that lingered on Bob was the winning bribe.

I stroked Max's fur, as if the gesture would ease the discomfort I'd had since lunch. Keeping Hunter's startling news about Erin's possible suicide from Izzie added to my stress. I didn't like imagining Erin's last moments, but the thought refused to leave my mind. At all costs, I'd promised Hunter to keep this information between us. This time, I planned to keep that promise, for now, anyway. Even when Izzie found out, which she would eventually, she'd be spitting mad at me. I wouldn't blame her, either.

When we'd first arrived at the park, Izzie got a phone call from the Whitmores' lawyer. Neither of us could believe the news. Our shop was one of the recipients of a generous donation from the Whitmore Foundation. On the surface, the gesture looked very selfless, but not to me. I suspected giving us money carried an unspoken message from the Whitmores, a warning to stay clear of the investigation into their daughter's murder. And I'd bet my last dollar that Alan had somehow found out I was the one in his study that evening. With an estate like theirs, security cameras had to be hidden all over. Mom and Hunter were right. I'd been foolish and had taken a huge risk.

"Hey! Would you look at that? Our favorite writer, who likes to boast of knowing all things about the Whitmores, is here and talking to Tito Alma, of all people. I'd love to hear *that* conversation," Izzie announced.

I glanced across the park grounds to where Izzie pointed. "Kind of strange, but then again, Storing seems the type who'd talk to anyone." Doubt crept in, just a bit. "He is a long way from home. Why come to Whisper Cove, just to see a movie?"

Arthur tugged on the leash of a brown and tan pug who seemed less excited about being here. The somewhat overweight canine took a few turns and then plopped down. His chest heaved from the effort.

"Maybe they know each other. Rather unlikely, but still possible." Izzie turned and waved at Brody as he and Rex walked toward us. "Be right back."

She sprinted across the lawn.

"What do you say we go for a walk to stretch our legs? Okay, buddy?" I patted Max's head. Only one way to find answers, I figured. Direct my questions to those involved.

Approaching the two men, I gazed at Arthur. "What a surprise to see you here, Mister Storing. It's definitely not a short drive from Buffalo."

"Oh, I stop by Whisper Cove quite often. Surprising we haven't run into each other, isn't it?" He fanned his arm across the park. "This place with its floating amphitheater, and now a movie where I can bring Rufus. I couldn't resist."

I glanced down at Max, who was sniffing Rufus in places he didn't seem to like. The pug stopped panting to let out a low but effective growl. Max backed away. "I thought you owned a cat?"

He chuckled. "You are correct. Rufus belongs to a friend who asked me to watch him for a few days while he's away on business."

I turned to face Tito. "I don't believe we've met?"

"Where are my manners. Chloe Abbington, meet Tito Alma." Arthur patted Tito on the shoulder while a satisfied grin stretched his lips. "He's been my inspiration for writing books on South American art. We go back decades, don't we, Tito?"

"Let's not exaggerate. We're hardly that ancient. It's a pleasure to meet you, Chloe." Tito took my hand and planted a kiss.

I hitched my breath and felt the heat rising to my face. The man was well aware of his good looks and the effect it had on women. "Welcome to Whisper Cove. I've heard a lot about you from my parents. You deal in art and antiquities." In truth, Dad wasn't a fan of Tito. According to him, even though Alma was one of the top dealers in the United States, he often cut corners and broke the rules to get the merchandise his clients wanted. Yet, as far as Dad knew, Tito never crossed the line by stealing or venturing into the black market.

"Ah, of course. Your parents are quite the pair, always turning up someplace in the art community. I've seen them at some of the auctions. In fact, they recommended this movie night event. What a unique idea. A floating amphitheater. Your town should be proud."

Max sniffed at Tito's pant leg. I gave the leash a tug, but he resisted. "Sorry about that. Max is too curious."

Tito extended an arm to give Max a pat on the head. "Hello, Max. Nice to meet you."

With a loud growl and bark, Max backed up. Tito laughed and threw up his hands. "Looks like his curiosity has expired." Tito checked his watch. "Sorry to cut this lovely conversation short, but I have to meet with a client soon. Arthur, I will see you in a couple of days." He tipped his hand and hurried away.

"He seems nice. And you're getting together again soon. Is he helping you with another project?" I struggled to keep from looking overly curious. Storing, from what I was able to gather, read people easily.

"Not exactly. But speaking of art reminds me. I want to write about local artists and their businesses. If you and your sister have some time to spare, I'd love for you to stop by the apartment to answer a few interview questions. I'd give you both a mention in the acknowledgements, of course," Storing said.

In my head, a couple of expletives spilled out. He had steered the conversation right past my question in one quick move. "Sure. Maybe tomorrow? We're driving into Buffalo for business. I'll talk to Izzie, but I'm sure she'll agree to come." I nodded, then watched as he turned to find his seat in a lawn chair.

"What do you make of that, Max? Tito and Storing are besties who happen to run into each other in Whisper Cove, of all places, and now Storing wants us to help with a book project. Strange developments, wouldn't you say?"

"Woof." Max pawed the air.

"Agreed." I patted him on the head before we strolled back to our blanket, where Izzie, Brody, and Rex sat. Max let out a few more barks with his tail wagging, excited to see his canine buddy.

Izzie pointed. "What was that conversation about?"

"Let me get settled first, then I'll tell you everything." Once seated, I pulled some drinks and sandwiches from the cooler. Soon, I began to recap what I'd learned, but cut the story short when the movie came to life. There would be time later to discuss what the relationship between Tito and Storing could mean, if anything. Right now, I'd enjoy the movie with family and friends.

The evening had turned out almost perfect, since Hunter had cancelled at the last minute because of work. The movie made people laugh and dogs bark, while the feline viewers mostly yawned and took naps. Definitely, cats were hard to please. As for me, I left the park totally relaxed and rejuvenated, ready for whatever came next. That included anything to do with Erin's murder. I might have been thrown and panicked by Hunter's latest news, but that feeling didn't last for long.

We turned into the drive. Stepping up to the porch, I said my goodbyes to Brody as he and Izzie walked around back to sit on the deck. I was suddenly exhausted, but not enough to keep me from checking out what I'd brought home from the Whitmore study.

I carried a sleepy-eyed Max upstairs and set him on my bed, tucked close to his favorite pillow. Pulling open the nightstand drawer, I fished out the trash I'd confiscated and spread out all the pieces on top of my comforter. A crumpled note with names and dates proved it was tossed recently, like in the last couple of days. The other torn bits I quickly recognized as parts to a photo. Arranging and rearranging, I worked the pieces like a puzzle. Soon, they formed a photo of Erin standing in the forefront. However, that's not what caused me to gasp.

I swallowed hard. If I took Erin out of the picture, the similarities were uncanny. The photo had been taken at a beach, overlooking the ocean, with a lighthouse off to the right. "Just like Clive's painting, only..." I peered closely at the tinier details. Gulls, like tiny specs of gray, soared above the water. And there was an orangish glow of the sun hanging low in the sky. "But no sign of a ship," I whispered, as if someone could be listening, while questions crowded my brain. Did Erin's search for answers about her brother's death lead her to this beach? The same one Clive had obviously visited at one time. Or maybe they had gone there together? Someone had been with her to take the photo. If not Clive, then who? Maybe her boyfriend, Peter, or one of her parents. Or was it someone else I couldn't think of? What if she'd seen the painting? That could've triggered a memory or given her a clue. I stared at the torn pieces. And who else but Alan would've torn the photo and thrown it away? No one else, I thought. The question was, why?

Chapter Fifteen

I stewed over my decision during breakfast, then again while getting dressed. Hunter needed to know about the torn photo. I groaned. This would be yet another confession to make. I picked up my phone and pressed the call button.

"Good morning. Why are you awake so…it's only six-thirty. Kind of early for you," Hunter teased.

"Funny you. Truth is, I couldn't sleep." I sat on the edge of my bed with my legs dangling.

"Why not?"

I heard the rustling of paper and smiled. The old-fashioned part of him insisted the only way to read the newspaper was by holding paper in your hands. Not on some phone app. "I have more news to share."

"Boy. You've been a busy lady. Is this another one of those moments when you tell me you've been places you shouldn't be or something?"

"How about we move past that and onto the more important stuff?" I scooted back and sat cross-legged.

"Hmm."

"Right. I found a photo. Well, sort of. It was torn into pieces, but I put them back together." I explained my discovery, including where I'd found it. "You see? Alan had to put it there. He's the only one who goes into the study. Other than the night Erin did, I mean." I took a breath. "What if it holds some kind of clue? Maybe he wanted to hide it because it makes him look guilty for some reason."

"Chloe. I can barely keep up with the information my team gathers. You piling on more is killing me." He paused. "But I do appreciate everything you've done. I keep saying the Captain should hire you and Izzie. Anyway, send me a snapshot of the photo. I'll take it from there."

"Will do. I promise to stop bringing you anything more about the case. Or at least I'll try. Love you." I hit the end call button, then sprinted downstairs. The pressure had lifted off my shoulders. Unloading that bit of news helped. Only a tiny twinge of guilt seeped in for adding more to Hunter's investigation. After all, he was the detective, and investigating was his job. I knew he could handle it.

I met Izzie in the foyer where she was putting on her jacket. "You ready for the trip to Buffalo?"

"Yep." She slung the strap of her bag over one shoulder. "We should be done at the art supply store in a half hour. On the way, shoot Storing a text to say we'll be at his place by ten. I'm really curious to know what he has in mind."

"More to it than writing a book on arts and crafts, I'll bet." I followed her down the drive to the Land Rover.

"I agree. He's up to something."

"Everybody we've met in this case is like that. Secrets, ulterior motives, and more. Totally hard to read." I buckled my seatbelt.

"Good thing we're the snoop sisters who can solve any crime." She grinned.

"Ha. Let's get going, snoop sister. We've got lots to do."

We also planned to stop at The Bistro for lunch. Hopefully, a conversation with Peter Fanning was on the menu. Hurrying back to the shop by three to finish a few work tasks before the monthly merchants' meeting started was the plan. After the break-in at Go Fly a Kite, Gwen Finch had suggested we should form a merchant watch program to look out for each other and our businesses on Artisan Alley. That idea eventually led to the monthly meetings to discuss all sorts of issues.

A quick stop at Maxine's Art Supply to put in our order, followed by a bit of browsing where we ogled the latest in art gadgets, left us ten minutes to reach Storing's apartment.

Izzie pulled next to the curb. "Let's do this."

Storing answered before we had a chance to ring the doorbell. "Come in. Come in. I'm so delighted to see you, ladies." His voice lilted in an almost sing-song way. "Have a seat. This time, I tidied up the place. More space to sit."

I glanced at Izzie and shrugged. At least he was in a great mood. "We're curious to hear what you are planning to write. A book on arts and crafts involves quite a lot."

"You mentioned something about focusing on local talent? How local? I mean, it could be as small as Whisper Cove or as big as all of New York state," Izzie sat on the sofa next to me.

"Goodness. Nothing as huge as that. I was thinking more along the lines of the Chautauqua Lake and Finger Lakes region. Big enough to attract lots of readers, but not too overwhelming for me to write, of course." He skirted around the counter to reach the kitchen. "Drinks? I have tea, soda, and juice."

"Iced tea would be nice," Izzie said.

"Same for me." I glanced at a boxed device sitting on the table in front of us. "Is that a tape recorder? I didn't think people used those any longer."

"Oh." He chuckled. "Call me old-fashioned. Or frugal. It works, so why not use it? Besides, I can't remember conversations like I used to. Can't write fast either. So, recording it is." He set the glasses on the table. "There. Now, shall we get started? Tell me about your shop. What made you think of paint parties? It's fascinating and so trendy."

He threw out one question after another, all of which we answered in detail. I had to admit, his excuse for bringing us here appeared legit. The notion we'd walk away without any information about him to help with Erin's murder case was discouraging.

"You've been very helpful, ladies. I plan to interview a couple of others along your alley. Any in particular you'd like to suggest?" Storing lifted his phone. "May I? I want photos in my book."

I stood up a bit too quickly, and my bag dropped from my lap. The contents scattered across the floor. "Oh, good grief. I'm such a klutz."

All three of us bent down to retrieve the items.

Storing stood straight and was eyeing the news article I'd kept about the murdered recluse and the art theft.

After Hunter's story about his investigation, I was curious to learn more, I explained.

Storing gave an exasperated sigh and shook his head. "Such a shame. That poor woman." He handed back the article. "Art theft is so common these days. Not very much effort on the thief's part, other than fear of getting caught. Did you know most small museums have very little security? No surveillance cameras. No motion detectors. Not even a decent burglar alarm. And would you be surprised to know that a good many heists are pulled off during open hours? Someone could just stuff the art in a bag and walk right out of the building without any guard noticing or security device triggering. A Rodin bust was stolen from a Danish museum in this way. Of course, the Mona Lisa theft was before modern security systems were installed. Thieves need to have sophisticated plans nowadays. In the Isabella Gardner museum heist, they disguised themselves as policeman."

I glimpsed the tape recorder once more, then turned to smile at him. "Wow. You certainly seem to know a lot about stolen art." My Spidey sense triggered.

He gestured with a careless wave to dismiss my comment. "I wrote a book on art heists."

I chuckled. "Of course you did. Everything's about art, isn't it?"

"Yes, and about the Whitmores, which does involve a lot of art, come to think of it. Now, how about that photo? He held up his phone as we posed. "Thank you. Now, who should I speak with next?" Storing sat back.

"Penny Swenson. She owns the aromatherapy shop, The Healing Touch. She'd love the publicity and is full of ideas," Izzie said.

"Oh, I know. What about our new shop owner on the alley? He could certainly use a little of that publicity." I glimpsed Izzie, who nodded. "His name is Remy Bouchere. He moved here recently from Louisiana and opened a place called Metallica."

Storing's brows knitted. "Isn't that a heavy metal group?"

I laughed. "Yes, Remy loves that group, but the reason for naming the shop

Metallica is because he works with metal."

"Ah. Clever choice. I will have to look him up." Storing stood up from his seat. "Thank you for coming and sharing your story."

"Glad to. Let us know if there's anything else we can do." Izzie grabbed her bag.

Storing held up his hand. "Now that you offer, there is something. After doing an online search about your business, I noticed you have an event tomorrow evening featuring a Taylor Swift theme. Swiftie Sweet Sixteen, isn't it?"

I blinked. "You know about Taylor Swift? I wouldn't think you listened to her type of music."

"You are right. I don't listen to her, but my niece does. She's a huge fan and would be thrilled to attend. If you have room to add another guest, that is." He folded his hands in a plea. "I know it's a lot to ask."

"Just so happens we have one spot open. She's welcome to join us," Izzie said.

I raced to add, "I almost forgot. Did you find another person to chaperon, Izzie? With thirty teenage girls, we need more than a couple." I worked out the details in my head. "Say, I know. Why don't you join us, Arthur? You can help us out while at the same time, getting personal insight into our business. What do you say?"

"I'd be delighted." He grinned. "Plus, it gives me an opportunity to be with my niece. We don't see each other often enough."

"Then it's settled. The event starts at six, but come early, if you like. You can observe how we set up an event," I added.

"We'll be there." Storing walked us to the door. "So, I almost forgot to ask. Did you get the opportunity to speak with Faith Whitmore? She's not very forthcoming, at least not with me. I'd love to hear anything she may have told you. To include in my next book, of course." His eyes gleamed.

And there it was. I wiped the knowing smile from my face. "Yes, she was very kind but sad, too. I got the hint she didn't want to talk about her daughter, so I didn't press." No way was I sharing what I'd learned from Faith or any other clues we'd gathered about the Whitmores.

"Too bad. I'm sure Faith is keeping some family secrets that the world would love to read about. Have a wonderful afternoon, and I'll see you this evening."

"What was that?" Izzie spoke in a breathy tone as she hurried alongside me to the car. "Why would you invite him to the event?"

"Oh, you know the saying about keeping your enemies closer. Like you, I don't trust Storing. He comes off way too secretive and sly. That's the vibe I get. Besides, spending more time with him might give us the clues to this case we need the most."

"You hope," she said.

"I do hope." I checked my watch. "Almost time for lunch and a chat with Peter Fanning."

Twenty minutes later, we parked in the lot next to The Bistro. The white brick exterior with huge windows framed in black was attractive. Inside, the industrial-style light fixtures hanging from the ceiling gave the place a modern look. Crowded with customers, and with almost every table and seat occupied, I worried Fanning would be too busy to talk.

"Table for two?" Izzie inquired. She gave the host her winning smile, even batting her eyelashes.

I wrinkled my nose as the young man, who couldn't be more than twenty, blushed. Men were too easy when it came to Izzie's charm.

"Right this way." He stumbled out his words, then quickly led the way to a booth near the front and by a window.

After ordering, I watched the comings and goings of the restaurant staff, hoping to catch a glimpse of the head chef. I'd found Peter Fanning's photo on The Bistro's website. The striking good looks would be hard to miss. Raven black hair, chiseled jaw, and a smile that could melt your heart. "What if he's not back from his trip?" I sipped my water.

"Then we enjoy our meal and see if one of his employees likes to gossip." Izzie nodded to a female server standing at the table close to us, who chatted nonstop with the guests. "She seems friendly enough."

"Needles in haystacks, Izzie. We need to speak with Fanning. Gossip won't do."

She sighed. "Let's deal with that problem when or if it happens."

The aroma of freshly baked rolls tickled my nose as the same chatty server approached and set glasses of water at our table.

"Welcome to The Bistro. My name is Addie, and I'll be serving your meal." She placed the basket of rolls, along with butter, in the center. "Is there anything else you need in the meantime?"

"I don't suppose the owner, Peter Fanning, is here today?" Izzie buttered a roll, keeping her gaze on Addie.

"Oh, absolutely. Guarantees your food will be delicious. Mister Fanning makes sure of it." Her voice carried in a bubbly, bouncy lilt.

I had to smile. "Thank you, Addie." After she walked away, I lowered my voice. "Well, at least he's here. Now, if only we can think of a way to get him out of the kitchen to talk."

"Don't worry. I have a plan." Izzie raised her chin.

Soon, our meals were served. The grilled steak sandwich on a hard roll, topped with cheese and a generous portion of mushrooms and onions, sent my appetite into overdrive. The sight and smell of it made my stomach growl, but oh my, the calories I'd need to burn off.

"At least the food is delicious. Try this." Izzie forked a bite of her spinach and tomato cheese omelet and held it to my lips.

I moaned. "Oh wow. Gotta say, Peter Fanning might not have Faith's approval because of his personality flaws, but his cooking skills are sublime."

Before long, our plates were empty. I dabbed my lips with the napkin and leaned back against the booth. "I'm stuffed and still waiting to see this plan of yours put into action."

"Watch this." Izzie waved to flag down our server, who made a quick route around tables to reach us. "Would the chef have a moment to speak? We'd love to compliment him on this fantastic meal."

"Oh, yes. Of course. I'll see if he's busy." Addie nodded, then hurried away.

"Clever." I pointed. "What do you plan to say to him, though? Something like 'hey, Peter. Did you happen to kill your girlfriend?' I don't think that'll work."

Izzie sniffed. "I'm clever. Isn't that what you said? Wait and see."

The blue-eyed, handsome chef, whose physique was just as impressive as his face, walked toward us. He wore the typical chef's white uniform that those in the high-end restaurants wore. Or at least restaurants that wanted to make a good impression on their customers.

"Good afternoon, ladies. I'm so glad you're enjoying your meal. It's always nice to hear praise from the customers." He smiled.

"So delicious. You should be proud. In fact, lots of people have recommended your place. One of them you might know. Erin Whitmore? She couldn't say enough good things about The Bistro." Izzie squeezed my hand. "Isn't that right, Chloe?"

I played along. "Absolutely. Such a sad tragedy about her death, though."

Peter's smile stiffened. Still, he managed to speak in a calm, even voice. "Yes, I knew Erin well. Her family is devastated. Now, if there's nothing else I can help you with, I should get back to the kitchen. Have a pleasant day." He snapped his fingers at Addie. "Addie, would you deliver two *mousse au chocolat* to this table? On the house, of course." In seconds, he disappeared through the kitchen door.

"Sorry. Peter can be a bit temperamental at times." Addie released a nervous titter. "If you prefer a different dessert, I can bring that out instead."

I studied her face. "Have you worked here long?"

"Four years this coming January." She cleared our plates.

"So, you know Peter pretty well?" I pushed, hoping to get more out of the chatty server.

"Umm, you could say that." She set the plates on the rolling tray beside her. With a quick glance at the kitchen doorway, just as Peter peered through a window. "Would you like your desserts in to-go boxes?"

"Sure. I think that will do," Izzie said.

As Addie hurried away, I whispered, "You look like the Cheshire Cat, all smug. He was totally thrown off when you mentioned Erin, but that only tells us what we already knew. We need more."

"I think we'll get that from our new friend." Izzie held up a note in her hand and chuckled. "A message from Addie asking us to meet her outside in the parking lot."

I gasped. "When did she give you that?"

"The fast hands of a server. I think when she took my plate, she dropped the note. It's not important. As soon as we pay the bill, we'll go wait around the corner where we can't be seen. She probably has to find a moment when Peter isn't watching."

We exited the restaurant, and, within minutes, the petite form of Addie appeared. She shifted her gaze side to side and behind her a couple of times. Her chest rose and fell in a rapid beat. The poor thing was terrified, I thought.

"Sorry. I don't want him to know I'm out here." She heaved a deep breath to calm herself. "Okay, so I heard you mention Erin Whitmore's name during your conversation with Peter. He didn't look too pleased. Of course, he wouldn't. He and Erin were tight once. Actually, for a long time. At least that's what I heard." She tapped the side of her head with one finger. "I'm pretty observant and I know plenty, see plenty of what goes on around here. Just ask any of the staff. If they want to know the scoop, I'm the one who can tell all."

"Yes, I see that." Izzie narrowed her gaze. "And what we'd like to learn is anything about Peter's and Erin's relationship."

Addie's eyes widened. "Oh, you heard about that, did you? The arguments, almost like shouting matches that went on in the past couple of months. The scene was pretty embarrassing." She clucked her tongue. "Not acceptable behavior for the workplace, is it? Anyway, this one time, and it was only a few days before she died, they had a huge blowout, right outside the restaurant door where anyone could see. Erin was crying and screaming. She accused Peter of never loving her and that he only dated her for her family's connections. A real gold digger. So sad, really. I mean, a year ago, they were like this perfect couple. Relationships. They are so dramatic at times."

"That is sad. Tell me, did Peter ever get physical with Erin? Shove her, slap her, or anything like that?" Izzie asked.

"Oh, wow. No. Never. Or at least nothing I've witnessed. Do you think…? Oh, God. Are you saying he killed her? That would be…" She gave her head a firm shake. "I can't imagine Peter doing something like murder. He does have a horrible temper, like sometimes he'll scream at his sous chef for ruining a dish. But murder? It's impossible to imagine." She twisted her hands.

"Impossible but probable. Like you said, relationships hold a lot of drama. Now, did Erin say more? Mention why she thought he was a gold digger?" Izzie asked.

I knew what Izzie was thinking. Faith had called Peter the same thing. Did Erin only repeat what her mother had said, or did Peter finally do something to make Erin realize Faith was right all along?

"Not that I remember." Addie wrinkled her brow. "But she did mention breaking up with Peter."

"I'm sure that didn't go over so well," I said.

"Not by a mile. Peter turned red, and after Erin stormed off, he screamed at all of us to mind our own business and get back to work. That's about it." Addie twisted her hands. "I should warn you, don't ever cross him and become his enemy. No telling what he'd do."

We thanked her for being brave enough to risk her job to tell us about Peter and Erin, then moved around the corner to the parking lot.

I pulled up short and splayed my fingers across Izzie's chest to hold her back. "Look. It's Fanning. He's standing close to our car."

Fanning leaned against a black truck, not more than six feet away from the Land Rover. He had legs crossed at the ankles and a cigarette in one hand. Taking a puff or two, he kept a steady gaze on us.

"No point in staying in this spot, is there? He may take his time, smoking for a long while. We can't wait," Izzie hissed, then moved to walk around me.

"And if he wants to talk, ask about our conversation with Addie? Then what?" I caught up to keep walking alongside her. I wasn't about to show Peter Fanning I was scared of him. And I wasn't. Mostly wasn't, anyway.

"Then we'll talk. I'm not going to back down. He's got to know that we won't." She set her jaw.

However, Fanning stayed in the same spot, keeping the same cross-legged stance and smoking his cigarette.

As I slid into my seat on the passenger side, I glimpsed him through my window. Closer now, the scowl and steely glare was more noticeable. He flicked the cigarette butt, then walked away without a word.

"I think Addie's warning about enemies comes too late." I gulped. "If he murdered Erin, he and his temper would do anything to anyone who could get close to the truth. Like us. I'm sure he knows who we are. I don't like this, Izzie."

"Yeah, neither do I." Izzie shifted into gear and raced out of the parking lot.

Chapter Sixteen

Max sprinted across the yard and back again, chasing the Frisbee. I leaned back to rest on my elbows. A chuckle escaped my lips. His energy gave mine a boost, which it needed. I hadn't slept well last night, worrying about Fanning and what Addie had told us. Erin's boyfriend was someone to keep an eye on and be wary of, at all times. Unless the server was lying or exaggerating. I had to consider that, too.

"We did the right thing. Mom and Dad shouldn't deal with this. Besides, once Erin's murder is solved, everything will be back to normal," Izzie said.

"I'm glad you agreed to not tell them. Mom and Dad have enough on their plate." The patrons of the arts group's president had asked them for a favor. Not a small one, either. Leading the next charity event at one of the art society's most influential organizations next month, plus hosting a small dinner party at our house? That nearly gave Mom hives, while Dad took charge to plan every detail. The dollar signs stacked up, but at least they had a huge budget to work with.

"Now, if we could only figure out exactly what caused the big rift between Erin and Peter, that would help." Izzie lay down and stared up at the sky.

"I'm confident something will show up when we're digging for clues." I got to my feet and brushed off the grass cuttings from my pants. "Meanwhile, we have an event this evening and possibly an opportunity to learn more from Arthur Storing."

After breakfast, we drove to the shop in my Mazda. The engine hummed quietly, and the AC worked. The tiniest things made me happy. Pulling into my usual spot, I heard my phone ring. "Hunter." I waved at Izzie as she gestured with her thumb toward the shop. Once she closed the car door, I opened the call.

"Hey, you handsome detective. Why are you calling so early? Let's see. Maybe you need my amateur sleuthing skills to help with a case? Or you just wanted to hear my voice?" I teased.

"Well, I do love to hear your voice, and your skills are impressive, but that's not why I called. Not exactly. Can you meet me at Spill the Beans around eleven? I need to share a few developments in Erin's case."

"Ah, so it is my detective abilities you're after. Okay then, my dear Watson, I'll be there at eleven."

"Hey, maybe I want to be Holmes."

"Sorry, that role is taken." I laughed. "See you at eleven."

Fresh-brewed coffee, Tom's delicious avocado Benny, and news about the case. Who could resist? It was like I told Izzie, something always popped up, and opportunity could be just around the corner. I hummed a Taylor Swift tune as I strolled down the path to our shop.

I passed through the doorway to find Izzie holding up two canvases, each with an image of Taylor Swift.

"Which do you think works best? The abstract in bold colors? Or the more detailed, realistic portrait in pastels? I can't decide." Izzie shifted her gaze back and forth, from one to the other, while chewing her bottom lip.

I sat on the stool. "I thought we already chose the abstract. You know, because it would be easier to draw? We're dealing with a group of teen girls, many of whom have little to no experience in art."

"Yeah, but this one has pizzazz and seems so stylish with the pastel colors," Izzie said.

"Pizzazz?" I chuckled. "I'm not so sure anyone our age uses that word, but I do see your point. I still say it comes down to which image is easier for the girls to draw and paint."

Izzie sighed and set down the one with pizzazz, as she called it.

I shook my head. "Why not save that one for a window display?"

"Great idea. Okay, so which one of us is going to paint the step-by-step canvases to hang on the wall?" She picked up a clean towel and wiped the counter clean.

"How about we flip for it?"

"Nice try. You always win a coin toss. Why don't I save us the effort and just offer to paint them myself?" Her lips spread into an impish grin.

I let go of an exaggerated sigh. "If you insist."

A wadded towel flew across the room and landed in my lap. "Funny you. Better get to work."

For the next hour, we stayed busy taking care of shop tasks and prep for the Swiftie event and sharing news about the latest happenings in Whisper Cove. There truly was nothing like work to keep your mind off problems.

A few minutes before eleven, I set aside my project for the next event and got out of my chair. "Time for me to meet Hunter. He's promised to share the latest about Erin's case."

"Good luck. And remember to return the favor," Izzie said.

I tilted my head and frowned.

"You should give him some details about our latest news, too." She nodded.

"Oh, you mean about Fanning? I'll see what Hunter has to offer first." I winked as I stepped outside.

After a brisk walk, I entered Spill the Beans a couple of minutes after eleven. A tune from the sixties, Tom Prichard's favorite era of music, played through the speakers. Hunter was already seated in a booth. I waved to Tom as I passed by. Leaning over for a quick smooch on Hunter's cheek, I then slid into the seat across from him. "Hello, Doctor Watson. Having a good morning, I hope?"

He rolled his eyes. "Yes, Holmes. It's been very eventful." Holding up the carafe, he added, "Coffee?"

"Yes, please." I stirred in a heavy dose of creamer. "So, what's this new development? Have you already solved the case?"

"Straight to business. Fine. I'm frustrated how slowly the lab results have been coming in. The department is swamped with too many cases. Anyway, the fingerprints we collected identified who we expected. Erin, Alan, Steele, but the identity of the fourth set threw me. Peter Fanning, the boyfriend you told me to take a look at." He sipped his coffee. "Why am I not surprised?

Anyway, he's earned a spot at the top of my who-to-investigate list. Thanks to you. My team is compiling a profile of Fanning as we speak."

I scratched the back of my neck. "Hunter, I have—"

"I know. You're about to say I told you so, but we're making progress. Seems Fanning and Erin had a huge argument in front of witnesses. She accused him of being a gold digger, using her for contacts to drum up business."

"Hunter, this is—"

"Yeah, it's a lot to take in. Erin's mother seems to agree with that opinion of Fanning. In fact, his staff at The Bistro—"

"Hunter!" I grabbed his hand. "Please, let me talk."

"Oh." He straightened. "I'm sorry. Did you want to add something?"

I shifted in my seat. "Yes, I do. Izzie and I know about the argument. We went to The Bistro yesterday and spoke with Fanning as well as with Addie, one of his servers."

A bemused hint of a smile surfaced. "I see. Busy ladies, huh? Then maybe I should be asking you about Fanning. Somehow, I get the impression you have my team beat."

I relaxed. "I very much doubt that." I recapped our visit to the restaurant. "What worries me is Addie's warning. She swears Fanning's temper gets out of control, especially when someone crosses him. Being his enemy is not healthy, and I'm pretty sure after yesterday, he considers us two of them."

"This is why I tell you what I do." His voice softened. "Be careful. Getting hurt isn't worth it. Not even to help a dear friend."

"You're probably right." I shrugged.

"Which means my advice falls on deaf ears." His hands splayed on the table as he pressed down. "That being said, I appreciate the info. Let's leave it at that."

Relieved to hear him move on, I asked, "Any news about the art theft at the storage facility?"

"Not very much. No sign of damage to the entrance door, and the security cameras were turned off. It leads me to think someone on the inside was part of their plan."

I recalled Storing's comments about art heists. He'd mentioned thieves needed creative ways to get away with their schemes. A flicker of an idea interrupted my thoughts, but then vanished. "Have you checked out the employees? Maybe one of them has a rap sheet."

Hunter chuckled. "Thinking like a detective and using lingo like rap sheet. Yes, we're working on that. The facility has a staff of twenty, both full-time and part-time. Good news is a traffic cam nearby caught a black van speeding through a red light. That was a few minutes after the call came in about the theft. Bad news is the plates were covered."

I gnawed on the pad of my thumb. I didn't say what Hunter must've been thinking. A black van tailed us the day Izzie and I delivered the painting to the facility. Probably a coincidence. Hundreds, maybe thousands, of black van owners in the Buffalo area. "Thank goodness I took photos of the seascape."

"And the photo you found in the Whitmores' study. That tells us Erin had a connection to Clive's painting. Details in both beach scenes are too similar to turn out as coincidental."

I sighed. "So many clues that haven't brought us any closer to solving the case." I ticked off the list of people who could be the killer. Had we eliminated any? Benson Brown. He had an alibi for the time of Clive's death, but not for Erin's, which kept him in play. Also, Faith, Alan, Storing, Fanning, and possibly Terence Ashe remained suspects. Izzie and I had to up our game and narrow down the possibilities. "Have you found anything on Terence Ashe? I know it's only been a couple of days since I told you about him, but I thought—"

"Give me time. Look. Don't worry so much. Sometimes, cases move slowly. And sometimes we get lucky."

"You mean like what Detective Winsell told me. Cases sometimes get solved by mere luck and not by detective work."

"Exactly. Now, how about dessert?" A mischievous grin crossed his mouth.

I moaned. "Why not?"

* * *

I set each of the tables with utensils, plates, napkins, and cups, then made a second pass to add blobs of the paints on the plates. Izzie stood at the front entrance, greeting each person who came through the doorway. I was anxious for Storing to step in and struggled to remain confident he'd show up.

At that moment, a teen girl with auburn hair and freckles walked up to me. "Hi, my name's Kristy, and this is my mom, Tina. My uncle Authur told me to tell you he's sorry he couldn't make it this evening. But we're here, and I'm so excited." She rose on the balls of her feet. "Taylor Swift is my hero. She's everything."

I smiled. Her voice squeaked with enthusiasm that only a teenager could feel. "Well, we're glad you could be here. We promise you'll love what we're painting." I pointed to the abstract image of Taylor and got another squealing response.

"This is so cool. Isn't it, Mom?" Kristy spread her grin from ear to ear, exposing a mouthful of shiny metal braces.

"It certainly is, honey." Tina rested a hand on her daughter's shoulder. "Thank you for inviting Kristy. She's spoken of nothing else since Arthur called yesterday to give us the news."

"Our pleasure. I'm sorry that Arthur couldn't make it. I hope everything is okay?"

"Oh, no. He's fine. Something about work is all he told me. Anyway, I'm glad to fill in as a chaperone, if you like."

"Sure. The other two chaperones are Gloria and Cherie." I pointed. "Standing next to the front counter, if you want to go over and introduce yourself." I glanced at Kristy. "Meanwhile, let's get you settled at one of the tables, okay?" Once I got her seated, I returned to stand next to the projector.

"What's going on?" Izzie stepped near. "Who's the red-haired girl?"

"Storing's niece, Kristy." I explained why Storing hadn't come.

"Really, it would've been difficult to find a moment to speak with him. We'll do it another time. Should we get started?" Izzie turned on the projector to let it warm up.

"Welcome, ladies. Or should I say, Swifties," I began the introductions. A chorus of giggles sounded at hearing me call them Swifties. "I'm Chloe. This is my sister, Izzie. If you have any questions along the way or need help, just call out to one of us."

The projector lit up the screen. Izzie pointed. "I'll be drawing each step of our painting project on the screen."

I crossed the room and pointed at the wall. "Here you'll find step-by-step paintings, and attached at the bottom are notes with tips on what to do. In case all of us are busy helping others, walk up there and take a look."

"Okay, Swiftie fans. Are you ready to have fun?" Izzie sang out.

A resounding yes echoed through the room.

The evening flew by with a ton of noise, but very satisfied and happy girls. The paintings turned out amazing, and I could see some artistic talent in a few. Future art majors, even. Besides their paintings, we gifted each girl with a Swiftie bracelet and took snapshots of them with their final projects to hang up around the room.

"I'll start gathering the trash if you wash the brushes," I said after the last guest left.

Walking up and down each row, I swiped paper plates, cups, and napkins into the wastebasket. Moving to the front, I gathered empty soda cans that some parents or girls had left behind on the counter. I thought about Fanning and what Hunter had told me.

His fingerprints in the study led to one obvious conclusion. He'd been in that room at some point. Was it to speak with Alan, perhaps about a business deal? Sure, Fanning was always hustling. Or what if he'd been there for something more personal, like Alan ordering him to stay away from Erin?

Of course, we had to consider the more damaging reason for him being in there. He could have murdered Erin in the study. Crime of passion? After what Hunter told me, it made sense. I pictured the scene. They argued. Maybe she fought for the gun, lost her grip, fell, and then what? He was so consumed with anger, he shot her? It seemed impossible to believe. I shuddered. My imagination would not let me sleep well tonight.

"Hey. Are you ready?" I jumped as Izzie walked up behind me.

"Good grief. Try not to sneak up on a person like that. All right?" I forced air in my lungs.

"What's got you so uptight?" She lowered her voice.

"It's just this case." I explained my disturbing scenario about Fanning.

"I can see that happening. Did Hunter say he would bring Fanning in for questioning? Would be nice to know if he has a solid alibi and isn't a killer." Izzie sat on a stool next to me.

"It never came up, but my guess is he'll ask him for an alibi and something to confirm it," I said.

Without comment, Izzie locked the door behind us.

"I can't wait to get home, take a shower, and snuggle with Max. I'm excited to watch that new mystery show this evening."

"I'll make popcorn and join you." Izzie followed me to the car. "What's this?" Once on the passenger side, she lifted the windshield wiper and picked up a note from underneath. "A note from Fanning. He wants to meet you tomorrow evening at seven and explain his side of the story about his relationship with Erin." Izzie hesitated, then handed me the note. "I'm coming along, and I'll get Brody for backup. Who knows what could happen?"

Shivers tickled my spine. How had the note got here? Had Fanning been following us? The idea concerned me more than a little. I studied the scribbling of words for a second before glancing up at her. "He says to meet at The Bistro at nine. A public place with lots of people. He wouldn't dare try anything."

"We're coming, and that's final." She stabbed the note with one finger. "The man with the hot temper who takes revenge on his enemies. No way you get to meet him alone."

The stubborn set of her jaw couldn't be ignored. I wouldn't try arguing. It never did any good. "Fine, but stay out of sight."

We traveled across town. Reaching our drive, I felt my phone vibrating in my back pocket where I'd placed it earlier. "What now?" I muttered. Parking the car, I shut off the engine before reading the message.

"Who's texting? Is Hunter sending you a goodnight kiss?" Izzie teased.

"No, the message is from Storing. It says something important came up, and he's sorry he couldn't come tonight but hopes the event was a success."

"You gotta wonder what was the something important. Like you said, he's too secretive and sly. He hasn't told us everything he knows about the Whitmores."

We walked up to the house. "I guess we'll have to wait and see. Right now, we focus on Peter Fanning. And I'm not telling Hunter about this meeting tomorrow. Not until I hear what the man with a hot temper has to say."

Chapter Seventeen

I shuffled the drawings, indecisive about which one worked best in the display window. "Hey, Izzie. Do you think these even work? Maybe we should switch to something more mysterious and dramatic. Black and white masks with some dark and brooding paintings and photos. You know, to fit the mood of a masquerade ball." I sat back with arms braced.

"We don't have any dark and brooding work. Only bright and happy ones." Izzie sat next to me. "Besides, guests will be wearing all sorts of costumes in many colors. Mysterious isn't limited to black and white."

"Yep. You're absolutely right." I swerved to the left to face her. "Speaking of the ball, isn't our town council president supposed to stop by with info about the event so we can create images for the posters to hang up around town? The ball is next Friday, only a week away."

Izzie tipped her head toward the door just as Justin Carpenter, the town council president himself, entered.

"Ladies, how are you?" Justin bellowed. The sound reverberated throughout the room. His cheeks had a rosy glow that never faded, as if to match his cheery personality. He waved a notepad in the air. "I'm sorry for getting to you so late, but with your talent, I'm sure you'll create something impressive, in no time."

"Sure. Let's see what you have in mind," Izzie said.

Peeking around her shoulder, I scanned the nearly three pages of notes. "This seems—"

"Totally doable, but with this amount of work involved, especially on a short deadline, we'll have to charge you more," Izzie blurted out.

I sensed the panic brewing under the surface, yet she hid it well with the calm smile on her face. "Maybe a twenty percent bump in price?" I glanced at Izzie, who nodded yes.

Justin frowned. "That seems a bit extreme."

Izzie held out the pad. "You're welcome to take the job somewhere else. Our schedule is pretty well full. Besides, we've already promised to come early Friday to help with the decorations."

Before he could respond, the door chimes announced another visitor. I puffed my cheeks with air, then slowly released it. Aunt Constance stormed in like a mad hornet.

"Would you believe—oh, hello, Mister Carpenter." She attempted a pleasant social greeting, but in an instant, turned to me and switched her tune. "Can you believe it? I've been robbed."

Both Izzie and I gasped, speechless.

"This is serious, Constance. Did you report the incident? Is there anything we can do to help?" Justin said.

"Are you okay?" I held her arm and guided her to sit in a chair. "I hope it's not too serious. What was stolen?"

She waved an arm. "Nothing like that. It's more—"

The chimes dinged again. Penny entered and stopped just inside the doorway, her legs apart in a deliberate stance. "I have questions." She pulled out the pencil stuck in her hair, and with tablet in hand, she added, "I've just got word that there's been new developments in the Whitmore murder case."

My mouth flapped, worried and waiting for the next person who'd charge through the door. "Um." I pressed my hand on Constance's shoulder. "Wait just a minute while I see what Penny wants. Okay?"

"Fine. I need a moment to recover." Constance gave me a sad-eyed look.

I threw up my hands and fixed my gaze on Izzie, who looked ready to blow a fuse and kick all three of them out of the shop. "Why don't you finish discussing details with Justin while I deal with Aunt Constance and Penny?"

Relief washed over Izzie's face. "Thanks."

"Penny, what is it? What have you heard?" I hid the impatience from my tone.

Her eyes flitted to gaze at each of us before landing on me. "Maybe I should come back when things aren't so busy."

"Aunt Constance will wait. She's resting for the moment. Why don't you tell me what this is about?" I was curious to know what she'd learned. More curious than hearing Aunt Constance's story told me I should get my priorities straight. On the other hand, she wasted no time getting on her phone, talking and laughing. Obviously, she wasn't that upset.

"I heard from a reliable source that a weapon was turned in to the police, one that could be the weapon used to murder Erin." She tipped her head, crinkling her brow. "I don't suppose you know anything about that?"

"Not confirmed a murder, yet, but I know the weapon is a pistol found in the Whitmores' study." I figured she already got those details from her niece's boyfriend. He worked in the department and was thought to have loose lips when it came to police business. Not exactly wise behavior if he wanted to keep his job.

"Um, hmm. That confirms what I heard. How about Martin Steele? I know his prints were found at the scene, and he was reportedly at the house the evening Erin died. Does this mean Hunter and the department will be taking a closer look at him?"

I shrugged. "Can't say. I only know Hunter says he's a suspect, until they verify his alibi."

She tapped the side of her nose. "This reporter will sniff out the story, sooner or later. Now, one more question." She shifted her weight. "I found out you received some of the donation money from the Whitmores' foundation to help local arts and crafts."

My stomach sank. I was afraid this news would get around. Penny couldn't hide the disappointment on her face. "Yes. We got the news from the Whitmores' lawyer. I guess you haven't heard about any others on Artisan Alley receiving donations?" I lifted my voice, hopeful the answer would be yes. If my hunch was right, Alan Whitmore used the gesture to shut me up about what I'd found in the study, but his ploy came too late. I'd already told Hunter at that point.

"Nada. But, it's early." She tapped the pencil. "One other thing to mention before I go. Do you know a guy named Arthur Storing? He called—sounded kind of flaky to me, which made me suspicious. You know how those spam calls can go. Anyway, he wants to meet and discuss my business."

"Oh! Yes, I almost forgot about that." I explained our association with Storing.

"Then I guess I'll get in touch. Only wanted to make sure he wasn't some kind of wacko. Thanks for the chat. See you soon." She waved and rushed out.

"Interesting. Maybe he is on the level," I mumbled while turning and nearly collided, chest to chest with Aunt Constance. "Good grief! I didn't know you were right behind me."

"Penny as a reporter. Well, I'm sure she does a good job. Otherwise, Wink wouldn't have hired her. Now, back to my problem. Can you believe it? That new shop owner, Remy something, stole my employee. And without a word, she up and quit." Her face reddened. "The nerve. What happened to the decency of the employer-employee relationship? A two-week notice would've been nice."

I relaxed. She hadn't been robbed, after all. "I thought you fired your employee. You told me a few months ago. Remember? You said you'd rather do the work yourself so it gets done right."

She batted her hand. "Never mind that. I was swamped, so I hired a young college girl who was anxious to make some money to help with her textbooks. Seems this Remy turned her pretty little head with his good looks and charm. Oh well, I won't have a problem finding someone to replace her. It just threw me off. Now, what's this I hear about the Whitmore donation?"

"It's not a big deal." I downplayed the Whitmores' gesture, purposefully leaving out the amount, which was extremely generous. Thankfully, Aunt Constance didn't ask.

She pursed her lips. "Be careful. The Whitmores are powerful people, and you don't want to owe them anything."

I tensed. "Mom said something similar. How do you know them?" Why did I get the feeling our family was hiding something?

"Let's just say there was a time your uncle David had a run-in with Alan Whitmore, more than once, in fact. Business with a Whitmore is never a good thing. Alan doesn't play by the rules." She poked my shoulder. "But that's all in the past. Right now, I say be careful. Avoid those people, if you can. I want my nieces to stay safe." She planted a kiss on my cheek, then left.

"Thank you, Mister Carpenter. We'll be in touch." Izzie escorted him to the door.

Justin nearly escaped, but Aunt Constance grabbed his arm and chattered on.

I chuckled. "Well, at least we're alone, now."

"Thank goodness." She moaned and sank into a chair. "We finally can get back to our real job."

"Finishing this display, and then preparing for this evening's jack-o-lantern event? I'm with you."

* * *

"You know I'll be careful. You don't have to tell me." As the light turned green, I pumped the gas. The event had run later than expected. We'd arrive at The Bistro with only five or so minutes to spare.

"I'm sorry. Call it nerves. I'm anxious, not knowing what to expect." Izzie fidgeted with her phone. She glanced in the side mirror. "At least we have Brody."

"Would you calm down? Nothing bad or dangerous is going to happen."

Up ahead, the restaurant sign flashed bold red and blue colors. As I turned onto a side street, I entered the rear parking lot. Outside, two employees wearing The Bistro uniforms seemed to be engaged in conversation. I recognized Addie as one of them.

"I think you should speak to her before going inside. Ask her what Fanning's mood is," Izzie suggested.

I stuffed my phone in my bag. "It doesn't matter what mood he's in. We're going to have that conversation about Erin. You sit tight. If I need you, I'll call." I didn't wait for any objections. Hurrying to the door, I stopped for a moment and followed along with Izzie's suggestion. "Hi, Addie. Remember me?"

Addie blinked. "Oh, wow. You're back. Don't tell me you want to go another round with the boss. Brave move." She gestured with her thumb pointed up.

"He called me, asking for a chance to tell his story about his relationship with Erin." I didn't move, hoping she'd dish out another comment about her boss.

"Good luck, but don't take everything he says as the truth. I've caught him in a lie several times. Peter is out for Peter. No one else."

"Thanks for the advice." I nodded, then stepped into the restaurant. I'd expected the place would be practically empty by nine, and I was right. No more than three or four sat at a table near the back. The bartender kept busy drying glasses and placing them back on the shelf. I moved toward his direction. "Hi. I'm supposed to meet Mister Fanning at nine for an appointment."

The muscular figure tensed his jaw and growled out a response I didn't catch. He hitched his thumb toward the back, where the kitchen door was located.

"Thanks." I headed that way, and as I reached the door, it swung open, nearly knocking me in the face. "Woah, there!" I hopped backwards, just in time.

Peter Fanning wiped his sweaty brow. "Sorry. I'm in a hurry to meet—" His eyes widened. "Oh, it's you. I, that is, won't you sit down?" He guided me to a booth on the opposite side of the room where the remaining customers had been sitting.

I watched them file out of the restaurant, one by one. As for the bartender, he tossed his apron on a chair and followed everyone out the door. We were totally alone, except for Izzie and Brody, who sat just outside. I licked my lips. "So, you wanted to talk?"

"Would you care for something to drink?" Before I could answer, he stood and reached over the bar counter to grab two bottles of water. Handing me one, he sat back down. "Sorry. My past two days have been hectic, to say the least." He managed a smile.

I studied his face. Not exactly relaxed, but he did say life was hectic. "I know the police have probably asked you about Erin."

He nodded. "Not surprising I'm on their list of people to investigate."

"Boyfriends and husbands. Police always look at them first. Anyway, I've spoken to Erin's mother. I'll be honest. She doesn't have anything nice to say about you. Can you tell me why?" I figured he was the type who preferred getting straight to the point.

He shook his head. "She never did like me. But I don't blame her. I didn't give any of the family a reason to trust me. And they were right. I was the worst when I first met Erin."

I was stunned. This hadn't been what I expected to hear. "That's quite a confession."

"Well, it's the truth." He raked fingers through his hair. "Look. I know I'm not the kind of guy who makes friends. I'm rude, abrupt even, and never engage in small talk."

"The exact opposite of friendly." I lifted the corners of my mouth. For some reason, I was finding humor in the situation. Sure, he could be dangerous, cagey, a real creep, but starting off with total honesty about himself? That didn't fit.

"No, you're right. I'm all the unpleasant stuff people tend to avoid." He leaned over the table. His arms rested on the surface. "What's more important and even more honest is that I fell in love with Erin. Not right away, but by the time I did, I think I'd already lost her. She stopped believing anything I said. I tried. I begged her to forgive me." He leaned back again, his body slouched in the seat. "She was the best thing that ever happened to me. I know it sounds cliché, but it's true. Unfortunately, I realized that too late."

"But why? What did you do to ruin things with her?" I had a strong hunch what he'd say, what Faith had said, and Addie. Yet, I needed to hear him say it.

"I was greedy. When I met her and found out who her family was, I saw opportunity. I'll admit I used her to make connections that only the

Whitmore name could give me. I went to all the parties and talked to all the right people. It didn't take long for those people to see me for who I was."

"A gold digger? That's what Faith Whitmore called you." He appreciated honesty. I was giving him that.

"Yes. I guess I was. Awful, isn't it?" He reached up to rub his neck. "Look. You probably won't trust anything I say, and I understand why."

He swiped his brow. "This whole situation has me rattled. Would you believe I spend every minute of my days worrying someone is watching me wherever I go? Last night I was locking up and noticed a car at the end of the street. Normally, I'd dismiss it as coincidence, but when I drove out of the parking lot, the car followed me. Paranoid, right? I just can't help it."

I struggled with what to say. I didn't know Peter Fanning, other than what people had told me about him. However, right now, it was hard to sympathize with his worry and paranoia. I took the conversation in a different direction. "Why don't you tell me what it was you loved about Erin."

His eyes grew brighter, and his smile could only be described as genuine.

"She was passionate and so loyal to those she loved. It broke her heart when Clive died. After that, Erin became obsessed with finding answers. She was determined to prove he was murdered. I think that was her undoing." The smile wavered. "We argued about it. I tried to convince her to stop. She disagreed, of course. It was then she accused me of hiding the truth, that I might have been involved in his death. That hurt more than anything." His chin quivered slightly. Taking a deep breath, he managed to continue.

"I admired her strength, but I worried what kind of danger she could fall into. That was what I'd meant. I wanted to protect her. Besides, Clive was like a brother to me. I'd never do him harm."

"So, you and Clive spent lots of time together?" The conversation had taken a turn.

"Yes. We both enjoyed following football and the Bills. Sometimes we'd take trips to see away games, even making it a weekend getaway and seeing some sites."

"And Erin? Would she go with you?" My mind worked fast. The photo of Erin at the beach.

"Not too often. When she could get away from work and if it was a place she'd like to see, she'd arrange to come along."

"How about the beach? Did she like trips where she could see the coast?"

He frowned and kept quiet for a brief moment. "I don't recall her visiting any places like that. Then again, I might be wrong."

Disappointed, I scrambled for something else to ask. "How about you and Clive? Did you go to the coast?" I was hesitant to tell him about the seascape or the photo of Erin.

"Ah, no. Again, I can't remember any trips to the coast." The creases in his forehead deepened. "Why are you asking about trips to the coast? Is that somehow important?"

"Oh, sorry. No, I just wondered. I think Faith mentioned something about family trips to the beach." I shrugged. "Revisiting childhood memories like vacations, you know. I figured maybe Erin and Clive would have felt like doing that." I relaxed my shoulders. This conversation had gone as far as it could. As if my thoughts sent a message to Izzie in some weird telepathic way, my phone buzzed, and her face appeared on the screen.

"Sorry. I should get this." I pointed at my phone, then slid out of the booth seat to walk several feet away from Fanning.

"What is taking you so long?" Izzie asked after I answered.

"I'm about ready to leave," I whispered while turning my back on Fanning.

"Just hurry up, okay?"

I heard the click as she ended the call. Returning to the booth, I smiled. "That was my sister. She needs me. Thank you for telling me about Erin and Clive."

He stood and shook my hand. "Well, maybe after our talk, you won't think of me as a villain in all this. I really did love her."

I tipped my chin. "Call me a sap when it comes to romance, but I believe you mean it. Have a good evening, Peter."

I rushed through the doorway, relieved to escape. I did believe he loved Erin, but everything else he told me, or perhaps intentionally held back, left me in doubt. Those details of his story could be a ruse and meant to throw me off. In any case, Peter Fanning would have to stay on our whodunnit list for now.

Chapter Eighteen

"I had to say it." Izzie broke down the empty boxes and stacked them next to the back door of the shop.

After our usual Sunday bagel breakfast, compliments of Claire's For Sweets Sake, and a pleasant conversation with Mom and Dad to talk about my birthday plans, we arrived at the shop.

"You really think we should put him at the top of our list?" I sipped more of my coffee. "He seemed so ashamed for the way he behaved at the beginning of their relationship and insisted how much he loved Erin. Not to mention, he might have a perfectly sound alibi."

"But you didn't ask him for one." Izzie pointed out.

"Because I didn't want to provoke his temper. I'll let Hunter take care of that detail," I argued.

"How about a crime of passion? You said it yourself. Someone could've killed Erin in a moment of anger, jealousy, or whatever heightened emotional state. Only, we didn't know who that someone could be. Now, I say Peter Fanning is the one." Izzie closed the cutting knife and stored it in the toolbox.

I stiffened. Talk about a struggle to keep a secret. I pictured Erin fighting for her life, struggling to get the gun away from her killer. Could it have been a crime of passion, after all? Maybe either Erin or Peter threatened to shoot, and that's when the struggle began. I shook my head. It was time Hunter and I had another talk. Keeping secrets was torturing me. Besides, it wasn't like Izzie would go blabbing the news to everyone. "I guess Fanning got to me. He certainly has me convinced of his innocence."

"Talk to Hunter. Tell him about last night's meeting with Fanning. You might be right that he has a solid alibi." Izzie lifted a thick stack of boxes and walked toward the back exit. "If that's the case, then we keep looking. Until Martin is in the clear, I won't stop."

"*We* won't stop. Say, after we finish tidying up the storage room, why don't we take a break for an hour or so and walk to the park? It's Sunday, and business is usually slow on Sundays. Closing up for a little bit won't hurt. Besides, we need to take our minds off murder." I hurried to open the door for her.

She heaved a sigh. "You always say the right thing."

Once the storage room was tidied, we locked up. Stepping onto the porch, I breathed in the brisk air that left an autumn feel to the day. Perfect September weather. We walked out of the alley area and toward the middle of town. Neither one of us spoke. Not talking about Erin's murder didn't mean I could stop thinking about it. I had a hunch Izzie felt the same way. I took the conversation in another direction. "I can't get that case Hunter and Winsell are investigating off my mind. You know, about art theft? Anyway, last night, I researched online about trafficking art, originals as well as fakes. Remember Hunter's mom said there's a lot of money in painting reproductions of famous art and selling them as originals. Unethical and totally illegal, but common practice."

Izzie slowed her pace and turned her head to stare. "You're thinking about Clive's painting. Or the hidden painting."

"Can you guess where are the hot spots for trafficking stolen art?"

She shrugged. "No idea."

"South America. Makes me think of someone we know."

"Who?" She skipped over a toy truck some child had left on the path leading into the park.

"The same man who visits all those South American countries for his business deals." I waited to let that hint sink in. When she didn't answer, I continued. "Tito Alma, Izzie. He's from Paraguay, which is a South American country."

Izzie widened her eyes and rubbed her arms. "Ooo, Chloe. I just got the tingles."

"And is it coincidence that Tito and Storing met during movie night at the park?"

"Yeah, I wonder. How does Storing fit into all this?"

"I haven't a clue, but I bet we're onto something. We only have to figure out what."

Izzie and I stood in front of the music-themed mural that was meant to advertise the floating amphitheater. A lump formed in my throat, thinking about my friend Lana. The creation of this mural was her vision. The musicians playing guitars with music notes floating all around them. Her talent was boundless.

I knelt down to clear away the dead leaves from the flowers I'd planted here two weeks ago. "If Clive's hidden painting, the fake Vermeer tronie, is behind all this, meaning both Clive's and Erin's deaths, could another connection be made to Tito? It seems like a stretch of logic, but still." I stood and took a few steps back.

"A huge mile-long stretch, if you ask me." Izzie swiveled on her heel to face me. "Why don't we ask him?"

"What?" My jaw dropped. "Ask him if he's part of art trafficking and the black market? Are you insane?"

Izzie threw back her head and laughed. "No. That's not what I meant. The true story of how he knows Storing would be a question I'd like an answer to."

"What else?"

"Let's put that discussion on hold for now. We don't even know for sure if the painting has anything to do with Erin's death." Izzie moved closer to the lake.

"I also searched for info on Terence Ashe. Would it surprise you to learn he runs a business in art restoration?" I said.

"No, not really. Everyone in the patrons of the arts group has something to do with art."

"True, but Ashe is more than your average art restorer. According to the bio on his business website, he graduated from one of the top schools with a master's degree in conservation, has years of experience working in prominent museums all over the globe, and, according to his reviews, he receives five-star ratings from most of his customers. All of this makes me ask why wouldn't he share any of it with the group? Carli told me he never talks about his business or his personal life."

"Maybe he's got secrets? I agree with you, though. Something about him doesn't add up."

"I'm not finished. We both are personally familiar with the term starving artist, but with Ashe's expertise and notoriety, you'd think he'd make a decent living. Right? Well, you'd be wrong. I looked up the address given on his website. Supposedly, he runs the business out of his apartment, which is tiny, and the building is ancient. I looked it up on Zillow."

Izzie shrugged. "Maybe it's to save money? Or because home is a convenient place to work at any hour of the day? Seriously, I think you're desperate to make a case about him. And weren't we supposed to give conversation about murder a rest?" She picked up a pebble and, with a strong pitch, skimmed it along the lake's surface.

"Absolutely." With finger and thumb, I swiped them across my lips. "All done. Let's feed the ducks and dip our toes in the water." I didn't admit it out loud, but no matter how unlikeable or secretive Terence Ashe was, that didn't mean he had anything to do with Erin's death. According to Carli, he argued with Erin, and he didn't like rich people. Those were the only two details we had to go on. I had to ask Mom and Dad about him. They might have a different view.

Within an hour, we were back at the shop. A couple of people sat on a bench across the alley. As soon as Izzie opened the door, they stood and walked toward us.

"Looks like we have customers," I said and stepped aside to let them enter first.

"Hello! Chloe, over here."

I shifted my gaze toward the parking area along the alley and spotted Mom with Max in the lead. The high-pitched bark as he lifted his front paws made me laugh. "What are you two doing here?"

"The weather is so inviting, and your dad is over at the Bixbys, having a beer with Tod. He won't be home until dark, if I know those two." She laughed.

"I hear you. I think Mister Bixby could talk nonstop for days, if you let him."

"Well, your dad can certainly keep up. Anyway, I got bored, and Max could use the exercise. Right, buddy?" She bent down to scratch his head.

"We just returned from the park. Had to take another look at the wall mural before it's stored away for the winter." I paused to swallow the lump in my throat. Any reference to Lana still hurts. "By the way, I wanted to ask you about Terence Ashe. Why don't we go over there and sit on the bench?"

"Terence Ashe." Mom's forehead creased as she took a seat. "He's mostly quiet during our meetings. However, there have been a few times that he'd have a lot to say."

"I heard from Carli that Ashe and the Whitmores don't get along." I picked up Max and cuddled him in my lap.

"I can't say she's wrong. However, when Alan Whitmore gets on his high horse and starts bragging about something like one of his many business ventures or the latest renovation of the family estate, I can understand why that provokes Terence. As for his argument with Erin, that makes little sense. She often criticized her parents in front of the group about rich people's entitlement and power."

"I've heard that about Erin from Arthur Storing. What I don't understand is why Terence would feel angry about the Whitmore money. Doesn't Ashe make a substantial income from his renovation work?" I quickly added how I'd done some research on him.

"It's hard for any of us in the group to know what he makes or if he's successful. He doesn't talk about things like that. Although Faith commented once about him. She couldn't imagine how he made a living in that business, which tells me she knows something the rest of the group doesn't." Mom tensed and leaned closer. "Don't tell me you think he had something to do with Erin's murder. Chloe, I swear you and Izzie are getting in too deep by playing detectives. Why not let Hunter and the authorities figure out the crime?"

I wrapped my hand around hers and squeezed gently. "Mom, I know you mean well, but Izzie and I can handle what we're doing, and I promise we won't get in too deep, as you put it. Okay?" I regretted bringing up the topic of Terence Ashe and vowed not to do it again. Moms worried incessantly about their children, even grown ones. I was wise to remember that.

"I'll hold you to that promise." She removed her hand from mine and picked up Max from my lap. "I'm going to take this little guy home and feed him. Besides, he looks ready for a nap."

As if to agree with her, Max yawned and licked Mom's arm.

I scratched under his chin. "Thanks for taking such great care of him."

"See you at dinner." She waved as Max tugged at the leash to hurry down the alley road.

The rest of the afternoon, I carried out work tasks without talking much. Most of what I had to say went on inside my head. After dinner, I'd taken a warm bath to soothe my mood and calm my nerves. Dressed in my jammies and flannel robe, I hurried downstairs to snuggle with Max and sit close to the fireplace. The temperature had dipped below forty, and the evening was perfect for a fire. After stacking the logs inside the hearth, Dad went up to bed. Supposedly, Tod Bixby had persuaded him to help chop up a fallen tree in exchange for a cord of wood. Dad could never pass up a deal like that.

Izzie stood and stretched her arms to yawn. "Don't stay up too late. You're all alone. In the dark. *Muahahaha!*" She widened her eyes and rounded her mouth.

I tossed a pillow at her and laughed. "Go to bed."

Her footsteps echoed as she climbed the stairs. The door squeaked as she closed it.

"At last. All alone." I hugged Max and planted a kiss on his head. Staring at the fire, I nearly dozed off. It had been a day. After Mom had left with Max, customers poured in, creating a total frenzy of activity. And on a Sunday. How unpredictable.

I raised the footrest and warmed my feet close to the flames. Soon, my eyes closed. The soft rumble of Max snoring coupled with the crackling fire lulled me to sleep until a knock at the front door startled me awake. "Who could that be at this hour?"

Max hopped down and let go of a cacophony of barking.

"Shhh. You'll wake up everybody, and Dad won't appreciate that." I hurried to open the door, just an inch or two, and kept it that way because I remained unnerved after today's events.

"Are you going to let me in? Or continue to stare at me like I'm some evil intruder." Hunter said while leaning closer to the door.

"Poor choice of words," I muttered while opening the door wider. Remembering my wet hair and pajamas, I blushed.

"Why? Have you been watching those scary Halloween movies again?" He circled his arm around my shoulders and pulled me closer. His warm breath tickled my neck as he tugged at a damp lock of my hair. "Love the wet look. Smells good, too." He growled under his breath. "I sure have missed you."

"Didn't we have brunch just two days ago?" I lifted my chin to stare at his face.

"Days seem like years when I'm not with you." He sighed and placed a hand over his chest.

I slugged his shoulder. "You are too sappy, but I love you anyway."

"I should hope so. Have any leftovers in the fridge? I'm starving." He moved down the hall.

"I see. Your appetite will always take first place while I come in a distant second," I teased.

"Not so. I'd say you and my appetite are in a tie." He removed a casserole dish from the shelf and took off the lid. "Lasagna. Do you mind?"

Max sniffed the air and circled around Hunter.

I shrugged. "Dad doesn't care for Mom's lasagna. It's made with cauliflower crust and organic something. I can't remember. So, yeah, go ahead. Izzie and I aren't fans of cauliflower anything."

He popped it in the microwave, then turned to face me. "So, I have some news."

"Me too. But you go first." I sat at the table.

The microwave dinged. Hunter removed the dish and brought it to the table, then sat across from me. "Ballistics report came back on the pistol you found. The only prints belong to Erin. More importantly, the weapon was fired and the magazine has one bullet missing. Chloe, it matches the one used on Erin."

"I see." My heart leaped. I'd found the murder weapon.

"The puzzling part in this is when I questioned Alan Whitmore about the gun. He swears Erin didn't like using them and never touched them." He shoveled lasagna in his mouth and chewed.

"If her fear about guns is true, that argues against the suicide theory, doesn't it?"

"And more to support, she was murdered. Looks like the coroner finally agrees. He's making it official in his report." He pointed his fork at me. "And how about this? The gun isn't registered."

I gasped. "So she bought it illegally? Wow. This *is* really puzzling."

"If she's the one who bought it." He nodded with his brows lifted.

"Great. More questions. I'm more frustrated than ever with figuring out what happened." I threw up my hands. At least suicide was no longer considered a possibility.

"Okay. Your turn. What's your news?" He sat back and massaged his stomach.

"You're probably not going to like what I'm about to tell you, but you should be used to it by now." I went on to describe the meeting with Fanning and what he had to say.

Hunter rinsed off the dish and placed it in the sink. Turning, he leaned against the counter. "Not buying his story. Those are like lines from a movie. Man confesses his undying love, swears his heart is broken now that she's gone, and how sorry he is for all the bad behavior. Nope. Not good enough."

"Did he give you an alibi?" For some reason, the romantic side of me wanted him to be innocent.

"An alibi? Yes. One we can confirm? Not yet. He claims after going to a food convention that ran late that evening, he spent the night at a friend's house near the Finger Lakes region."

"Let me guess. You haven't been able to question that friend."

"No, I got an answer. She corroborated the story."

I shifted in my seat. "Then what's the problem?"

"The friend could be lying to cover for Fanning. I got my team checking his car's GPS. If that proves his story, then I'll be satisfied."

We said goodnight at the door. Climbing the stairs, I whistled for Max. I couldn't bring myself to totally agree with Hunter. No doubt, I was a sucker for romance and wanted Fanning's story of his feelings for Erin to be real. I turned out the light and got into bed, snuggling Max closer to my side. "We'll just have to do more sleuthing to prove I'm right, won't we, buddy?" I closed my eyes and left all those thoughts behind.

Chapter Nineteen

I sat in the patio chair and sipped coffee from my mug, amused by Max, who chased a rabbit around in circles until the furry creature found refuge underneath a lilac bush. As the sun peeked from behind the clouds, I squinted. "Where are my sunglasses?" I turned side to side, then leaned over to find them on the stone floor.

"With no event scheduled, I think we can do dinner at the winery this evening," Izzie said.

"The group would love to have you attend, but I bet your motive has nothing to do with enjoying our company." Mom cocked her head and cast a knowing glance.

"You'd be right. We're anxious to meet Terence Ashe." I finished my coffee and set the mug on the floor, waiting for the lecture.

"That's fine. I know nothing I say will stop you two from snooping. At least your dad and I will be at the winery to keep an eye on things." Mom's lips pursed.

I popped up from my chair and leaned in for a hug.

"I can't breathe, Chloe." Mom's voice muffled into my chest.

"Oh, sorry. I love your concern. It's part of what makes you a great mom, *Mom*." I planted a sloppy kiss on her cheek.

"Stop. You don't have to act so happy. I'm concerned for your safety. That's all."

"We are, too," Izzie said. "Everything will be fine."

"To cover up, we'll tell the group you're thinking of becoming members. No one will doubt you." Dad grabbed another slice of turkey bacon off the serving dish.

"Then it's settled." I gripped the arms of my chair and pushed off to stand. Whistling for Max, I then turned to Izzie. "What time do you plan to head to the shop?"

Izzie checked her watch. "In a half hour. I want to take care of something else first." She shifted her eyes sideways toward the back door, gesturing for me to follow.

Once inside the kitchen, I caught her arm. "What's with the hushed behavior?"

"I didn't want Mom and Dad to hear." She wrung her hands and sat at the table. "I'm worried about Martin. It's been a week since we last spoke, and he chased us away. I know we promised, but I think maybe I should reach out? Call him to make sure he's doing okay."

I pressed my grip on her arm. "No. We promised. Anyway, no news is good news. Right?"

"That's a stupid saying. People get good news all the time," she griped.

"Sometimes they don't. If he was in trouble, don't you think we'd hear about it?"

"Yeah, I guess. But he could be suffering emotionally. I don't like to think of him like that." A pout turned down the corners of her mouth.

Once I'd told her the coroner had determined Erin's death a homicide, her worries about Martin spiked. At least she hadn't been too upset when I shared Hunter's news about powder burns on Erin's hand and clothes. It was a load off my chest to finally let go of that secret.

"Okay, tell you what. I'll mention it to Hunter when I see him or talk to him next time. He'll probably let me know if Martin's still a suspect."

"I guess I have no choice. Phillip always answers the phone, and if Martin gave him orders, he won't let me speak to him. This is so frustrating." Izzie paced the room.

"Give Martin time to figure things out by himself, Izzie. That's what he'd want."

"It's fine. I'm going upstairs to change. Meet you back here in a half hour."

The discouraged look on her face made me sad. Frustration was not an easy mood to process. Even though I'd suggested Hunter would open up to me, I had my doubts. He'd decide Izzie and I were too personally involved with Martin. Unless he could tell me Martin had been cleared and eliminated as a suspect, he'd keep quiet. I shrugged. One of those good news moments Izzie mentioned certainly would be nice to hear.

I dressed, fed Max, and took him on a quick walk. By the time we returned home, Izzie came down the stairs. Somehow, I always got more done in less time than she ever did. I eyed her coiffed hair and carefully applied makeup, along with painted nails and stylish outfit, then glanced in the hall mirror at my jeans and t-shirt, a face freshly scrubbed but minus any coverup, and my straight hair clipped back. Yeah, it made perfect sense.

Approaching the shop, I caught sight of Penny. She stood on the front step, tapping her foot as if nerves or impatience got to her. The moment she turned, both arms flew up, then flopped to her sides.

"About time. I thought you opened by nine," she said, squinting through her oversized orange-tinted glasses.

"What's with the seventies fashion look?" Izzie pointed at the spectacles.

Leave it to Izzie to know her history of fashion trends, I thought.

"Oh." She fingered the frames. "I've been on a kick listening to Elton John. Made me think of those wild glasses he'd wear. And the seventies. Crazy but fun times. From what I've heard, of course."

I unlocked the door. "We only open at nine during the summer months. Unless there's a holiday or some kind of town event."

"I'm too impatient, I guess. There's a big opportunity to get my name on the front page of the Gazette. I need comments or maybe a quote from you." Her voice pitched with excitement.

Izzie frowned. "I thought you already had enough from us the last time we talked."

Thunder rumbled in the distance while a gust of wind swayed the tree branches.

"Let's get inside before it pours," I suggested.

Penny sat on a stool nearest the door. "The latest news has busted this case wide open, and I want to be the first to write about it. Now, I thought you could give me some background information. You know, where he was born, how he made his money, and what connects him to the Whitmores." She poised pencil on paper.

Izzie and I glanced at each other and shrugged. "Background about who? We're confused."

Her eyes widened. "Oh! I'm guessing you haven't heard the latest. Martin Steele has been arrested and is in custody at the Chautauqua County precinct."

"Are you kidding me? They won't quit. What have they got on him now?" Izzie ranted. "I swear, he didn't kill Erin Whitmore."

Penny shook her head. "It's not that. He's been arrested for possessing stolen art. My source told me that police obtained a search warrant and found a painting that was reported stolen from a museum in upstate New York a few months ago."

Izzie crossed her arms and scowled. "That's ridiculous. Steele is many things, but not a thief. He respects art and the art community. There's your quote."

Penny scribbled on the pad, unaffected by Izzie's annoyance. "Thanks, ladies. I'll be in touch if anything changes and I need more comments." With that, she flew out of the shop and down the alley.

"I can't believe it. This is insane. Martin must be furious. I know how proud he is of his reputation in the art community." Izzie sank into a chair with her shoulders slouched.

I sat next to her. "I don't understand why Hunter didn't tell me. It's only been a few hours since we spoke. He never mentioned one word about Martin."

"I think we both have a good reason to visit the precinct. Don't you?" Izzie said.

I checked the time and made a decision. "We have to put that on hold. Let's say if we close up by three, that will leave us enough time to pay a visit, see what the situation is with Martin, then drive home to join Mom and Dad for our trip to the winery. What do you say?"

"I say Martin and Hunter have lots to explain, and I want to hear every detail."

Without another word, we got to work. The next event was Wednesday. This time, in keeping with Whisper Cove holiday tradition, our guests would be painting a lake scene with our very own ghostly figure, Abigail Bellows. It was said she haunted Chautauqua Lake on Hallows Eve. The town celebrated with a festival that evening. Vendors set up food tents, while people wearing costumes brought flashlights and binoculars, hoping to get a glimpse of the Lady of Chautauqua Lake.

At three sharp, I flipped the sign on the door to message we were closed. We scuttled outside to the Land Rover and sped north on Whisper Cove Boulevard. With only a thirty-minute drive, we arrived at the Chautauqua precinct. I sensed Izzie's agitated mood and hot temper simmering just under the surface.

"How about let me talk to whoever is in charge to ask about Martin?" I raised my brow.

"Fine. Good idea. I'd probably start off shouting, and that would get us nowhere but kicked to the curb and banned for life." Izzie patted her face with a moistened toilette.

Once inside, I search for a familiar face. People, coming and going, filled the waiting area, which made my task a challenge. The service window came into view. A female officer I recognized stood behind a plastic shield.

Tall, brown eyes, and a full mane of hair I'd die for motioned to me. "Chloe Abbington and her sister Izzie. It's been a while since you stepped foot inside our building." She grinned ear to ear.

"Hi, Rachel. It's nice to see you," I said.

"You here to see your guy? Hunter's not in, but he should be back around six, if you want to stick around."

"Oh, no. Actually, we were hoping to speak with a man you have in custody. Martin Steele?"

Rachel frowned. "Sorry. No can do. He's with his lawyer at the moment."

"Do you have any idea how long that will take?" Izzie leaned around my shoulder and spoke calmly.

"Not a clue. This lawyer is big league and has a lot of influence in the department. He could take a few minutes or maybe a few hours. His choice. I'd say in Steele's case, their meeting would fall under the latter. Would you like a cup of coffee or a soda while you wait? I mean, if you're thinking of waiting." She lifted her mug to gesture. "Piping hot and actually quite good for an office brew."

I opened my mouth to speak when Izzie tapped my shoulder.

"I see Phillip. Let's go speak with him," she said, then, without waiting, circled around a line of people to reach the other side of the room.

"Guess we'll pass on the coffee, after all. Thanks, Rachel." I smiled.

"Okay. You want me to give Hunter a message?"

"Um, no. In fact, maybe it would be better not to mention we were here?" I nodded my head in Izzie's direction. "My sister is really upset about her friend, and if Hunter spoke to her about coming here, that might put her over the edge. You understand."

"Of course." She slid one of her arms underneath the shield and squeezed my hand. "Give your sister my best, and let's hope for things to turn out well."

I thanked her, then hurried through the crowd to where Izzie and Phillip stood. "What did I miss? Is Martin holding it together?" I stared at Phillip. We knew he was aware of everything about his boss and attended to his needs, night or day. It was difficult to imagine when the man found time to sleep.

"He's incredibly calm. I don't know how he can be, but then again, we're talking about Martin Steele," Phillip said.

It was true. From the stories Izzie had told me, the man could master anything, overcome any obstacle, and achieve satisfaction. "That's a relief."

"What I don't understand is what brought police to his house in the first place? How did that happen?" Izzie asked.

"An anonymous caller claimed to have seen a painting that he suspected was stolen from a museum in New York. He described the painting down to the tiniest detail. It was enough for authorities to obtain a search warrant." Phillip shrugged. "Very strange."

"But Martin would never possess a stolen painting, not knowingly." Izzie scratched her chin. "Could someone actually sneak into the house and leave the painting for police to find?"

"Not possible. No one could bypass our security system. Besides, the painting in question, the one police confiscated, is a reproduction given to Mister Steele by a close friend." He checked his watch.

"Are you sure it's a reproduction?" I asked. Both Izzie and Phillip stared at me with eyes widened, as if I'd lost my mind. "I get it. Martin knows a fake from a genuine work of art. Sorry."

"I need to make a call, but please, ladies, don't worry. As soon as the painting is examined, the authorities will have to release Mister Steele. By then, they will be asking a different question."

"Which is?" I curled my brow.

"Who would want to frame Mister Steele and why? I think we all can answer the why part. The authorities need to figure out who." He tipped his hand and walked to a corner of the room.

"Well, it's obvious the person framing Martin is the killer." Izzie huffed and led the way back out to the car.

The air blew out of me, and my confidence in solving this murder went along for the ride. It felt like we'd take a few steps forward, but then something discouraging would happen to send us that many more in reverse. Whoever we were dealing with was proving to be extremely clever. Secondly, he or she must have done their homework on Martin and somehow known about the painting in question. Another thought came to mind. What if this person knew him personally? Even been inside his home? I shivered and slipped into my seat while Izzie powered on the Land Rover. Not a comfortable thought to imagine someone close to Martin was a killer. "I wonder if the police have any leads as to who gave them the tip?"

Without waiting for a response, I clicked open my contacts and called Hunter. I heard the rustling of paper as he answered.

"Hey! I was just about to call you." He mumbled.

"Eating on the job?" I guessed and listened to a garbled yes. "Do you have a minute to talk about Martin?" I pressed the speaker button so Izzie could hear.

A groan came across the receiver. "I know what you're going to say. Why didn't I call to let you know about his arrest?"

"I wish you had. Instead, we learned about it from Penny, of all people."

"I'm sorry, but in my defense, the arrest happened late last night. I mean, really late. And this morning, I've been chasing down leads in a dozen other cases I have on my plate. Give me a pass on this one, please?"

The whiny plea in his voice made me smile. "Fine. You're forgiven. But if you really want to make it up to me, will you share any leads you have? Like, who called with the anonymous tip?"

"That's not exactly what happened. The Captain got a call from an investigator who tracks down stolen art. He received the anonymous tip, which then led us to obtain a warrant to search Steele's house. You know the rest."

"Are you sure the investigator is legit? I thought the FBI's Art Crime Team took care of stolen art cases," I argued. Those were valid questions.

"He's legit. Supposedly, the FBI contracts with independent investigators when necessary."

"Sounds fishy."

"Maybe, but a painting fitting that description was stolen. Too coincidental not to be something real."

"Or the whole thing is fake and meant to place Martin at the top of your list, again." I struggled to keep from sounding cranky because that's how I was feeling. Tired, cranky, and beyond resentful in how Martin was being treated by the police.

"He insists the painting is a fake. Sounded convincing, but we'll see what the lab has to say."

I tapped the edge of my phone. The strain in his voice told me to let the issue go for now. "I should let you get back to work. Izzie and I are attending one of Mom and Dad's art group meetings at a winery this evening, but if you get any updates, call me. Okay?"

After the call, I settled back in my seat. "What do you think?"

"Like you said. Something's fishy about the whole incident." She gripped the steering wheel. "Now what?"

"We go to the winery and see if we can have a talk with Ashe."

* * *

"Would you listen to yourselves? None of us knows the truth. We can only speculate." The formidable figure of Tito Alma straightened. He sipped his wine while shifting his gaze to land on each and every person at the table.

Izzie and I had been speechless when we walked into Gritos Wine and Spirits with our parents. Seeing Tito, standing next to the wine bar as he chatted with one of the group's members, was surprising but not totally unexpected. For someone who seldom attended the meetings, two in a row gave me pause.

Gritos was one of my favorite wineries. Unique compared to others, the business was housed in a repurposed early twentieth-century barn. Massive wood beams formed a V in the ceiling while centerpieces made with vintage wine bottles gave the atmosphere a warm and cozy feel. Wrought iron trim, wood plaques with burned engravings, and framed photos of wine-making history completed the décor.

"I know Martin Steele personally," Tito added. "He is well-respected in the art community. One of the top dealers. His clients have nothing but praise for him."

"Yes, but even those at the top sometimes fall from their glorified pedestals and do horrible things." The surly voice came from behind us.

I turned. A man with dusty blond hair and a slim build walked into the winery. As he moved closer to the table, the bloodshot eyes and sunken cheekbones of what once could've been a handsome face became evident. Terence Ashe. I recognized him from the photos I'd found online. But this man appeared a ghost of himself.

Terence took a seat at the table and signaled to the server, who brought him a glass. "Leave the bottle," he growled. "Now, where were we? Ah, yes. The glorified elite. Those entitled souls never once take accountability for their actions. Isn't that right, Mister Alma?"

"Perhaps you've imbibed enough for one day. Mister Ashe, is it?" Tito's lips curled as he punctuated the word mister.

Terence tipped his glass. "Not nearly enough."

"Are you saying you believe Martin Steele is guilty?" Tito continued.

"I'm saying all self-absorbed, entitled people can make mistakes."

Next to me, Izzie tensed. She squeezed my hand, and I instinctively wrapped my fingers around hers. "Don't," I warned. "We came to listen and observe. Remember?"

"Sorry." She cleared her throat. "Terence Ashe. So glad to finally meet you. My name is Izzie Abbington, and Martin Steele happens to be a close friend of mine." She pulled her hand from my grip. "I'm guessing you do believe Martin murdered Erin Whitmore?"

Ashe shook his head. "I'm not saying one way or the other. And it's a pleasure to finally meet you, Miss Abbington. What I am suggesting is many of those entitled people can say or do most anything and get away with it. For instance, they might fabricate a story to accuse someone of a crime."

I hitched my breath. It was easy to understand what he implied. Not to mention who that person fabricating stories would be.

"You're speaking of Alan Whitmore." Tito lifted his chin. "I've heard the rumors. By the sound of it, you have as well."

"I wouldn't be surprised if he's found a way to frame Steele. He's done far worse." Ashe picked up the bottle and poured to fill his empty glass. "If you'll excuse me? I need some fresh air." He stood and carefully made his way outside to the back patio.

The memory of Carli's words about Terence filled my thoughts. I found her seated at the far end of the table. She hadn't said a word so far this evening, but her eyes told me plenty. She tipped her chin with barely a nod at me. The message was clear. No need to hear her say I told you so. My question was why? If Ashe only knew the Whitmores through this group or even had a casual business relationship with them, why the extreme animosity? Or could we be misreading him? His attitude might be only a generalized hate for all rich people. Still...

Conversation veered in another direction, prompted by Dad, who announced the fall festival committee in Whisper Cove was seeking donations from any art-affiliated businesses.

I listened and watched as Tito stood up and took steps toward the patio where Ashe remained seated. If the two acted as gentlemen, apologies would be made. I certainly hoped so. Sure enough, after what looked like a brief exchange of words, they shook hands and Tito returned to the group.

I touched Izzie's arm. "I'm going out there to speak with Ashe. Can you cover for me, in case Mom or Dad asks where I am?"

She nodded. "Let's hope you can learn something from him. I'm getting worried Martin will be charged with Erin's murder and soon."

With my glass in hand, I circled around tables to weave my way to the patio door. A cool breeze kicked up. The sun had disappeared under the line of trees bordering the winery. I rubbed my one arm, wishing I'd worn a sweater.

"Allow me." Terence slid his jacket off and draped it over my shoulders as I sat on the concrete bench next to him.

"Thank you." I clutched the lapels of his jacket and pulled them together. "I'm sorry if we upset you. All this talk about Martin's arrest has us on edge."

He waved his arm. "Nothing to do with you and your sister. She is your sister, right? I can tell some family resemblance."

My brows lifted. "Really? I sure can't." Tall, long, brown hair, runway model pretty? And me, short, dark, cropped hair, and maybe a bit too curvy. Or at least not the model type.

"I'm not talking about looks. Your gestures, the smiles, even the way you both tilt your heads when someone says something you take an interest in. I notice things like that." He shrugged. "Sorry. I was observing the group through the front window for a while before gathering my courage to join you all." He stared at me for a second longer, then turned to pour more in his glass.

Courage to join. That was a strange comment. "No one's ever said that. Thanks. Anyway, I still apologize." I rubbed my finger across my glass hard enough to make it squeak. "Sorry."

"I'm not wrong, you know."

"About?"

"Alan Whitmore. I wouldn't put it past him to try and frame Martin Steele or anyone else for his daughter's murder."

"I see." I stared at the almost empty wine bottle and scrambled for what else to say. His words left me wanting to know more, but in his present state, I was unsure how he'd respond.

"I know his type. In fact, I probably know Alan Whitmore better than anyone in that room." He motioned to our group's table.

"How? What do you know about him?" My voice came in a breathy whisper, not quite confident to ask.

"Let's just say, in my line of business and his penchant for collectibles make us likely to cross paths more than once." He tipped his glass to drain the contents. "We should go back inside."

"One more question?" I gently tapped his arm. "I'll admit I've read articles about your restoration work. Truly remarkable. You should be proud."

"Yes, well, that's not a question." He paused. "What do you want to know?"

"My Mom has told me you never mention your business during group meetings, never hand out your card, or ask the members to pass along the information to anyone wanting restorations done. Why?"

He shrugged. "Because that's not why a became a member. I enjoy talking with like-minded people. At least, I used to enjoy it until the Whitmores joined."

At once, his face reddened like anger fueled it. I shuddered. "You're right. We should go back inside." I handed him his jacket, then led the way, anxious to put distance between us. It didn't take a mind reader to know how deep his resentment for the Whitmores went or to guess if Alan felt the same about Ashe. I, for one, didn't want to get caught in the crosshairs of their supposed feud.

I pushed open the patio door and hurried to the table. This murder case with such a growing number of players was more challenging than a game of Clue. It made me wonder. Would we ever figure out who killed Erin?

Chapter Twenty

I crossed my arms while bouncing one leg. The heel of my shoe tapped the floor in a nervous tempo. Izzie and I had gone back and forth discussing the possible scenarios of murder. Each suspect had their own story. None of them completely plausible.

"We need to narrow down this list. It's been two weeks since we started, and I'm ready to lose my mind." I pressed down on my knee with both hands to stop the nervous leg movement.

"Fine, but who goes first?" Izzie pointed at the desk computer in Dad's study. Our list had been typed in forty-sized letters with a bold font.

"Well." I tapped my lip. "How about Terence Ashe? The only thing incriminating we have on him is his hatred of rich people, specifically the Whitmores."

"Correction. He hates Alan Whitmore. Notice how he never mentioned Faith's name? Or Erin's, for that matter."

"I never noticed. So, do we cross his name off the list? That would leave us with the Whitmores and Peter Fanning."

"What if we search for more information, like where he was the night of Erin's murder? Hunter might know. And don't forget about the huge argument he had with Erin at the bar. She told Carli how Ashe was despicable," she argued. "That's definitely incriminating."

I scratched behind one ear. "Being despicable doesn't make you a killer. It just makes it hard to have friends."

Izzie pushed the mouse to delete Terence Ashe from the list. "If we find out anything suspicious, though, his name goes right back on here. Deal?"

"Absolutely." I scooted forward to the edge of the sofa. "What about Storing?"

"As Erin's killer? He is peculiar, but other than that, what makes him capable? He's looking for a scoop on the Whitmores, something juicy to put in his next book, which means he'd want to keep them alive. There's nothing to learn from a dead person," Izzie reasoned.

"Harshly put, but I see your point."

Izzie's fingers tapped furiously on the keyboard. "Let's add him, just in case. He can be our dark horse."

"I like that." I read down the list. Not too many, but still not narrow enough. Alan and Faith Whitmore, Peter Fanning, and Arthur Storing. I wanted to tell her we should add Martin's name because his alibi for that night still hadn't been confirmed. She was hardly objective in the situation. Still, I kept my mouth shut.

Max trotted into the room and hopped up in my lap. I scratched the top of his head while replaying the evidence we had gathered on each of those names. "There's more we could look for. How about we start with exploring how the photo of Erin I found connects to Clive's painting? There can't be that many beaches along the northern coast with lighthouses." I set Max on the floor. "What about Shannon at the library? She's always talking about traveling to locales on the coast. If we show her the photo, she might recognize that beach."

"Which gets us to finding the killer, how? Chloe, I'm frustrated." Izzie sank into a chair. "We can do what you suggest. On the other hand, maybe our time would be better spent snooping into our suspects' lives."

"We'll do both. Spend our free time searching for everything we can. I know it's exhausting, but what choice do we have other than to call it quits and let the authorities do all." I reasoned out loud because it was true, and Izzie knew it.

"I'll start researching for more background on Terence Ashe."

I smiled. Izzie's way of answering my question was to move into action. "Great. First, let me talk with Hunter and get some updates. Then I'll give Shannon a call and see if she has time to meet with me."

Enthused to get started, I got on my phone while sprinting upstairs to my bedroom. We had a free day until late this afternoon while the shop was being given a fresh coat of paint. Ralph from Paint and Plaster offered a great deal that fit our budget. He'd attend to the inside job today, then work on the outside tomorrow.

It was too early to try the library, so I called Hunter instead. "Hey. Good morning," I greeted.

"Chloe? What time is it?" A rustling noise interrupted his comment. "Sorry. Just getting up. What's wrong? Are you okay?"

I chuckled. "I'm fine. Sorry for calling so early, again. Izzie and I are getting ready for a very busy day." I sat on my bed, legs crossed and feet tucked under.

"Oh? Busy how?"

I heard the edgy tone. "Calm down. Just doing some research. Nothing dangerous. Thinking of ways to help with Erin's case. Speaking of, has Martin posted bail?"

"Not yet. There's been a new development. Turns out security cameras around the Whitmore estate show Steele had returned to the house the night of Erin's murder, just a few minutes after midnight. It shows him slipping in through a side entrance that goes directly into the study. Unfortunately, the view of who lets him in is hidden."

"That explains why no one else, including the housekeeper, would've seen him enter." I worked to picture the scene and how it played out. "What did Martin have to say about it?"

"He's refusing to answer why he returned. However, the footage shows a lapse of twenty minutes from the time he entered the house and left."

I frowned, realizing how bad this looked for Martin. He had plenty of opportunity to do the deed and leave without anyone knowing. Except the security camera puzzled me. Surely, Martin would have considered the Whitmore estate had plenty of them. Why would he murder Erin, knowing he'd be identified on the camera?

"You're not saying anything."

"I'm still processing. Why come back a second time? If he was going to kill her, why not on the first visit? And let's agree he had to consider the security cameras being there. Risky business, knowing that, and to still do the crime. Nope. This theory doesn't add up."

"Maybe not, but the judge seemed to think it was enough to keep him in custody and not allow bail."

I dragged fingers through my hair. "I don't suppose you've spoken to Terence Ashe yet?"

"It's on my to-do list. What I can tell you is his name doesn't come up in the crime database."

"That's a relief."

"Look, since I'm awake, I might as well get started on my day, too. Good luck with your, what did you call it?" Research?" He cleared his throat. "Stay safe, Chloe."

"Always." I rested the phone in my lap and stared at my reflection in the mirror. "You can do this." Taking a breath to relax, I hopped off the bed and made my way downstairs. Izzie sat at Dad's computer, staring at the screen. "Hey. I talked to Hunter." I rushed to recap the conversation before she could interrupt. "I'm sure the video isn't too damning. Martin's lawyer will figure out how to work with the judge. I bet Martin will be home by dinnertime." I kept cheer in my voice, but from the look on her face, it wasn't working.

"Why wouldn't he tell me? All these secrets he's keeping. I can't understand. How are we supposed to help him, if we don't know the whole story?" Her voice cracked. She stood and paced the room.

"Hey, now. What's all this commotion?" Dad stepped in from the hallway. His face creased with concern.

I explained the situation with Martin. "Anyway, it looks like he stays behind bars for now."

He studied Izzie's face. "Sweetheart, I'm sure Martin can handle himself. Besides, didn't he ask you not to get involved? He worries about you two, as much as I do." His arm wrapped around Izzie's shoulders. "If he kept this or anything else from you, most likely it was done to protect you." He stepped back. "Now, in my experience, there can be more than one side to a story. Things aren't always as they appear to be. That video might look incriminating, but why not wait to hear what Martin has to say?"

"Yeah, but wait for how long? I don't have much faith in him explaining anything anymore." Izzie moved to sit behind the computer once again. She fingered the mouse, clicking on the screen. "Right now, I'll keep working to find answers. Whether he likes it or not."

I sighed. Izzie only knew one way to get over her mood. Work to keep her mind off her worries. And if that didn't help? Yoga. Mom's answer to calm the body. It had its benefits. I waited until Dad left the room. "Did you find anything more on Ashe?"

"It's strange. The site I'm on should tell me more than it does. No record of where he lived before moving to Jamestown, and that was only five years ago. And remember all that information you found on his education and employment? Well, I can't find any record to back up that claim. There are only a half dozen top schools where he could've received his master's in art restoration. I checked alumni records, and no one named Terence Ashe pops up."

"Maybe he embellished the bio on his website to attract business?" I shrugged. "It is strange, though."

"Suspicious, too. I can't stop wondering about his connection to the Whitmores. I tell you, Chloe. Something about him doesn't add up." She shut down the computer and stood. "Want to take a trip to Jamestown? I got a call. Our costumes for the masked ball came in. We could pick them up and then swing by that party supply store to get the decorations Justin Carpenter asked for. He promised the town council would reimburse us."

I wagged a finger. "You aren't fooling me, sister. You want to see where Ashe lives, don't you?"

She blushed. "Nothing like getting firsthand evidence about a person. Right?"

I chuckled. "Lead the way, snoop sister."

We made a quick stop at For Sweets Sake to grab coffees and breakfast croissants before heading out of town. Soon, the cluster of lights ahead announced the city limits of Jamestown. The sun had made its way above the horizon to brighten the sky and shout good morning. The rays of light touched the dew-covered grass and flowers, making them sparkle.

I snuggled in my seat, letting the steam from my coffee bathe my face. "We have time to kill before the shops open. Why don't we stop by the city park? We can finish our breakfast and talk."

"You mean the park that's across from the apartment building Ashe supposedly lives in?" She curled her lips. "You are worse than me, always thinking of the next move."

"Enjoying the park and surrounding view. That's all." I sipped my coffee and avoided her pointed stare.

"Uh, huh. Okay. Let's do that." She turned onto the bridge that led us into town and the park.

I spotted no more than a dozen or so visitors, mostly seniors who likely had their days and time free to enjoy the quiet morning and sunrise. Getting out of the Land Rover, I grabbed the bag of leftover croissants and hoisted the strap of my bag over one shoulder.

We walked the path leading to several benches, then picked one that had a perfect view of the tall building across the street. "You know the odds are incredibly small," I said.

"Of seeing Ashe? Oh, I'm sure they are."

"Still, it's a beautiful morning to sit in the park." I munched on my second croissant and stared at the multi-storied apartment structure. A few people exited carrying bags, umbrellas, or briefcases, probably on their way to work. Ashe's workplace was inside, though. No reason to leave, other than for a delivery to a client. The odds of catching sight of him were more like one in a gazillion.

I stiffened and nearly dropped my croissant, my rambling thoughts interrupted. "Well, that's certainly unexpected."

Izzie gasped. "Faith Whitmore? Holy wow."

The familiar figure with that confident walk stood at the front of the building. She turned side to side, as if anxious to find anyone watching. Within seconds, she hurried across the street and got inside a car.

"I have so many questions, starting with why she would be coming out of the building where Ashe lives. Doesn't he despise everything she stands for?

What reason could they possibly have to meet?"

Izzie's jaw dropped. "You don't think they're having an affair, do you?"

"Good grief. That's a horrible thought." I paused. "But what if they are? That would explain all his animosity toward Alan. Boyfriend who hates the husband since, you know, he's married to the woman and the boyfriend isn't?" How convoluted was that? I refused to go down that road.

"Oh, look! There's Ashe. He's carrying…" She squinted. "Looks like the large bags we use to put paintings in."

"Could be he's delivering a painting he restored to a client."

"Yeah, makes sense. What doesn't make sense is Faith Whitmore." She got up to toss her cup in the trash bin. She emptied crumbs from the croissant bag into the palm of her hand, then scattered them on the lawn. Birds swarmed to the site and pecked at the ground.

"We should follow him." I landed on my feet and picked up my bag.

Izzie shook her head. "No time. We have errands to take care of. Besides, what are we supposed to do? Confront him and ask why he's sneaking around with Faith? I doubt he'd answer truthfully."

"I was thinking more along the lines of where he's going and whoever he's meeting." As a cool breeze kicked up, I buttoned my jacket. We had enough to think about. Faith and Terence in a relationship? Most unlikely and hard to prove unless we caught them in the act. I shuddered and swallowed the sour taste in my mouth. "Let's go pick up our costumes, then head to the supply store. I'm done with all the soap opera images playing in my head."

Chapter Twenty-One

Yesterday ended without any further soap opera drama. Work at the shop until five, family dinner coupled with pleasant conversation, and early to bed. The way it should be. I felt relaxed and ready to tackle a new day.

The aroma of fresh-brewed coffee teased my nose and my appetite. Conversation hummed while dishes clanked and clattered, echoing from the kitchen. I'd arrived at eight and ahead of Hunter, even though he'd set the meeting time. I inhaled the delicious scent of bacon as a customer passed by my table with his plate.

Izzie was at home with a migraine, so I was running solo this morning.

"Hey, beautiful. Sorry I'm late." Hunter came from behind me and leaned over to plant a kiss on my cheek.

"Not too late, but my empty stomach is protesting a bit." I laughed. "I hope you're ready to order food."

"Then, let's go." He pulled out my chair and linked his arm with mine.

"So, what's the news on the case?"

"Nope. It can wait. The morning is full of sunshine, I'm relaxed, and I don't want to ruin this moment with you by talking shop. Not just yet. K?" He hugged me.

My brow creased. "That doesn't sound promising. I want promising, Hunter. It's been almost nothing but disappointing for over two weeks."

He whispered. "First, order breakfast. After your belly's full, then we'll talk."

What choice did I have? However, the anxiety from waiting gave me indigestion, and I hadn't even eaten yet. "Did you read about our masked ball in the paper? Looks like some pretty important people will be attending, including the relatives of that woman who was murdered in Sinclairville. The case you're investigating? Burnell is the name, I think."

"Right. That case. And no, I haven't read the article, but our pal Winsell has. In fact, he's all over the place with investigating that art theft."

"Has he come up with any leads?" More than one way to make him talk. I avoided eye contact, in case my expression hinted too much at my overly curious mind.

"Ah, I see what you're doing." He took his tray and mine, then led the way to our table. "But no, there's absolutely no evidence of a connection to Burnell's stolen art and your hidden painting."

"It's not my painting. It's not anybody's painting. That's the problem. We don't know who wants it or what Clive planned to do with it."

"Or Martin planned. Let's not forget he's somehow involved."

"Having the painting in his possession doesn't make him involved. If that was the case, then Izzie and I are involved too." I saw the look, that set jaw, and his lack of response. "Seriously? You think we're involved in art theft?"

"I didn't say that." He took a bite of his egg sandwich.

I grumbled and munched on a slice of bacon. "I thought we weren't going to talk about this until after breakfast."

"Hey, you asked first. Now, let's eat. Preferably without talking because that topic will obviously come up again."

"Obviously."

We did eat in silence, other than an exchanged greeting or two with locals who recognized us. I drained my cup and stood. "You want a refill? Or should we talk, now?"

"A refill, then talk." He took the cup out of my hand. "Relax. Enjoy the view. I'll be right back."

I studied the room. I loved passing the time people-watching. When my gaze landed on the far corner, I grinned. "What do you know?"

Megan and Remy held hands across the table with the brightest smiles on their faces. Megan deserved a piece of happiness in her life.

"Izzie could be Cupid or start a match-making business, for sure." Actually, both of us recognized the spark of interest Megan displayed from the moment we met Remy. How nice that Remy felt the same way.

Hunter set the filled cup in front of me. "What'd I miss?" He followed my gaze and twisted around to look.

"Oh, just admiring a romance in bloom." I tipped my chin and let the steam bathe my face. "Tom's coffee is the absolute best."

Hunter moved past asking questions about romance and who makes the best coffee. He settled into his seat. "Now, to the case. I have good news and bad."

I wiggled in my seat. "Let's get the bad news out of the way."

"Until five years ago, Terence Ashe didn't exist."

"What do you mean? That's not possible."

"As far as any records go, it is. We checked every database possible. No place of residence, no birth, death, or school records that could be a match. Nothing. It's like Ashe was born five years ago."

"That's exactly what Izzie ran into. So, now what? Have you spoken to him yet? I'd love to know what his alibi is." I pictured the image of Faith exiting the apartment building.

"I did. He's not a very talkative man."

"Seems to be a popular opinion."

"Anyway, he claims to have been home alone that evening. Problem is can we find anyone in the building or crucial evidence to verify that."

"I spoke with him the other night at the art group meeting." I recapped my conversation with Ashe.

"It fits what he told me. Obviously, the man has a grudge against the Whitmores."

"Against Alan, not necessarily Faith." I described the trip to Jamestown and seeing Faith come out of the apartment building, only minutes before Ashe did.

"That certainly raises a lot of questions."

"An affair? It's what Izzie and I are thinking."

"Well, it would seem the most obvious."

"Don't you think it puts a different spin on all his protests about Whitmore wealth, especially when all his complaining is directed at Alan?" I needed him to say what I was thinking.

He scratched his chin, staring at me without speaking for several seconds. "If there's an affair going on, Terence Ashe would resent Alan Whitmore."

I nodded. "Jealous that he is married to her? It would make perfect sense."

"Puts all his talk about the entitled elite in a different light."

"Exactly." I finished my coffee and slid my chair away from the table.

"I'll have one of my men check with other residents in the apartment building. Maybe someone has seen them together or knows more about the relationship, if there is one."

"What if you go straight to the source? Confront Ashe."

"He won't talk. Besides, I've got plenty else to investigate. This case is bogged down with suspects and leads."

"I get it. Anyway, you're probably right about him. Okay, I need to go open up the shop." I stood on tiptoes and kissed him goodbye. "Thanks for breakfast and the conversation."

"And thank you. We make a great team, don't we?" He grinned.

"When you're not lecturing me to stay out of your cases, we do," I teased. "See you later." I waved, then hurried outside.

By midday, Izzie came to the shop, sans migraine. We had everything checked off on our list of items for this evening's event, so we worked on decorations for the masked ball. Colored streamers, ghost, witch, and skeleton appliques, die-cut letters, black eye masks, and 3-D crepe paper pumpkins were spread out on the floor.

"I think we should spray everything with gold glitter. Give it a more magical look," Izzie said.

"How about we only glitter the appliques and letters? That would make them stand out more against the streamers. And the pumpkins are fancy enough as is." I massaged the back of my neck. "Now we just have to figure out where to display everything in the casino."

"Good call. I like the idea of contrasting." She picked up one of the pumpkins. "How about we sketch the casino with all this in it? That'll make things go faster when we get there."

"I think this will work. Do you want to start on the sketch? I'll organize these decorations into separate containers. Give me a yell if you need help." I gathered the pile of die-cut letters and placed them in a plastic box.

"What's this? Are you decorating your shop window for Halloween?" Gwen walked inside, holding an envelope. She wore a bright orange sweater and brown slacks, looking like the perfect picture of autumn. Her face flushed as she swiped her brow.

"Afternoon, Gwen. It's been a week or so. Where have you been? The kite shop almost looked abandoned," I said.

"Yes, well, Winston and I took a trip to visit his family in Maryland. Such lovely people. It's nice to feel a part of a family." She sniffed.

I didn't comment on her troubled past and issues with her ex-husband. "Yes, it is nice to belong. Anyway, we're taking all these to decorate the casino for Friday's masked ball."

"Ooo! Wonderful idea. Do you need help? Winston is busy during the day with work, but I can make myself free for a couple of hours Friday afternoon." Her eyes brightened.

"I think Izzie and I can handle it, but if you're bored, your help is certainly welcome." I gestured with one hand. "What's in the envelope?"

She hurried over. "Winston took photos of our mixed event at the park. I made copies for you and Izzie."

I stood and took the envelope from her hand. "Thanks, Gwen. That's very thoughtful."

"You're welcome. I wish I could stick around, but I have a hair appointment at three." She patted her head. "Maybe I'll see you at the casino Friday afternoon."

I waited until the door closed, then slid the photos from the envelope. It had been a beautiful, sunny day for our kite paint party. I remembered how busy the park was with people strolling along the walking path or feeding the ducks, children at the playground laughing and squealing, and so many boats out on the lake. The park was popular that day. I shuffled through the photos and admired all the work we'd put into the event.

"Well, what's all this? Decorating for the holiday?" Penny stepped through the doorway.

"Nope. Decorations are for the masked ball. How's the article going? Anything new, besides murder?" I smiled.

"Not enough. Let's put it that way. I came here hoping you'd have something to share." Penny plopped in a chair and fanned her face. "Unseasonably warm today, don't you think?"

I shrugged. "Let me turn on the ceiling fan." We'd stopped using the AC last month to save utility costs. Days like this made it a challenge. At least by evening, when we held most of our events, the temperatures cooled.

"What are those photos of?" She pointed to my hand.

"Oh yeah. These were taken at the park a couple of weeks ago for our kite paint party with Gwen." I handed them to her. "Maybe looking at these will give you some ideas to write an article on Gwen's kite-making."

While she looked at the photos, I finished filling the boxes with all the decorations. I grabbed another container and put a couple of cans of spray glitter in it.

"Hey, take a look at this one." Penny nudged my shoulder.

I took the photo from her hand and studied its contents. It was a view of the lake in the background, and our projector with Gwen standing nearby, demonstrating how to make a kite. However, it was a couple off to the far left and a few feet behind Gwen that caught my eye. I gripped the photo and took a sharp breath.

"You recognize her, don't you? I certainly do." Penny's face grew smug.

"Erin Whitmore." I leaned closer and squinted. "Who's the man with her? Do you know him?" I turned to Penny, waiting for an answer. Why in the world would she have been in Whisper Cove? It was only hours later that she was murdered. I rubbed my arm, feeling a sudden chill.

"The hat pulled low over his forehead makes it hard to guess. But he, or she, I can't really tell with that slender build, which is kind of feminine, now that I think of it. Anyway, looks like the person is saying something private to Erin. See how close to each other they're standing?"

"Odd. Why visit the park?" I rubbed the edge of the photo while attempting to come up with an explanation.

"To see the sights? Like the amphitheater. Everybody loves the amphitheater."

I blinked. "I guess, but there has to be more to the story. Coincidence in the timing. That day was only hours before she was murdered. What if the person with her is the killer?" My voice trembled. The very idea I could be right was unsettling.

"Guess we'll never know why she was there. She can't talk."

I stared. Penny made her comment in a matter-of-fact manner and without emotion. Was that what becoming a news journalist did to a person? In her case, I assumed it did.

She handed the photos back to me and left after a quick goodbye.

"Was that Penny?" Izzie came out of the storage room with a drawing in her hand.

"Yeah, Penny. She was all business."

"Really? What did she say?"

"I'll explain later. Yay! You finished the layout of the casino room." I pointed at her hand.

"Yep. All done." She frowned. "What's that you're holding?"

"Photos from our kite event. Gwen dropped them off. Here. Trade you." We exchanged items. "Take a close look at the photo on top and see if you recognize anyone."

It took no more than ten seconds. Izzie's eyes widened as she snapped her head up to stare. "Erin Whitmore? Who's the guy with her?"

"Or woman. It's hard to tell. We need to figure it out. That and why they were at our park, of all places."

A sudden gust of wind blew through the open window, and the sky darkened. A streak of light followed by a thunderous boom. I shivered. Talk about a dramatic overture to match our thoughts. Could the person with Erin be her killer? That was another question we needed to answer.

As if the ominous moment came in human form, a man threw open the door, allowing the pelting rain inside.

I gasped at the sight of Tito Alma standing in our doorway.

"Ladies, could we talk?"

"Mister Alma. Please, come inside," I said. The grim expression and solemn tone of voice hinted this wasn't a mere social call. He gripped a piece of paper in his hand.

"Please, take a seat." Izzie gestured. "Would you care for a water or tea?"

"No. I'm fine." He leaned forward and held out the paper he'd held so tightly. "You need to see this."

"What is it?" I took the paper from him and unfolded it. A newspaper article.

"I know you are friends with Martin Steele, and your parents mentioned you've been working with the police to help solve Erin Whitmore's murder." His voice lifted at the end.

"Working with the police might be a stretch. More like alongside them," I interjected.

"Or outside, like freelancers," Izzie added.

Tito frowned, as if puzzled. "It really doesn't matter in what capacity you're doing this. What is important is your encounter with Terence Ashe. You should know, he's not who you think."

"Oh, we know something's not right about his hatred for the Whitmores," Izzie started.

I took a moment to glance at the article. My heart raced as I studied the photo and the caption underneath. "Izzie."

"In fact, we went to Jamestown this morning and you'd never guess who we saw," Izzie said.

"Izzie." I spoke sharply and a bit louder, which caught her attention. "Terence Ashe isn't Terence Ashe." I passed her the article.

She took a moment, her head shifted back and forth before lifting to stare. "Todd Ameling? Terence Ashe is Todd Ameling?"

"That's what I came here to tell you. Be careful, ladies. Anyone who hides his identity must have secrets, maybe dangerous secrets." Tito heaved a breath. "The other night at your group meeting, something triggered my memory. I recognized the man whom you call Terence Ashe from one of my business trips to Cleveland. Slightly heavier, no beard, and his eye color has changed. Maybe he wears contacts? Anyway, I thought you might share this with your police department. I would do this. However, for some personal reasons which I won't explain, I'd rather not."

Izzie and I didn't speak. Maybe Tito had some secrets of his own.

The article didn't tell me much. The write-up was about an art foundation I hadn't heard of, located in Cleveland, which Todd Ameling had organized. Unless he had a twin or doppelganger, Terence Ashe was hiding his true identity, most likely to keep his past in the past. I settled back in my seat. Terence, aka Todd Ameling, had become a very interesting person.

Chapter Twenty-Two

"What should we do about this?" Izzie held up the news article. There had been no time to talk about it after Tito left the shop because people had begun trailing in for the event. "Todd Ameling? It's like Tito said. If he found it necessary to change his name, he must have secrets about his past."

"I do have an idea, but it's risky." I yawned. The paint event last night hadn't gone smoothly. Rain poured for hours, and lightning killed our electricity for at least twenty minutes. We'd finally managed to finish up, but the weather had made it almost impossible for guests to leave with their paintings. Fortunately, we scraped together enough plastic bags to cover their precious cargoes and keep them from ruin.

"I'm listening." She sat on my bed.

"We could try tailing him. Go to his apartment and wait for him to leave. That way we might catch him going someplace or meeting someone that gives us a clue, or several, to figure out what he's been hiding."

"Risky and maybe pointless. I mean, is tailing him a good use of our time? I feel like we have so little left. We could end up with nothing and waste our morning," Izzie argued.

"Then, what do you suggest? We confront him, ask why he changed his name to Terence Ashe, and what he's hiding about his past?" The idea sounded crazy as I said it.

"Yes. We do exactly that." Izzie bounced off my bed and paced. "We tell him who we saw coming out of his apartment yesterday. That news coupled with saying his real name, or his Cleveland name—who knows how many aliases he has—should get a reaction and maybe a confession."

I pointed. "That just might work. Oh! And let's tell him we took pictures of him and Faith together."

"But we didn't. We didn't take pictures, and we didn't see them together."

"He doesn't know that. We could probably say we witnessed them canoodling in the park, and he'd be scared enough to believe it."

Izzie snorted. "Canoodling? You sound like Dad. What you say makes sense, though. A few white lies to get the truth out of him is worth a shot."

"Yes, so we have a plan."

"Then why are you looking so glum?"

"I was looking forward to putting on a disguise and tailing him. That's exciting stuff."

"I thought you said it was risky?" She tipped her head.

"Risky, exciting, dangerous, they're all the same and make this snooping business fun."

She rolled her eyes before turning to walk out of my room. "Whatever you say."

I reached around the corner of my bed to grab my shoes. The movement caused Max to wake up and stretch. "Hey, sleepyhead. How about we go outside for a walk? Fresh air and exercise will be good for both of us."

He covered his eyes with his front paws as if to say he was too tired to bother. I laughed. "Not this time, buddy." I scooped him up in my arms and set him on the floor. Once I slipped on my sneakers, I walked out to the hall. Turning, I added, "Let's go, Max Abbington. We're burning daylight."

"Another Dad expression? That's so you," Izzie called out from her bedroom.

"I'll take that as a compliment." I grinned as I passed by, then skipped down the stairs with Max trotting right behind me. "Be back in twenty!"

I objected to Izzie's idea. She wanted to call Ashe, aka Ameling, before paying him a visit. Much better to catch him by surprise and not give him time to invent some story of lies to keep his secrets safe.

I drove us to Jamestown. We'd reached the city limits a little after nine, hoping the time would be early enough to catch him at home. The elevator lit each floor number as we ascended. My heartbeat doubled its pace as the tiny cubicle dinged and the door slid open.

"We're here," Izzie whispered.

I blinked. "Why are you whispering?"

"I don't know." She shrugged. "I'm nervous, I guess."

We had no idea what to expect when he answered his door. Or if he was at home. Anticipation of the unknown made me anxious. I pressed the doorbell, then stepped a comfortable distance away. Izzie's mood was definitely getting to me. However, I remembered Hunter's opinion. Todd Ameling would be reluctant to talk. We had to push hard and make him.

"Just a minute." A voice spoke, and steps pounded. The door swung open as he added, "I wasn't expecting you for another half hour. I hope you brought the money because—" He paused and his eyes widened. "Oh! I'm sorry. I thought…" He shook his head. "Never mind. Can I help you?"

"Hi, I, that is, we thought maybe you have a moment to talk?" I stammered, but quickly realized by the puzzled look he didn't remember us. "Chloe and Izzie Abbington? We met the other night at the patrons of the arts meeting at Gritos?"

"Ah." He snapped his fingers and pointed at us. "Yes. You are Joe and Kate's daughters."

"Yes, we are." I managed a genuine smile. "Could we talk, Mister Ameling?"

He stepped back but kept his grip on the door frame. "I don't know what you mean. Who's Ameling?"

"Come on, Terence, aka Todd. You know the answer. You're Todd Ameling. At least you were when you lived in Cleveland, Ohio, five years ago." I grew bolder with each word. He looked frightened and unsettled. Fair or not, this was exactly where we needed him to be, if we wanted to get to the truth.

He pushed the door forward a few inches. "I don't know what your game is, but I think you should leave."

"Not just yet." I pressed my hand against the door before he could close it. "We have questions."

"And if you don't answer them, we'll go straight to the police with the photos we took," Izzie added.

"Of you and Faith Whitmore coming out of your apartment building, looking a little too chummy." I couldn't help but feel a tiny twinge of guilt for causing the look of fear that spread across his face. Playing hardball wasn't easy.

His shoulders dropped, and he motioned for us to come inside. "It's not what you think it is. Trust me."

The apartment was small and dated, with fixtures that would be perfect for a movie set in the sixties. I took a seat on the sofa, and Izzie sat next to me, so close we practically knocked knees. "Let's start with why you changed your name."

He settled into a chair across from us and then picked up a liquor glass from the end table. Taking a sip, he held up the glass. "I'm being rude. Would either of you like something to drink?"

We both shook our heads and waited for him to answer.

"I made some enemies back in Cleveland. Not very nice people, you see. I didn't want them to find me. That's about it."

I raised my chin. A sketchy explanation at the very least. There had to be more to the story. "Powerful, rich people?"

"Some. Business associates. I should've known better." He took another swig.

I opened my mouth to ask for more, but then I glimpsed Izzie, who gave her head a tiny shake. She was right. He probably wouldn't say anything more about Cleveland.

"What about Faith Whitmore? I thought you despised the family. Why would we see you two together like that?" I said.

"I never said anything directly about her. Alan is another story. Besides, my animosity toward rich and privileged people is more of a general opinion."

I detected the mild blush on his cheeks. He was embarrassed, but why?

"Why were you together, though? Unless you two have become friends, it makes no sense," Izzie reasoned aloud.

"She hired me to refurbish an antique frame and restore the painting. Like I said, not at all what you must be thinking." He narrowed his gaze.

I bit down on my lip. "Wasn't she concerned how her husband would feel?

I mean, you have been pretty open with your opinion of him."

He grinned. "That's what made the business deal so appealing. Look. Faith Whitmore isn't on the best terms with her husband. I got that impression from the moment I met her." He shrugged. "Besides, business is business. As long as I'm getting paid, that's what counts."

I lifted my brow. "Keep your feelings about people and your business dealings separate. Is that it?" He wasn't fooling me, not a person with that much hatred for someone.

"Right." He stood. "Now, if that's all, I have a client who should be arriving in about ten minutes." He gestured toward the door.

We left the apartment and got into the elevator. He'd said so much and yet so little. To put it another way, Todd Ameling hadn't given up all his secrets. That much I was sure of.

"What do you think?" Izzie pressed the first-floor button.

"I think we need to speak with Faith Whitmore."

"And use the same tactics. Photos and maybe add canoodling." She grinned.

"Whatever. What we don't tell her is Ameling's story. We want to see how much or how little hers matches his."

We got into the car once more. I let the engine idle while I got on the phone. "Hey, Mom. Do you happen to have Faith Whitmore's phone number? I remember you said you worked with her on a few of the group events. Maybe you talked on the phone?" I chewed on my fingernail, hoping for a number.

"Oh, of course I do, but what do you need it for? You aren't planning to call and pester the poor woman. She's still grieving," Mom said.

"I promise. We don't plan to pester her. She's um…" I raced to come up with an excuse. "We wanted to ask her about donating some items for the charity auction at the masked ball."

"Oh, I already did. She's got everything ready to deliver."

I rolled my eyes. "That's great. We're close to Buffalo and can swing by to pick up the items so she won't have to deliver them. Less to stress about. Since she's grieving and all."

"That's such a kind gesture. I have wonderful, caring daughters. We're so proud of you both."

"Thanks, Mom. Can you tell me her number so I can write it down?"

Within seconds, I had what I needed. Hanging up, I turned to Izzie. "You want to call while I drive? If we're lucky, she'll agree to meet at a place close by. Something tells me she'd prefer keeping her husband out of the conversation."

"Give me the number." Izzie punched in the keys. "I have an idea. How about we use picking up the charity items as an excuse to meet rather than starting the conversation with what we know about her and Ameling? We want to avoid scaring her off." She placed the phone in her lap, waiting for me to answer.

"You're probably right. Mom will be expecting the donations when we get home." I nodded. "Not too much deception to feel guilty about."

"So what if our visit should turn into a conversation about Ameling. It's totally believable." Izzie winked.

"We are so devious." I sighed.

"So very devious." Izzie laughed, then pressed the call button.

Soon, we turned into the parking lot of Lala's, a French restaurant only twenty minutes from the Whitmore estate. Faith had seemed relieved to hear our offer and promised to bring the items along to the meeting so we wouldn't have to stop at her place. No surprise there.

A part of me felt sad to think she could be involved in any way with Erin's murder or with what I now strongly believed was a stolen painting that Clive had carefully hidden. Keeping my outlook positive, I hoped she was merely an innocent player in all of this.

The exterior of Lala's was deceiving. Plain and rather worn stucco with chipped painted letters in the sign over the door. The only trendy feature it displayed was the chalkboard listing today's specials sitting on a tripod stand in front of one window. However the interior was another story. It was like stepping into a picturesque scene of Paris, reminding me of the many cafes and restaurants I'd gone to while living there. I felt right at home.

"*Bienvenue, Mesdames.* Table for two?" The hostess, dressed in a white blouse and black trousers, stood just inside the doorway.

"Actually, we're meeting someone." I peered around her and spotted Faith near the back seated in a booth.

"Madame Whitmore? She's expecting you. Right this way." She wove her way around tables to the other side of the room.

Faith stood and smiled. "Chloe, Izzie, so nice to see you again." She held out her hand to shake. Afterward, she quickly sat down. "I'll admit, I was surprised to hear from you."

"Well, Mom had mentioned you were donating items for the charity ball," I said.

"And we were in Jamestown on business this morning, so we thought, why not help you out?" Izzie added.

"Very nice of you. Thanks." She fingered the menu in front of her. "Todd called me a half hour ago. He said you might be paying a visit. Or maybe I should say he warned me." Her gaze fixated on us. "Nothing personal is going on between us."

"Okay. That was unexpected." I expelled a lengthy breath. Our element of surprise disappeared in an instant. Now what, I wondered?

"I don't know what he told you. We didn't stay on the phone for more than a minute." She leaned back. "So, I'd be more than happy to tell you my side of things."

"Should we order lunch first? I'm famished." Izzie picked up her menu and scanned the contents, avoiding eye contact with Faith.

I kept my attention on the conversation. "We'd be glad to listen, as long as what you tell us is the truth."

"I plan to." She waved to the server, who rushed over to our booth within seconds.

During the entire meal, Faith refused to talk about Ameling. Once the server cleared our plates and refilled our drinks, she dabbed her lips with a napkin, then told us her version of things. "Todd Ameling is blackmailing us."

I choked on the sip of my iced tea and set down the glass. "Excuse me? Did you say blackmail?"

"Yes. Todd knows about my husband's business deals, the ones that aren't completely what you'd call honest. He threatened to go to the authorities, claiming he has proof. Unfortunately, that's true. You see, he was one of my husband's so-called victims in a deal that went badly. People lost thousands, and for some, their reputations."

I swallowed, my mouth suddenly dry. How did we go from murder to art theft and now to blackmail? I was reminded of my concern in the beginning, how maybe the case was too complicated for us to handle. It just got a whole lot worse.

"So, Todd Ameling has personal reasons for wanting to blackmail you," Izzie said with a head shake. "Like he's out for revenge."

"Exactly." She blinked away tears. "Only my husband is totally unaware of this. I couldn't give him the chance to do anything…drastic." She paused. "Alan can be ruthless when pushed. He'd refuse to pay a blackmailer, and I'm afraid in this case he'd do even worse. Let's say he likes to teach people who cross him a lesson."

"You mean hurt Todd?" Izzie's voice shook.

"He has caused plenty of problems in the past. I couldn't go through that again. Not now." She lifted her chin. "Besides, I refuse to let the Whitmore name be damaged more than it already has. The deaths of our two children have taken a toll on us. Isn't that enough suffering?" She sniffed and rummaged through her bag to pull out a tissue.

Her emotional reaction seemed genuine. I wasn't a parent, but I understood losing a loved one and the heartbreak it caused. At this point, her version of the relationship with Ameling was more convincing than his. "I do have one question. Todd claims you commissioned him to complete a project. If it's true, and he's blackmailing you, why hire him?"

She folded her hands and set them on the table. "Isn't it obvious? It's my alibi for meeting with him. If anyone noticed us together, like you have, the idea of blackmail would never occur to them."

Good answer, I decided. "Did you know about those shady deals, especially the one that involved Ameling?" If she was complicit, I wasn't certain she'd answer truthfully.

She narrowed her gaze. "And if I said yes, would that satisfy you? I can't confess to knowing every business deal of my husband's, but I'd be blind not to notice there were details that gave me reason to believe how he sometimes crossed a line."

"Nothing more you can tell us about what went wrong with Ameling, is there?" Izzie said.

Faith removed a credit card from her bag, then got up from her seat. "I think I've said all I want to." She paused before walking away. "I should warn you, my husband isn't someone to cross. Most anyone, including you, would never stand a chance."

Without another word, from any of us, she left the restaurant.

"Whew. That was a lot," Izzie said.

"You got that right. Raises lots of questions. It's what she didn't say that leaves us nowhere. Do we consider her guilty of anything? Other than being married to a despicable, corrupt man. And as far as Todd Ameling goes, he's more like Alan Whitmore's victim. Makes it easy to understand why he'd want to blackmail him." I set my card in the tray, along with the bill.

"True, but the details of how exactly he became a victim isn't clear. She didn't tell us much about that. In fact, I'm not convinced he's guilty of anything but blackmail. Not a sound connection to murder or art theft, is it?"

"I guess not. Unless…" I teetered my head side to side. "Unless his revenge runs so deep he'd go so far as to kill Erin because she was a Whitmore."

Izzie scowled. "A bit farfetched. Or how about this?" She shifted around to face me. "What if Erin learned about the blackmail, confronted Ameling, and they got into a heated argument that ended in him killing her?"

I reared back my head. "Also far-fetched. Let's put the guessing aside and think about what to do next."

Once we took care of our bill, we left the restaurant. I couldn't stop the dozens of questions and theories crowding my brain. Ameling and the Whitmores had a long, albeit troubling, history. He resented them for some business deal gone bad. Obviously, we needed more information about that. Also, his alibi about being home alone the night Erin was murdered wasn't much of an alibi. "Or maybe he wasn't home alone," I thought aloud.

"Who?" Izzie got into the passenger seat.

"Ameling told Hunter he'd been home alone the night Erin died."

"So? It's weak, but still an alibi."

I started the engine but didn't move. "Great," I mumbled.

"We forgot about the charity items. I wonder if she's still in the parking lot." I shifted into gear and slowly cruised past the cars.

"She's probably gone. We'll have to call and make other arrangements, although I doubt she'd want to see us again." Izzie pouted.

"We'll think of some excuse to tell Mom. Now, where was I?"

"A theory about Ameling?"

"Right. Okay, so both he and Faith implied there's nothing going on between them, meaning in the bedroom. But what if there was? They'd want to keep it a secret, especially from Angry Alan."

Izzie widened her eyes. "You think they might have been together that night. That's brilliant. And so classic, like it came right out of a movie."

I maneuvered the car to take the highway entrance when my phone rang. Glimpsing the dashboard display showed Hunter was calling. I pressed to answer. "Hello, detective. Making progress on the case, I hope?"

"No hello or how are you? All work and no play makes you no fun." He laughed.

"I'm plenty of fun. Just not at the moment." I recapped what we'd learned from Tito and our meetings with Ameling and Faith.

"Well, that goes with what I discovered in the database," he said.

"How?"

"The name Ameling gave us new results."

"What do you mean?" I frowned.

"Todd Ameling served two years in jail for embezzlement. In court, he'd pleaded not guilty, insisting he was framed by the Whitmore Foundation, but the jury didn't believe him. Also on record are the numerous phone calls he'd made from prison, threatening the Whitmores. The family filed a report, so we have proof. Looks like Ameling is a loose cannon."

I pulled to the side of the road. My hands were shaking so hard, I couldn't drive. Izzie's expression mirrored mine. Frightened beyond belief, I couldn't get past how we'd spent time alone with a criminal, a dangerous one at that.

Chapter Twenty-Three

We didn't have any time to process Hunter's news about Ameling's criminal past because Martin called soon after. He wanted to meet at the jail, saying he was ready to share everything concerning Clive, Erin, and what he'd been doing before his arrest…this time. As it was, we couldn't visit until this morning. Our day's schedule was certainly full. I mentally perused the agenda. First, our visit with Martin, followed by a couple of hours at the casino to decorate. Afterward, we'd head home for dinner and get ready for the ball.

Fortunately, Mom didn't make much of a fuss about us not bringing the items donated by Faith. By the time we got home from Buffalo, Mom had received notice that a delivery service had dropped them off at the casino.

"What do you think he'll have to say?" I questioned while pondering my own scenarios, every one of them proving his innocence because that's what I believed. Martin Steele was guilty of nothing more than being a loyal friend to all those he cared about. Like Clive, but he couldn't stop him from dying. Maybe that's why he worked so hard to help Erin. He didn't want to fail again. Sadly, fate had other plans, none of which were in Martin's control.

"I guess we'll know soon enough." Izzie pulled alongside the curb to park in front of the sheriff's building.

I studied her face. It was stoic, and she lifted her chin in confidence or maybe in defiance. She still carried a lot of hurt because Martin had kept his secrets from her, right from the beginning. She viewed herself as one of his closest friends. She expected him to confide in her, no matter how difficult the situation was.

Without another word, I got out of the Land Rover and stepped toward the entrance, pausing only to wait for Izzie to catch up.

The judge had decided Martin should remain in jail until they'd heard from the expert about the painting confiscated from the Steele home. Martin promised Izzie the painting was a reproduction, not an original. He assured her that's what the report would say.

Entering the building, we were confronted at once by Martin's assistant. Phillip's eyes were bloodshot, and his haggard face caused the lines to deepen.

"Hi, Phillip." Izzie leaned to hug him. "Have you been getting any sleep? You shouldn't worry so much. It's not healthy. Martin can take care of himself."

I screwed my mouth shut. Wasn't that the advice I'd been giving her? "Have you heard any further news from the lawyer about Martin's release? It's been too long."

"Five days *is* a long time to sit and wait for the judge to come to his senses," Izzie griped.

He gestured to follow him to the far corner of the room. "The woman who can confirm Mister Steele's alibi has returned from her business trip. She's arranged to meet the judge and give her testimony. That should carry some weight. Of course, there's the video of him returning to the Whitmore estate." He scowled. "Foolish thing to do."

Izzie sighed. "Then there's still the issue of the painting he has."

"As you said. It's been five days. I'm sure the report will be coming anytime now." Phillip lifted his brows. "Are you ready to visit with him? He's anxious to explain everything and answer any questions you have."

"Yes. I'm anxious, too." Izzie pulled back her shoulders.

Phillip nodded to Rachel at the front desk. A buzzer sounded, and one of the deputies held open the door leading to the jail chamber.

I'd seen no sign of Hunter, which didn't surprise me. As a detective, he spent most of his time out of the building to investigate his cases.

Martin sat in the last cell—there were only four—with his back resting against the wall and eyes closed. He straightened as we approached.

The deputy opened the cell door and stepped away to let us inside. "I guess

I don't have to worry about you making a great escape, do I?" He smiled wryly and walked to the front without locking us in.

"Oh, Martin." Izzie squeezed him tightly, then kissed his cheek. "What are we going to do with you?"

He chuckled. "I don't believe you need to do anything. I'm in full control of the situation."

"Really?" She reared back her head. "And yet, here you sit."

"It's good to see you, Martin." I took hold of his arm. "Don't let her fool you. She's done nothing but worry about you these past few weeks."

"Sit." He gestured at the bench across from him. "I have lots to share."

Anxious to learn what he had to say, we took our seats and gave him our complete attention.

"First, I meant what I said about being in control. I will be out of here by tomorrow. My alibi, Claudia Montaire, has flown in from France and will vouch for me. As for my painting reported as stolen, my new friend, Jeremy, says the report has arrived. He took a peek and assured me it's all good news. So, there's that. But I'm getting ahead of myself. Let's start with the gift from Clive. The day I received it, I knew something was wrong. Not about the gift. Clive had always been a generous person and a good friend." He stopped to take a breath.

And to regain his composure, I assumed. Losing a close friend, as I well knew, was like a blow to your heart that you hope will pass in time. It hadn't yet for me. I'm sure it hadn't for him.

"The seascape was eerily familiar. And Clive's note, mentioning our wild college days, finally triggered a memory. It's amazing how well everything came together. In an instant, I was back in college. It was summer break. Clive and I had decided to go on a road trip to see as many art museums as we could." He laughed. "Those were such good times." His voice trembled ever so slightly.

"It was in Boston. First, we had to stop at the beach. The lighthouse gave the scene just the right touch. Serene yet haunting, don't you think? The ocean liner in the distance was not there when we visited. I puzzled over why he'd included it, until it hit me. That date he painted on the ship.

March eighteenth. Boston. Nineteen-ninety. While the entire city was celebrating Saint Patrick's Day well into the night, thieves dressed as guards broke into the museum and orchestrated the biggest, most famous heist in history. Clive and I weren't there at the time, of course. We were only boys then. However, we had learned all about the robbery in an art history class. Thirteen masterpieces were stolen from the Isabella Stewart Gardner Museum and never recovered."

"Let me guess. One of the paintings was a Vermeer," Izzie said.

"Yes. A Vermeer, a Rembrandt, a Manet, and others."

I frowned. "But the painting hidden behind Clive's seascape isn't an authentic Vermeer. It can't be the one stolen from the Boston Museum."

"That's where you'd be wrong. At least about it being authentic. At first, I thought the same thing. A talented imitation of one of Vermeer's tronies. It's well known the master only painted the set of four. At least, that's what the world believes, to this day. I did, until I spoke with Claudia and then another dealer in France, who both confirmed our hidden painting is a genuine Vermeer.

"The story had been told to a local news reporter by a descendant of the family, but was never proven true. Supposedly, Vermeer had painted the first in a new series of tronies and stored the painting, hoping to sell it to a wealthy collector. But then Vermeer took ill and died. The painting remained hidden for centuries, behind a wall in a false compartment. That's where Clive comes into the story."

The deputy approached, carrying a tray with three cups of coffee and a small container of cream. "Thought you all might need some."

"Thank you, Jeremy. That's very considerate," Martin said.

Something told me Martin had made himself quite comfortable in jail and was treated well. "But why would Clive lead you to the Boston Museum, if this painting wasn't stolen from there?"

"I don't think Clive wanted to make it obvious. He'd created clues that only I would be able to decipher. The funny part is I didn't. Until you told me, I wasn't even aware the painting was hidden behind Clive's. At least, I recognized the coastal view from the details in his seascape. From the note,

I eventually was able to figure out the reference to the museum and the heist, but that's as far as I got. Until I spoke with Erin, that is."

"Clive told her, didn't he? What he had been doing and how he obtained the Vermeer." Izzie nodded.

"She asked me to meet her. She had concerns and wanted to discuss them." Martin sighed. He stirred cream in his coffee and took a sip. "I was disappointed to learn she thought I'd gotten Clive killed by involving him in a shady deal. I didn't, of course. She also strongly believed he was murdered. I had felt the same. However, discouraging as it was, I reminded her that the authorities investigated and found no foul play. I assured her I loved her brother and would never harm him. I'm not convinced she believed me."

I checked my watch. "What else was she concerned about?"

"She told me Clive's story. He'd been in financial trouble and was desperate to make quick money. As if luck was with him, while on a buying trip in France, he visited one of those markets where street art is sold and spotted the painting. Everyone he spoke with assumed it was a pastiche, imitating Vermeer's style. Clive knew better. To be sure, my friend was very discerning and had a keen eye when it came to art. That's why he called an associate in Holland to discuss the matter and learned about the story told by Vermeer's descendant. Clive quickly purchased the painting for practically nothing.

"Enter player number three. Antoine. I'll tell you more about him later in my story. Let's just say he's an unscrupulous dealer and has many connections in the black market. Clive knew him through business, unfortunately. I don't want to speculate any further. I'd like to remember my friend as an honest man. Anyway, according to Erin, Clive knew someone—he never told her his name—who had clients with deep pockets. She learned later these were the type of people who would deal with the black market in order to get their hands on a coveted work of art. Remember, Clive needed money and a lot of it." Martin finished his coffee.

"So, what I eventually learned was how Clive began to spin a story. One that Antoine would tell to his clients and make them all fight over the Vermeer. The artist's final painting, hidden for centuries, and one that the world has never seen. The foolish part was that my dear friend ignored the fact he was playing with some very dangerous people. He threw caution to the wind, as they say.

"According to Erin, Clive admitted he was worried that he wouldn't get the money to pay his debtors in time. However, his mood changed when she saw him the next day. He said his contact, that is Antoine, had called him to say he had a buyer who would pay seven figures. Clive was relieved, and Erin was happy for him. He told Erin that soon he'd be able to free himself from their father's power. Everything was working out, or so he believed."

"Wait." Izzie leaned forward. "Clive needed money. He learned about the Vermeer that everyone thought was a pastiche. He bought it, then made a deal with Antoine's help to sell the painting for a seven-figure sum. But for some reason, the painting ended up in your hands, and poor Clive died in a horrible accident. I don't understand. Why didn't Clive sell it to the buyer instead of giving it to you?"

"I don't know. I don't know why he sent it to me. I can make an educated guess. Perhaps the arranged deal went south in some way. What I can tell you is Antoine is a very dangerous man."

"You know him?" I said, feeling surprised.

"I met with him. Only once." Martin's eyes turned dark, almost black.

I shuddered, refusing to think of what Martin didn't say.

"He won't be a problem. I threatened to return to France and bury him in the ground, if anything happened to Erin. Sadly, when I got home, I learned what had happened."

"But the painting? We still don't know why he didn't sell it or who it was promised to?" Izzie asked.

"That is what Erin was searching for: answers to those questions. She had no idea what happened to the priceless painting Clive planned to sell, but she wouldn't give up, no matter what I said or her parents or her friends said. She refused to listen." In one instant, he aged twenty years. His sagging face folded and creased as if it could swallow him up.

"The photo." I snapped my fingers. "I found a photo torn to pieces in Alan's study. It showed Erin standing on a beach with a view of the ocean behind her. The lighthouse, the same lighthouse as in Clive's painting, is off to the right. She went there, Martin. Maybe not alone. Someone would've taken the photo."

Martin came alive once more. "That is interesting. It means she figured out the scene in the painting. Clive must have told her about our trip that summer. She'd certainly remember the stories."

"But that would mean she'd seen the painting before it was sent to you." I searched my mind for what else I knew. "Arthur Storing said Erin claimed Clive was excited about a painting he planned to sell. He also said Clive talked about a painting he'd finished and planned to give to you. What if Clive showed the seascape to Erin, but she kept quiet about it?"

"That's possible. Storing. Now, there's an odd man. Always into everyone's business, personal or otherwise." Martin fingered his coffee cup.

"Especially anything about the Whitmores," Izzie added. "Why did you return to the Whitmore estate, Martin? The sheriff has you on video, and it's close to the time Erin was murdered. That doesn't look promising for you and not the kind of risk you'd take. Can you explain?" She stared without so much as a flutter of her eyelids, waiting for his answer.

He stroked his chin while all three of us remained quiet. So quiet that the murmur of voices from the front echoed down the hall and to our corner.

I heard Rachel's deep belly laugh and wished the mood in this jail cell could be that cheerful instead of our solemn one with the heavy conversation about murder.

"I'd pulled in my drive when my phone rang. A frantic call from Erin. Remember I mentioned Antoine? He is the reason I returned to the Whitmore estate. Erin had received a threatening call from him. He told her his name and demanded to know why he hadn't received the painting from Clive. When she explained he was dead, Antoine threatened her. He had a very temperamental client who was anxious to get his Vermeer. Of course, Erin didn't know where the painting was and told Antoine as much. I won't repeat what Antoine said he would do to Erin if she didn't turn over the painting at once. Erin feared for her life, and I promised I would help." He drew in a deep breath. "So, yes. I returned to give her a gun. A pistol that's totally untraceable, which is what I'm sure your detective discovered."

CHAPTER TWENTY-THREE

He nodded.

"The pistol I found in the closet." I swallowed the lump lodged in my throat.

"From what I hear, yes." He gripped his knees. "If only I hadn't, she might still be…" His voice faltered.

"Stop. It's not your fault." Izzie came to his side and wrapped an arm around him.

"I keep thinking. Who could've done this? Her killer can't be Antoine. He was in France at the time. When I got off the plane, Claudia was waiting to take me to his place. There's no way he could've flown to the states, murdered Erin, then return to his home." He stood and circled around his cell from one side to the other. Once he stopped, he pointed at us.

"There is possibly one player we are forgetting. One whose name and identity we don't know. Another buyer. I'm not speaking of Antoine's arrangement. Clive could have changed his mind, despite the risk of angering Antoine. What if he found someone else to purchase the painting, someone who offered to pay more?"

"Sounds believable, but then we keep coming back to the question of why he sent the painting to you instead," Izzie said.

"I asked her if anyone else contacted her about the painting. Someone other than Antoine. She answered no. However, Erin was a talker. It would've been easy for someone to overhear her argue that Clive was murdered because of an art deal and put that claim together with our Vermeer."

He sat once more. "The problem is, I have no idea who in the community would go to such lengths to get the painting. Murder? Not likely. How could she give someone information on the painting's whereabouts if she was dead?"

"A crime of passion. Erin refused or insisted she didn't know the location of the painting, and the killer was so enraged, he, or she, killed her." I shuddered.

"Possibly." Martin shrugged. "Our conversation during that second meeting ended with me promising to find answers about Clive's death, which is why I flew to Paris. Of course, at the time, I didn't know where the

Vermeer was hidden. I told Erin about Clive's seascape, how I was taking good care of it and would give it to her when I could. It seemed like the right thing to do. Then, I left the pistol with her and told her to be watchful. Anyway, I flew to Paris that night and called Claudia, asking her to meet me at the airport."

"Here's a thought. What if Antoine hired someone living here to find the painting? And that person came to the house and murdered Erin," I suggested.

Martin shook his head. "I doubt it. When I spoke with Antoine, I would've known if he lied. Trust me."

I certainly did. Swallowing hard, I stood. "I'm glad all is working out for you. Being in this jail cell can't be comfortable."

"Not like home, but it has its perks." He winked.

"You mean like Jeremy waiting on you constantly bringing coffee and take-out food from Delmonico's, I imagine," Izzie teased.

"Definitely a perk. See you soon on the outside."

We hugged goodbye and called for Jeremy to lock the cell door. There was some protocol that needed to be followed, after all.

Chapter Twenty-Four

I adjusted my mask as we entered the casino. The cat costume I'd picked out was comfortable and my perfect style. Easy to move in and no flowing dress to trip over. Black from top to toe with a white-tipped tail and ears. Indeed, I felt like Cat Woman ready to do battle with the Joker, the Riddler, or even Batman if necessary.

Izzie, true to her personality, had chosen to be Elsa from *Frozen*. An ice blue gown with a flowing train flattered her willowy figure. She was a perfect match for the character. In fact, everyone at the ball, having donned character-themed costumes, made the room feel like a Hollywood studio set. Exactly what the town council had been hoping to achieve.

I glanced at Hunter and smiled. He wore a Robin Hood costume and looked every bit the part of a do-good thief, ready to rob the rich and give to the poor. "Where are your bow and arrows, Mister Hood? Kind of hard to defend yourself without them." I winked.

He tugged at his tunic. "I don't need weapons. This costume will scare anyone off."

"I think you look handsome, in a roguish way." I stroked his arm. Even though I carried on our light conversation, my mind took my thoughts elsewhere. The case never left me. I couldn't stop sifting through the details we'd gathered, sorting them, dropping them into boxes that matched appropriately to each suspect, and then creating scenarios about who killed Erin.

"You don't fool me." He touched my chin, lifting it with one finger. "You haven't stopped thinking about Erin's case the entire evening. Don't you think your mind deserves to rest a bit? Relax and enjoy the moment." His expression almost hinted at disappointment.

I wasn't exactly the date he deserved. My attention should be on him and the ball. I smiled. "Let's dance."

"That's more like it, kitty cat." He took my hand and guided me out to the dance floor.

I pressed the side of my head to his chest. At least, this way, he couldn't see my face. The ideas continued churning, as if they refused to be silenced. Despite Hunter's advice, I had to sort this out. Whoever murdered Erin needed to be caught before harm came to anyone else. I was certain the killer would go to any lengths to keep from being discovered.

I lifted my head as the music stopped. "Do you think Erin was killed because of the painting, or was the motive more personal?"

Hunter sighed. "I guess there's no persuading you to stop. So, to answer your question, I don't have an opinion. At least, not yet." He took my arm. "Let's go outside and cool off. The casino is unseasonably stuffy."

I walked with him to the far end of the room, where doors led out to the patio overlooking the lake. We sat on two wrought iron chairs that had been covered with cushions for this evening's occasion. The breeze, with scents of algae and driftwood, carried from the shore. "I can't stop thinking about that question." The tail of my costume wiggled out from under my seat, and I stroked it mindlessly. "If Fanning did it, that would make it personal. He has a quick temper and must've been angry with Erin when she broke up with him."

Hunter shook his head. "We got a call today from the friend who lives in the Finger Lakes area. Remember? The one Fanning claims he spent the night with after that food convention? She says she'll get back to me with proof he was there."

"Wow. Stalling for time. That's another way to cover up." I crossed off his name on my list of possibilities, just in case. "What about Todd Ameling? He's a textbook case of mystery and secrets. He has the revenge motive, and his alibi hasn't been proven. I mean, come on. At home alone all evening? That's the classic alibi that nobody believes."

"Hmm." Hunter tapped his chair in thought. "The revenge motive is strong. It looks like he had plenty to be angry about, being framed and serving jail time. He's made no secret of believing the Whitmores are to blame."

The tingling of excitement lifted my voice. "Oh! And he could've known about Clive and the hidden painting. What if attempting to steal it was his way of revenge? Maybe he'd gone to see Erin that night, and things went wrong, and he murdered her. A stretch, but possible. Or she found out about the blackmail and threatened to tell the authorities. Panicked and worried that he'd be sent back to jail, he murdered her on the spot." I swallowed hard. These gruesome scenarios were becoming too easy. I didn't like the new side of me. Where was the happy, carefree me? She was disappearing by delving into all these murders in the past year and a half.

Hunter's face tensed with worry. "Watch it. You're losing that soft side of you I love so much. Don't become too cynical. The world needs more innocence and people who have faith in the good of others."

"Hard to do when that goodness won't show up. Lots of ugly players in this case." I scowled and kicked at a stray pebble on the patio floor.

He wrapped an arm around me and squeezed. "I'm taking you to Disney World when this case is over. You need a strong dose of the magic kingdom's dreams."

"Funny. I may hold you to that promise." I thought a moment. "You know, if someone's trying to frame Martin to tie him to Erin's murder, the killer would have to know a lot about Martin. Right?"

"True."

"Also, when Martin gave us the painting to deliver to the storage facility, he was worried someone had been following him. That could be the killer," I reasoned aloud.

"Right again. I see where you're going with this. The killer might have guessed or knew Clive hid the Vermeer behind the seascape, then followed the trail to where the painting ended up with Martin."

Something nagged at me. A detail that kept itself hidden outside of my conscious thoughts. I was sure it had nothing to do with Ameling or Fanning or Alan Whitmore. But who?

A phone rang and startled me back to the present. I turned to find Hunter pulling his phone from under his tunic.

"Detective Barrett." He kept his voice low, then stood to walk to the far edge of the patio where no one was close by. Once he'd finished the call, he hurried back to me. "I'm sorry, but I have to leave. Brody can take you and Izzie home."

"Why? What's happened? Is it about the case?" I walked with him back inside the casino.

"I hope so. I had one of my tech people look back over the past two weeks to find any traffic reports that involved a black van in the Buffalo area. That was the call I just got. Back on Tuesday evening, September twentieth, a woman reported a man driving a black van, license plate AUTR7125, dinged her car. Supposedly, when she confronted him, the man shouted to mind her own business and then sped away without exchanging insurance info."

I gasped. "That's the vehicle that followed us from the storage facility."

"And the accident happened the same day the storage facility was broken into. Now, here's where it gets interesting. The woman got a glance at the inside of his van. She reported a black ski mask sitting on top of a large picture frame. I tell you, this woman has a sharp memory. After the storage facility break-in that local news had reported on, she remembered what she'd seen in the backseat of the van. So, she called the BPD again. This time, to give them a tip about the robbery. Somebody else likes to play detective, it seems." He winked, then gave me a kiss on the cheek. "I'll keep you posted. I want to pay that dear woman a visit. See if she can tell us more about the man. Stay here, and try to enjoy yourself."

"Uh, huh. Sure. Be careful." I tugged at his tunic. "Robin Hood in action."

He blushed. "When I show up in this? The guys will never let me live it down."

"I'll bet." My heart pounded as I watched him leave through the front doorway. We were getting close. I searched the room for an ice blue gown and spotted Izzie standing next to Brody dressed as Prince Charming. Holding the cat tail in my hand so it didn't sway and smack somebody, I rushed to the other side. Grabbing her arm, I pulled Izzie to the front foyer where we'd have more privacy, and then gestured at Brody to follow.

"What on earth is going on? You look white as a sheet." Izzie removed her mask.

"It's news. Good news. Maybe, but definitely news." My mouth flapped until I anchored it shut for a second before taking a deep breath to calm myself. "Hunter got a call from the precinct. They might have a lead on who drives the black van, which would be the person who took part in stealing the painting and who knows what else. We're so, so getting closer. Don't you think?" I smiled, but was sure it looked maniacal.

"Explain, please." Izzie leveled her voice.

"Sure." I retold everything Hunter had to say.

"Holy wow. This could be the break we've been searching for." Izzie squeezed my hand.

"What's Hunter doing now?" Brody asked.

"Following up. He's going to see if the woman who filed the report can tell him anything more."

"Any ideas? If this is the one who stole the painting, and he turns out to be the killer, do any of the people you've been suspecting fit?" Brody unfastened the top button of his shirt and rolled up his sleeves. "Stuffy in here."

"I'm still in the dark. Maybe if Hunter gets a description from the woman, that would help," I said.

"Definitely would help. Still, we aren't sure yet if this goes beyond stealing a painting. Could be totally unrelated and a mere coincidence," Izzie said.

I groaned. "Which would put us back to square one when it comes to Erin's murder."

"You want to get out of here? Doesn't seem like any of us are in a mood to party, after hearing that story," Brody suggested.

"Yeah. I'm certainly ready to go home and turn in for the night. I'm exhausted from playing detective in my head. Just let me grab my jacket. I left it at our table."

I hurried back across the casino floor to where our table was situated. Grabbing my jacket, I turned and spotted Alan and Faith Whitmore. They sat alone along the back wall. Faith had her hands folded in her lap, and her mouth drew a solemn line. She didn't look happy to be here. I thought about what she'd said while we sat at Gritos. How she talked about Alan didn't sound like a woman in love. It was more like a wife who feared her husband.

My jaw tensed. I felt the heat rise to flush my face. Men like Alan Whitmore, the ones who believed the world owed them, that they were always in the right, and in every situation, played by their own rules, deserved the kind of anger Todd Ameling possessed or the criticism and disrespect Erin and Clive felt.

I clenched my fists and marched over to where Alan stood, letting my tail swing back and forth, wielding it almost like a weapon. I smiled that maniacal grin again. "Good evening, Alan. How are you enjoying the party?" I didn't bother with protocol and his surname. He didn't deserve it.

He curled his lips. "Miss Abbington. What a pleasure to see you somewhere other than my private study."

I let that one pass. "I wanted to thank you for the generous donation to our business, but also to say it won't work."

"What do you mean?" He appeared genuinely puzzled.

"You can't buy my silence or my cooperation. Not with any amount." I turned away, but his words stopped me.

"I hear your friend is still behind bars. I hope he rots in jail for murdering my daughter."

I gasped. Granddad would tell me to walk away and that no good came from arguing with a snake. You'd only get bit. Granddad was too kind. I pivoted on my cat heels. "Why don't you tell the truth? Erin didn't tell you she thought Martin caused Clive's death. In fact, Martin only wanted to help Erin find answers. What did you do to help? Nothing. In fact, I'd bet you made up the whole story in order to frame Martin because you feel guilty for failing both your son and daughter. You're a failure. As a father." I glanced at Faith. "And as a husband."

I couldn't take another minute to look at his face. Before he could answer, I walked away. Keeping my head down, I avoided all the stares. "Sorry, Granddad. I couldn't help it," I muttered. The memory of him and the love of Kate and Joe filled me with the warmth I needed. I wanted to be that innocent, kind person Hunter spoke of.

I pulled my phone out of my bag and pressed Hunter's number. I couldn't wait a second longer. Maybe he'd already spoken to the woman. He answered on the first ring.

"I was just about to call you."

"Did she say anything? What the driver looked like? Anything?" I gulped air and sat in the nearest chair. I could see Izzie and Brody standing in the foyer, waiting.

"She described very little. It was getting dark, and the man wore a hooded jacket that nearly covered his forehead. Medium height, slender build. She says he wore glasses and kept sliding them up his nose, like it was a nervous habit."

"Great." My hopes deflated. How was that going to help? Lots of men wore glasses, and medium height was average. Slender build didn't stand out as unique.

"She did mention one odd thing, though. She said when she approached him, he was kicking the bumper and mumbling something about his brother who'd be furious when he found out. Anyway, that's all she could tell me. Not much help, is it?"

"No, I guess not."

"Don't give up. BPD is cooperating and will check all the traffic cam footage from that day and see if anything helps track his whereabouts. Unfortunately, as I said before, after Evelyn Parsell died, there's no record at the DMV."

"He's made sure he won't be found easily. Look, we're getting ready to leave. I'm anxious to tuck myself into bed and get some much-needed sleep. Love you."

"Looking forward to doing the same. Love you, cat lady. You are purrfect." He chuckled.

"And you're so corny, Robin Hood." I ended the call and stuffed my phone inside my bag. The lead didn't give me confidence. The incident happened more than two weeks ago. What were the odds the guy had skipped town with the stolen paintings? Most likely, he was long gone and never coming back. I certainly wouldn't.

"Okay. I'm ready to go." I put on my happy face and lifted my voice, hoping to fool Izzie. The truth was, my head was pounding. Confronting Alan wasn't the best timing. I reeled with the information Hunter had given me, trying to work out who the driver of the black van could be. Fear nagged at me, like it was thumping me hard on the chest, telling me to hurry up and figure it out. Problem was, I couldn't seem to get there. I sighed and followed behind Izzie and Brody, hoping for some miraculous revelation to hit me in the head.

Chapter Twenty-Five

I slid into the backseat of Brody's car as Izzie shifted sideways to stare at me with those inquisitive eyes. "What?" I tried looking clueless. That didn't work either. "Fine. I had a major blowout with Alan Whitmore. I told him off, called him a lousy parent and husband, which he is, and to top it off, I accused him of lying about Martin. Not my finest moment."

"Good. If you hadn't said it, I would have. Now, what else?"

"I called Hunter." I relayed the details of his conversation with the woman from the night of the accident.

"Okay. That sounds promising." She let out the words slowly.

"No, it doesn't."

She sighed. "It really doesn't. So, now what?"

"I bet BPD will check traffic cam footage from that day. See if they can get a location of where the driver went," Brody said.

"Ha. Now who's playing detective?" I laughed.

"I'm learning a few things by hanging around you two. Seriously, though, that next step makes sense."

"It does, and BPD is already on it. Let's hope they get something." I leaned back against the seat and closed my eyes. I sorted bits and pieces of information to form a plausible explanation, one that identified who that man driving the van could be. Beyond the obvious, the van puzzled me, like a thought that refused to come out and show itself but seemed important. Black van. The woman described the accident scene in detail. Like Hunter said, she had a sharp memory.

I opened my eyes and turned to stare out the window. Dark, choppy water lapped the shore as the wind kicked up. I stared at the lighthouse beacon shining across the lake. She'd mentioned the driver was of medium height and slender. Neither Fanning nor Ameling fit that description. They were both tall, and Ameling had a more muscular build. But what if the woman was significantly tall? From that perspective, he could've looked average height.

Her observation of what she called a nervous habit puzzled me, too. Playing with his glasses wasn't odd, though. I'd done it when I was anxious or nervous. The driver obviously had been feeling that way. She said he'd kicked the tire and griped how his brother was going to be angry when he found out. About the damage to the van? That had to be why. Maybe it was his brother's van.

I jerked and sat up straight. Why hadn't I thought of it before? I thumped Izzie's shoulder.

"Ouch! What the—I was just about to doze off." She turned her head sideways. "Why did you do that?"

"Listen. Do you remember Storing complaining about his situation? How he was tired of not having enough money or something. And how his car was in the shop, so he had to borrow his brother's vehicle?"

"Ah, yeah. I remember he said he couldn't afford the repairs. Oh, and how he couldn't wait to move out of his dilapidated apartment. I don't blame him. That place is shameful. I mean, who does the maintenance? It needs—"

"Izzie!" I smacked the back of her seat. "Focus. Do you remember anything else about him when we visited? Like any gestures or words he used that stood out? You know, nervous habits, for instance?" I didn't want to say the answer. I needed her to have noticed.

She squirmed in her seat and twisted around to face me. Her dress crinkled and rustled as if it protested the movement. "Well, he didn't say any words that I'd call a habit." Her jaw dropped. "Yes! There was something. He kept fiddling with his glasses."

"Sliding them up his nose?" I bobbed my head up and down.

"Yes. And fingering the edges to adjust them, as if they'd fall off his face." She frowned. "Why? What are you thinking?"

I held up a finger. "Wait." I held my phone and pressed the call button. Totally anxious, I tapped my foot on the floor. "I knew something was odd when he spouted off all that stuff about art heists. Who was he trying to fool? I bet he never wrote a book on it." I smacked the back of Izzie's seat. "Why didn't we check? We just went along with his story. Stupid. Stupid." I cursed under my breath as the call went to voicemail. "Just great. He's not answering." I waited for the beep. "Hunter. Hi. It's me. Listen. Check and see if Storing has a brother living in the area. I believe…no, I'm sure the black van belongs to him, and Arthur Storing is our thief." I hung up and locked eyes with Izzie. I sensed we were thinking the same thing. Arthur Storing had been driving that black van. He was one of the thieves who broke into the storage facility and stole Clive's painting. I had no doubts about that, but could he be Erin's killer?

"Izzie, I think your dark horse just crossed the finish line." I shivered, thinking back over the past two weeks, how Storing played a part in our search. All the while, we assumed he was merely an eccentric writer who was obsessed with the Whitmores, maybe envious because they had everything he didn't. Never once did we think he had what it would take to murder someone. Izzie had called him the dark horse, the least likely suspect. Appearances definitely could fool you, and did in this case.

Brody pulled into our drive. As the car idled, he fixed his gaze on Izzie, then me. "If this was Hunter talking, I'd warn you to stay put and not do anything stupid. So, don't do anything stupid, okay?" His voice strained.

I noticed the worry in his eyes and reached up to pat his arm. "We won't. There's really nothing we can do to help. Hunter will listen to my voicemail and then go straight to Storing's apartment to arrest him. We've done our part." I pushed open the door. "Come on, Izzie. We should get a good night's sleep. Something tells me tomorrow is going to be a busy day."

Izzie gave Brody a kiss and said a few words that echoed mine, then walked with me to the front door. "We aren't going to bed, are we?"

"Not a chance. We're going to Arthur Storing's apartment." I unlocked the door.

"Because Hunter can't take care of this? What are you thinking, Chloe?

Everything you said to Brody makes sense. More sense than us trying to handle Storing. Besides, it's late. Too late to make the drive to Buffalo."

"What if Hunter doesn't listen to the voicemail in time? What if Storing is planning to make a getaway and fly out of Buffalo to someplace where we'd never find him? And what if that leaves Martin with a murder conviction hanging over him? What about that?" I ran out of breath by rambling on with my "what if" scenarios.

"And what do we do if we find Storing at home? Arrest him with our water pistol? Zap him with the Taser we don't have?" She pointed at my bottom. "Swat him with your Cat Woman's tail?"

"We'll figure that out when we get there." I stepped into the foyer. Without turning on the light, I tiptoed upstairs and waved my arm for Izzie to follow.

"Oh, sure. Great plan." Izzie whispered with obvious sarcasm.

We reached our bedroom doorways. "Come on, Izzie. What happened to snoop sisters in action?"

"This snoop sister wants to call it a night and let the real cops handle the matter." She slouched against her door.

"And Martin? You're okay with him being accused of murder?"

"Of course not." She scowled.

"Then, come with me. We'll make sure Storing doesn't escape. And I promise, we can sit outside his apartment, safe in our car, and wait for the police to arrive. No dangerous escapades involved."

When she nodded, the breath that had caught in my throat released. "Meet you downstairs in five minutes. We change clothes and head to Buffalo."

It was nearly ten on a Friday night. Football games were wrapping up. Cheers from a stadium and the pounding of drums echoed from the nearby high school. I leaned forward to concentrate on the road. Pitch black, with only the beam of headlights to guide me. A slight mist dotted the windshield, not even enough wet to trigger the wipers.

I pulled onto Storing's street and inched along until reaching the front of his apartment building. I parked along the curb and peered out the side window. "There. That must be his car. It's parked in front of his door."

"Not the black van," Izzie whispered.

"Makes sense. I'd ditch the van and find another ride, in case the police were looking for me."

She turned to me and blinked. "You thinking like a criminal is kind of scary."

I rolled my eyes. "It's just common sense."

"Look! You can see him through the front window. He's on his phone and pacing back and forth. I wonder who he's talking to?"

"How about the buyer who wants the painting?"

"Or his band of thieves, planning their getaway." Izzie hunched in her seat. "I'm not comfortable with being here, Chloe. What if he has a gun and tries to shoot us?"

"He hasn't even seen us." I straightened and leaned around Izzie to get a better look. "Is that a suitcase on the porch?"

"Ah, it is." Izzie whistled. "You were right. He's leaving tonight and will get away before the police arrive. What do we do now?"

"Hold tight." I swung my door open and hopped out, then sprinted across the drive to peek inside Storing's car. In the backseat lay a large canvas bag, that judging by its shape and size contained the missing painting. I hurried back to the car and got behind the wheel. "The painting's in the backseat," I panted. Getting my phone out, I tried Hunter once more. This time he answered.

"All tucked in for the night, I hope. Did I miss anything interesting at the ball? I sure had my eye on that statue. It would've fit perfectly in my mom's study. How much—"

"Hunter, I don't have time for statues and masked ball drama." I blurted out to interrupt as my gaze fixed on the window of Storing's apartment. He'd disappeared from view.

"Okay." He dragged out the last syllable. "What's going on? You sound agitated."

I rushed to explain where we were and how Storing looked like he was ready to make the great escape. "He's got the painting in his back seat, and there's no sign of the van."

"That's because it's here in an abandoned warehouse parking lot on the east side of Buffalo."

"Didn't you listen to my voicemail? Storing borrowed the van from his brother. We pieced together a conversation we had with him. He complained about not having enough money to fix his car, so he borrowed his brother's. And that weird quirk of fidgeting with his glasses? He does that. Oh, and it never once crossed our minds his talk about a huge project wasn't for a book deal. It must be the painting. He and probably others are responsible for the storage facility heist. I'm sure of it." I glanced at Izzie, who nodded in agreement.

"Chloe, don't you and Izzie do anything foolish. Just drive away before he sees you, and let BPD take it from here. Please. I'm begging you this time. Don't."

I heard the door slam and snapped my head around as Izzie gasped.

"He's leaving. Start the car, Chloe. We can't let him get away." Izzie gripped my arm and tugged.

"Sorry, Hunter. He's leaving now." I switched on the ignition, but turned off the headlights.

"Chloe," he started.

"We can't let him get away with this. I'll call you with updates."

"Chloe, I'm telling you."

"Talk soon." I ended the call. BPD couldn't get here fast enough. I was certain Storing had an escape plan that would evade the police. He would've taken that into consideration, especially after the fender bender incident. That was two weeks ago. Most likely, he abandoned the van and got his car back from the shop, leaving the authorities no chance of identifying him.

"He's getting in his car," Izzie said and buckled up.

I shifted into gear, letting him get to the end of the block before pulling away from the curb. With any luck, he wouldn't spot us. We'd underestimated Storing. Turned out he was clever and disguised his behavior well. I recalled the rather confused man we first met. Absentminded and scatterbrained in his words and actions had made us think he couldn't be much help, let alone carry out a master plan of a heist and possibly commit murder. The two crimes could be unrelated, but my bet was on Storing having committed both. Poor Erin. Most likely, she never saw him as the enemy, but rather as a confidant. Someone she could share her secrets with. I thought of the poem about the spider and the fly. Storing must have enticed and flattered Erin to gain her trust. The perfect trap.

"He's turning off the main highway. Where in the world is this supposed to go?" Izzie said.

The car bumped over the uneven surface, jarring my teeth. I grumbled with a few curse words. "Obviously not the road to the airport."

An inky blackness soon surrounded us as we left the comfort of the tiny dots of light from the street lamps behind. With another turn, I slowed the car to navigate while gripping the steering wheel and watching for any potholes or unfamiliar objects lying in the road. Where was Storing leading us? I had a sudden suspicion he'd guessed we were tailing him. "Do me a favor. Get on your phone and drop Hunter a pin so he knows where we are."

Izzie's teeth chattered as she pushed buttons on her phone. "Remind me again why we're here? And not at home safe in bed?"

I didn't answer. There was no time. A tree branch slapped the windshield, and my breath caught as I skidded to a stop. "Maybe we should—" Before I could finish, Storing put on his brakes and killed the engine, blanketing his car in total darkness.

In seconds, he appeared in our beam of lights, his palm extended to block the glare. I shuddered at the angry scowl pinching his brow. All at once, he lifted his arm and pointed a gun, then moved toward us.

"Chloe!" Izzie shouted. "Reverse. Put the car into reverse!" She slapped my arm.

"Stop hitting." I shifted and stomped on the gas pedal. We traveled maybe ten yards before the wheels came to a stop. I pressed the pedal to the floor, all while fixing my gaze on Storing, who kept coming. The whine of the engine grew louder, but we weren't moving.

"We're stuck. This can't be happening. Chloe, we need to move," Izzie shouted as she opened the door, ready to bolt out.

"Wait." I pulled on her arm. "He might shoot if he sees you." I prayed the headlights would be blinding enough to keep him from taking aim.

"Why didn't you just stay out of it?" Storing shouted. As if his legs couldn't handle more, he stopped. "I never wanted to harm anyone, and now you've left me no choice." He dropped his arm but kept a tight hold of the gun. "I have to deliver the painting. Can you understand? I need the money. I can't live this way any longer." He shielded his eyes from the headlights. "I just can't do this. I'm not really a bad person. I never meant…" In the next second, he tossed the gun to the ground, then turned to get back in his car but didn't attempt to drive away.

A cloud of dust stirred on the road behind us, and I heard the scream of sirens grow louder as police cruisers approached.

"It's okay. We're okay." I wrapped an arm around Izzie's shoulders and pulled her tight. I kept my eye on the rearview mirror, waiting anxiously. At the sight of Hunter jogging down the dirt path toward us, relief took over my emotions. "It's over, Izzie. We're going to be fine."

Chapter Twenty-Six

I lifted my chin to breathe in the lake air. Sitting next to Hunter, I smiled. He shoveled potato salad in his mouth and chewed. All around me were the faces I loved. Izzie, Mom, Dad, Hunter, even Brody and Martin shared in this special moment on the rock. My birthday celebration that I wanted to have here on this tiny sliver of land was perfect. No presents, loud music, or any of the other fanfare that came with birthday bashes. I had wanted this and only this. I ruffled Max's furry head as he lay sleeping in the sun.

With all my effort, I tried erasing the troubling details of Erin's death and Storing's despicable acts that ended in true dramatic fashion. However, my brain wasn't wired that way. I had to know answers, the reasons for everything that happened.

"I still can't believe Storing managed to put together such an elaborate plan to steal the Vermeer painting and think he could get away with it. You said it yourself, Martin. Those people in the black market can be dangerous to deal with." I pointed my fork. We did have cake, despite me telling Mom not to fuss. She didn't. She had Claire from the bakery make it. And it was delicious. I took another bite.

Dad groaned. "I thought this was supposed to be a pleasant celebration and not involve talk about murder and stolen goods."

"Sorry, but my mind won't let go. Plus, it's my birthday." I straightened. "Shouldn't I decide what we talk about?" I teased him with a wink.

"Whatever you wish, shortcake." He chuckled.

"Storing didn't bargain for such sharp detectives working the case." Hunter grinned.

"Why, thank you." I bowed my head.

"I was talking about me and my team, but go ahead. Take the credit," he quipped.

"Come on. Izzie and I figured out the owner of the van. Or I should say, illegal owner. Does criminal behavior run in the Storing family? Anyway, if it wasn't for that tiny detail, Storing could be halfway across the world by now."

"True. Surprisingly, his mouth was like a running faucet during the interrogation. Gave up everything but the person known as the buyer. At least we know the guard helped get them into the storage facility. Police are looking for him, but he hasn't been at work since the day of the heist."

"And what about the guys who were in on the robbery?" I asked.

"We're still working on finding them, too." Hunter set his plate aside.

"I can't get over how he coaxed all that information out of Erin, like news about the painting and her plan to meet with Martin that night. He even convinced her that he'd help find out more about Clive's death. Then led her on a wild chase that went nowhere," Izzie said. "Too bad she never got the answers she wanted."

"Until we find evidence to the contrary, his death remains classified as an accident." Hunter looked away for a second, then continued. "That day you spotted her at your kite painting event in the park? Storing was the man with her. He learned that day about her meeting with Martin to discuss Clive's death and his important discovery, one that was worth millions. It was only after following Martin to the Whitmore estate that evening that he learned Clive's discovery was a priceless painting," Hunter explained.

"Wait. At that point, Martin didn't know where the Vermeer was hidden. Right? So how could Storing know? Brody asked.

"True. But after hearing Martin tell Erin about the seascape, Storing made a calculated guess but wanted to make sure Erin wasn't hiding any information." Hunter nodded.

"So, when he got the chance, after Martin left that second time, Storing came inside the study and confronted Erin. Poor Erin. When she didn't cooperate and tried to fight him off, he killed her," I said. "He must've placed the gun in her hand to make it look like suicide."

Hunter held up a finger. "There's more. Storing claims he found a ledger belonging to Clive in Erin's purse. It has dozens of names. People he'd done business with, and many of them in the black market."

Martin sighed. "Little did I know Clive had been dealing with that horrible side of the art world for years. He'd kept it a secret from me."

"Most likely, he did that because he was ashamed and didn't want you to think less of him." Izzie patted his arm.

"Yes. I suppose that's true, but I wouldn't have. He was my friend. I would've helped him somehow. Friends do that for each other, don't they?" Martin smiled at Izzie.

Izzie sniffed. "Now, stop it. Don't you dare make me cry."

"Who wants more cake?" Mom interrupted.

Everyone held out their plates for her to add a slice, except for me. My stomach was full, for once. Obviously, Mom didn't want a replay of what happened in the study that night. Erin had fought for her life, but in the end, Storing was too quick, too strong, and too desperate.

"Do you think Clive's ledger will help you figure out who Storing intended to sell the painting to?" Izzie asked.

"I'm not sure about that, but we'll turn it over to the FBI's Art Crime Division. Detective Winsell is working with them on the Burnell case. They'll be thrilled to see all those names. My guess is there will be plenty of arrests in the near future. Even a connection to the Burnell's theft. Who knows?" Hunter gave a thumbs-up. "Score for the FBI."

Martin cleared his throat. "I might be able to help."

All of us stared. Like everyone else, I was curious what he had to say.

"Antoine mentioned a name or two of his best clients. He assured me they'd ask no questions, if I ever had a valuable art piece that was acquired by whatever means. I got the gist of his comment and told him I didn't do business that way." Martin paused. "He also mentioned a dealer I should watch out for. Someone who's not choosy, as long as the profit is high and he remains anonymous to those involved. Antoine claims the dealer uses a nom de plume. Though he is certain the man is from somewhere in South America." Martin paused again. This time with a pointed stare at me and Izzie.

My breath caught. What was he implying? I found it difficult to fathom, yet the hint was there. Martin was an astute judge of character. I'd bet his opinion being right, any day.

"Anyway," Martin continued. "A nom de plume makes this very mysterious and entirely untraceable. Doesn't it? Antoine says the dealer is contacted through a P.O. box and never once by phone. His commission is more than the usual, but he gets results. No matter how and to what lengths he has to go, he closes the deal. No doubt, it reeks of unsavory and criminal behavior."

"Holy wow," Izzie exclaimed.

"Yeah, I second that. Is there any way you can work with that information?" I studied Hunter's face and considered whether he'd read into Martin's comment like I had. Tito Alma as the anonymous dealer? It seemed impossible, yet he was here in the area. He came to the art group's meeting at Gritos. He was at the movie night in the park and talking to Storing, no less. In plain sight, yet nowhere that would make us suspect he was the infamous dealer. Sure, Izzie and I had discussed how he could be involved in some small way. But as the dealer after the Vermeer?

I glanced down at Max and chuckled. That evening at the park, when Tito had tried to pet him, Max growled as if he knew something wasn't right. Maybe it was true. Dogs did have a way of knowing who to trust.

"I'd say this dealer has gone to great lengths to keep his identity a secret. Probably been doing it for years. I don't hold out any hope for solving that case," Hunter said.

His face gave nothing away. "Then I guess we'll never know who Storing was doing business with." I waited a moment. "Come to think of it, even Storing doesn't know."

Hunter leaned forward. "Storing claims he was scheduled to drop off the painting at midnight last night. Someone was supposed to meet him. Doubt it would've been the dealer himself."

"Did you go to the meeting place?" I asked.

He nodded. "No one was there. My guess is this dealer learned about Storing's arrest and has left town, or maybe never was in town. Who knows?"

We all fell into our own thoughts and made no comment for the moment. Overhead, geese formed a perfect V and squawked to bid farewell as they flew south.

"He had a flight pass in his pocket," Hunter said, as if it was an afterthought. "To Cypris."

"No extradition." Martin chuckled. "You have to admire the effort and his detailed planning."

"The mind of a killer, you mean," Izzie sniffed. "Sorry. I can't get over how we missed it. Storing, of all people."

"Like, how did he get away with shooting her, and no one in the house hears it? Makes no sense," I added.

"Actually, it does. After speaking with Alan again, he admitted that both he and Faith hadn't been at home when the shot would've been fired. His story about Martin was a total lie. He didn't see him arrive. He admitted Erin never told him Martin was responsible for Clive's death. In fact, no one but Erin was home when Storing visited. The housekeeper had left at nine." Hunter glanced at Martin. "Sorry, Martin. I was just doing my job."

Martin looked out at the lake for a brief moment, then turned. "I appreciate all you've done to find Erin's killer. That was most important." He shrugged. "Besides, I enjoyed my time behind bars. Your deputy, Jeremy, was a wonderful host."

"You are an amazing man, Martin. Despite that looming charge of murder, you manage to find humor in the situation." Izzie gave him a brief hug.

"Did you ask Alan about the photo? I keep wondering who was behind the camera." Maybe it didn't matter, but I loved tying up those loose ends.

"Yes, he tore up the photo. He seemed honest and sincere. Emotional over losing both his children, he locked himself in his study to have a cry. He didn't want Faith to see him that way. Searching through his desk drawer, he found the photo among some others. Claiming the likeness of Erin, looking so happy, made him overwhelmed with guilt. He felt like a failure as a parent and husband. He ripped up the photo, saying he wished he had listened to her and helped Clive. As for who held the camera, he has no idea."

"And the gun? How did it end up in the closet where I found it?"

"Alan also confessed he put it there. He'd found the pistol in Erin's hand and panicked. Of course, he worried how the pistol could lead to more problems for the family. Always thinking about his reputation, I guess." Hunter shook his head in disgust. "So, he hid it in the bedroom. Worried Faith might find it, he placed it in the study closet the next day."

"Speaking of Faith. What's the deal with her story? Was she telling the truth about blackmail?" Dad asked Hunter.

"She was. When Ameling approached her—he figured she'd be easier to manipulate—Faith paid the sum, leaving Alan out of it. Not for the reasons you'd think. She wanted to protect the family, but also her money. Turns out she's the wealthy one, not Alan. When they married, she inherited the family trust worth millions. Alan brought only his business savvy to the marriage." He scratched his jaw. "Why she put up with him all these years is beyond me. But that's all over. She told me she'd filed for divorce last month. She's leaving him and guess who's taking Alan's place?"

"Good grief. Don't tell me. It's Ameling, isn't it?" I slapped my thigh. "I was right. From blackmail to a love affair."

"Trading one bad boy for another, it seems. If I were Ameling, I'd keep an eye on her," Martin said. "She's a shrewd woman with power and money."

"Oh, stop. Don't you believe in romance?" Mom retorted.

"I do!" A laugh burst out of me. "And birthday celebrations, and beautiful fall days like this one, and friends who turn into more." I winked at Hunter.

"Speaking of birthdays, how about we end all this talk about murder and celebrate? It's why we're all here, isn't it?" Mom raised her glass of punch. "To happy times ahead."

We echoed her sentiment and eased into pleasant conversation about the goings-on happening in Whisper Cove. Moments like these gave us hope. I certainly hoped no more murders were in the foreseeable future, but that was a tall order. I glanced at the guy sitting next to me, and the sight of him warmed my heart. "Say, we almost forgot our rock tradition."

"Yes." Izzie pointed. "You go first, Chloe."

CHAPTER TWENTY-SIX

"What are we talking about?" Martin asked.

"We each reflect on this past year and share one thing we are grateful for. Our granddad started this, so in his memory, I want to say how much I appreciate my family and friends. Without your love and support, I wouldn't have survived all the challenges and craziness with a murder or two thrown in—sorry, Mom. I had to say the word because it has been a part of our lives. Anyway, that's what, or I should say who, I'm most grateful for."

"My turn!" Izzie waved her hand.

I grinned. The perfect celebration. What more could a girl ask for on her special day of the year? I glimpsed each face, reflecting on how these people fit into my life. Not money, not even Faith's millions, could promise happiness. I found my happiness right here, in this moment, with all these people. I glanced up at the sky and said a heartfelt thank you to Granddad. At least for this day, all was right with the world.

Acknowledgments

As with many fiction books, there may be factual details or references, but adding variations of the truth is what can make the story more enticing. *A Tint of Murder* involves a stolen painting that references the famous 1990 art heist at Boston's Isabella Stewart Gardner Museum, which occurred during the early morning hours after St. Patrick's Day. Thirteen priceless items, including paintings by Rembrandt and Vermeer, were stolen and to this day never recovered. That event is fact. However, my story about a hidden Vermeer painting is total fabrication. The artist did indeed paint a set of four tronies but no others. (A tronie is a type of work that depicts an exaggerated or characteristic facial expression.) The world of art heists and lucrative black market deals to sell fake paintings are also very true. Sadly, only ten percent of stolen art is recovered. A difficult task for the FBI Art Crime investigators since many stolen pieces end up in private collections owned by wealthy collectors and are easily hidden.

As always, I must give a shout out to the awesome author group I belong to—your support and advice are priceless.

And of course, the team at Level Best Books—my editor, Shawn Reilly Simmons, Deb Well, a marketing guru, and all the other wonderful people at LBB who make this whole writing and publishing process a smooth endeavor.

To those in my life—family, friends, and the author community—you have given me the peptalks, not to mention virtual hugs, when I needed them. I'm eternally grateful. And of course, to my muse, my furry pal, Max. You are a star in this series and a light in my life.

About the Author

Bailee Abbott is a native Ohioan who spends her days plotting murder and writing mysteries. She's a member of Sisters in Crime, International Thriller Writers, and Mystery Writers of America. Bailee lives with her husband and furry friend Max in the quiet suburbs of Green, Ohio. Visits to Bemus Point, a town along the Chautauqua Lake in southwest New York inspired the setting for the Paint by Murder mystery series. Bailee also writes the Sierra Pines B&B mystery series under the name Kathryn Long.

AUTHOR WEBSITE:

https://www.baileeabbott.com

SOCIAL MEDIA HANDLES:

Twitter: https://twitter.com/BaileeAbbott1

Facebook Page: https://www.facebook.com/BaileeAbbottBooks

Goodreads: https://www.goodreads.com/author/show/21094675.Bailee_Abbott

Instagram: @baileeabbottbooks

Also by Bailee Abbott

<u>WRITING AS BAILEE ABBOTT</u>

Paint By Murder Mysteries:
  #1 A Brush With Murder
  #2 Kill Them With Canvas
  #3 Easier Dead Than Drawn

<u>WRITING AS KATHRYN LONG</u>

Sierra Pines B&B Mysteries:
  #1 Boarding with Murder
  #2 Snowed Under Murder
  #3 Blooming with Murder

Mackenzie Blue Mysteries:
  #1 Buried In Sin
  #2 Played By Death

A Deadly Deed Grows

When I Choose

Dying To Dream